THE BEST OF
MARTINUS PUBLISHING
2013

www.martinus.us

Cover art by Jessica Hale

First Edition, Released December 2013

Table of Contents:

A Thursday Night at Doctor What's Time and Relative Dimensional Space Bar and Grill
By Bruno Lombardi

"Who else has killed Hitler?"

I looked up from cleaning a beer glass at the sound of that question—and then groaned inwardly when I realized who had said it.

Of *course* it would be Wells who would say that. Leave it to him to always be the one to make my life difficult.

I took a quick look around, taking in the entire room in one glance—every good bartender learns real quick how to scope out his entire bar using just one quick glance—and looking for any trouble.

For once, there wasn't.

Soames was at a table with Rogers, comparing scars again. Stargard was doing his usual *uber*-Poland spiel/rant to whoever would listen to him, this time a bored looking guy in a monk costume. Taylor sat by himself, nursing a large scotch. Even from here, I could hear him mumbling to himself about how 'those maniacs blew it up' and how they should all 'be damned to hell.' Hey, at least he wasn't going on about the 'Omega virus' or whatever the hell he was calling it, so I'm cutting him some slack tonight. Tony and Doug—looking quite dashing in their clothes (green turtleneck and grey slacks for Tony; a conservative Norfolk suit for Doug)—were babbling on about the Titanic *again*, this time to the new guy, Frank Parker. Parker wasn't paying much attention to them, mainly because he was ogling that cute girl, Cameron. Emmett was sitting alone in a corner of the counter, still slowly sipping his first—and only—shot of whiskey of the night. Emmett's a nice guy, but he really can't hold his liquor and he knows it.

All in all, just a normal Thursday night in Doctor What's Time and Relative Dimensional Space Bar and Grill, the universe's only time-traveler's bar.

* * *

As you may have guessed, I'm not just the barkeep—I also own the place. Have done so for just under ten years (personal time frame), or

4,000,000,000,000,000,000,001 years (universe time frame).

It's a pretty cool gig, all in all. Hours are great, although some of the actual minutes leave a *lot* to be desired. Mind you, that gets made up (for the most part) with all the cool stories and people, so it kind of evens out overall.

As for why I run this joint—hey, 'invisible hand' and all that jazz. You've got time travelers running around all over the space-time continuum; they're going to want to have a place to kick back, drink a few beers and hang out with old/new/future/past friends and fellow travelers. I got in on the 'ground floor,' so to speak, with opening night being three hours after the Big Bang.

Why the Big Bang? Simple; one of the very first thoughts that a time traveler has after they invent their time machine is *'Gosh- I can be the first person to actually witness the Big Bang—think of the scientific discoveries!'* The thing is, well, *everyone* in all of space and time has *exactly* the same thought.

Ever see those pictures of LA traffic jams? Yeah, that's what's waiting for you there. Freakin' Sardine City. Just FYI.

I figured that, after being stuck in gridlock for a few hours, one will end up getting *mighty* thirsty. So off I went with my time machine/bar.

Had to get a new front door; the hordes practically *ripped* it off the hinges going through it to get to the beer. Within four hours of opening, I was already making a profit. Haven't looked back (or forward, as the case may be) since.

I move the place around a lot—it's always nice to see new scenery. Right 'now' we're in the year 2237 AD, Armstrong City, Luna.

Anyway...

"Who else has killed Hitler?" repeated Wells, this time a bit more loudly and clearer.

All around the bar, a few ears perked up.

I groaned.

I *hate* it when someone brings up that question.

"Well?" asked Wells.

A dozen hands shot up, more or less at the same time.

Well, there goes my quiet night...

Remember how I told you that one of the first things that a time traveler does after they invent their time machine is to go to the Big Bang? Well—guess what the second thing they come up with is. Yup, *'I can kill Hitler!'*

Why not? Makes sense, doesn't it? Stop WWII, prevent the Holocaust, save millions of people, alter the entire course of the Cold War, etcetera, etcetera, etcetera. You know the drill.

Unfortunately, it doesn't *quite* work that way. I should know—I tried it myself once. Didn't work then, won't work now. It *never* works—but that doesn't stop everyone from finding out the hard way.

Everyone has their own story—and in each and every case it blew up in their faces. Every. Single. Time.

Why is Hitler so impossible to kill? No idea. I've heard a million crazy theories explaining why—and trust me, some of them are *really* out there—but, quite honestly, I don't know which one is true or not. Don't care, to be honest.

Old-timers are smart enough to not even bother trying to do it at this point. But you still have all the newbies and n00bs and youngsters and Kool Kidz and all those other idiots trying anyway. And then we have to hear them all *whining…*

As for why I hate it when they start talking about it? Just watch…

"April 19, 1942," said this one guy—young dude in a red biker costume named Swann, I think. "Hitler was doing some tour of some factory. Figured that would be the perfect time to take him out."

I rolled my eyes. Yeah, like nobody ever thought of *that* one before. I shrugged my shoulders and started getting a few shots ready—I make a mean *Beam Me Up Scotty* and my *Mind Eraser* is listed as a WMD in 13th century Paris—and leaned back. People were going to need them in a minute.

"So, anyways," continued Swann, "I'm hiding in the rafters with a sniper rifle. I have an absolutely clean shot here. Absolutely clean! And just as I pull the trigger..." Swann paused, like he couldn't believe what he was about to say next. (I'm willing to bet a hundred dollars in the currency of any time period you choose that that's *exactly* what was going through his mind.)

Swann got it together, at least for a few seconds. "Stupid rat," he said, shaking his head in dismay.

"Rat?" called out someone in the crowd.

"A *rat* drops right down on my arm, just as I pull the trigger!" screamed Swann. Most of the newbies in the crowd were staring at Swann with open mouths of shock and going '*Whoa, no way, dude!*' All the old-timers, on the other hand, were just nodding their heads and muttering, 'Yup, uh-huh.'

"So what happened next?" called someone else.

"I miss his head by a good five feet, that's what!" screamed Swann. "Next thing I know, half the LSSAH regiment is shooting at me and I barely jump out of there in time!" Swann ended with an expletive and shook his head with a loud sigh, then leaned his head down and started pounding it on the table. I nodded at the waitress and passed a tray of assorted shooters to her. With practiced ease, she rushed over and placed the tray in front of him. Swann stared at the tray for a moment, then shrugged his shoulders and started downing them, one after the other.

I added an extra twenty dollars to Swann's already impressive tab and started making another batch of shooters.

"1936, Berlin," said this cute looking middle-aged blonde woman by the name of Sapphire, speaking with a haughty English accent I couldn't quite place. "Opening ceremonies of the Olympic games. Took a bit of doing but managed to take the place of one of Leni Riefenstahl's camera crew. Plan was obvious; follow Hitler around and then, when the right moment shows up, blow him away with the gun secreted in the lens of the camera."

I smirked; you have *no* idea how many time-travelers were running around Berlin during the '36 games. How many, you ask? Let me put it this way; the *Olympiastadion* could seat 65,000 people when it was built. Take a guess how many time travelers there were in the crowd. Go ahead, guess.

Give up?

Everyone in the stadium on opening day was either a time traveler, a local working for a time traveler, or someone looking for a time traveler. *Everyone.*

Damn tourists.

Anyway...

"So I'm all lined up and I pull the trigger—and I *succeed!*" There were gasps of surprise and/or confusion from the crowd of newbies again. A couple of the old-timers just nodded their heads knowingly and muttered *'here it comes'* or *'wait for it'* or *'taking bets now, man;'* stuff like that.

I nodded my head as well. That's the *other* part of the sordid mess with killing Hitler.

"Wait—you actually *killed* him?!" exclaimed someone in the audience.

Sapphire just nodded her head and took a deep breath. "Yeah, I killed him. Unfortunate..." Here she paused to let out a very long sigh. "Unfortunately, the bullet went right through Hitler's head and hit Jessie Owens just as he was walking by!"

I rolled my eyes. Believe me, I can *totally* believe that happening. Trust me, that ain't the silliest thing I've heard.

"Wait, Owens got killed *too*?!" yelled a different neophyte, stating the obvious.

Sapphire just nodded her head. "So now I have to go back and fix it so Owens stays away from Hitler when I shoot Hitler. But now there's two versions of me running around, so I have to be extra careful I don't cross my own timestream. So I convince Owens to take a different path, but unfortunately, now Jackie Robinson—who was in the stadium to see his brother compete—gets killed instead! So now I have to go back a *third* time to clean up the mess, and now a random spectator in the audience gets hit. Except that spectator is the ancestor of the woman who discovers cold fusion, so now I have to go back a *fourth* time..." At this point Sapphire just shook her head in frustration. "*Eighteen* times I went back, and each time somebody important got killed! Eventually—with so many alternates of myself running around—I just had to quit before I ripped the time-space continuum or something!" With a loud sigh, she collapsed into a chair.

I sent over a large scotch and added it to her tab.

Poor lady. I remained pretty blasé about it, but I knew how something like that could mess with someone. I really did sympathize with her.

You see, that's the other thing with trying to kill Hitler. Sometimes you actually succeed, but you screw up so badly that you have no choice but to go back and *save* Hitler from getting killed in the first place. Yeah, I know, major bummer, but there you go. Nobody said time travel was easy.

People were starting to get bummed out. That's both a good thing and a bad thing in the bar business.

Let's be honest; bartenders *love* it when their customers come in all depressed. Depressed customers sit quietly in a corner and drink until they're plastered or broke; either way, we like that. But there's a fine line between 'depressed' and 'totally bummed out.' Depressed people spend money and stay quiet; that's good. Totally bummed out people start complaining loudly and spend all their time just staring at their drinks instead of actually, you know, *drinking.* That's bad.

By now, about half the crowd was in the *'mildly depressed'* stage but about a third were edging into the *'totally bummed'* stage.

This was going to be a long night.

"I can top that," said this guy, standing up. I recognized him. He wasn't exactly a regular, but he hung around here a lot and tended to keep to himself, which made my life easier. He jumped around a fair bit and he had some *really* out there stories. Oddly enough, he wasn't a scientist like most of the guys here. Apparently he started off writing stories for *'confession magazines'* for young, confused women before he got into the time-travel business. Called himself the Unmarried Mother (hey, I've heard weirder names). Also claimed to be both his own mother and father, so, like, whatever, man.

Anyway, he kept talking.

"October 1916," he said. "Battle of the Somme. Hitler is a young corporal working as a runner on the front lines. In the original timeline, he gets wounded in the leg and spends a few months in a hospital near Berlin. Figured that would be the perfect time to take him out."

Oh yeah, the 'Kill Hitler during World War One' shtick. That's a *bit* cleverer than the usual 'Kill Hitler' plan. I'm always surprised that only one in ten time-travelers comes up with that plan.

"So," continued the Unmarried Mother. "I decide not to pussy-foot around here. I've got a high-powered rifle, sniper scope, the works. I'm all set up to shoot when there's this big flash of light, and that's when another time-traveler—with exactly the same idea I had—jumps in!" He paused for a moment, giving us all the death glare. "Right on top of me!"

Unmarried Mother threw up his hands in disgust. "And guess what happens? It turns out that *I'm* the one who gave Hitler the leg wound! *I'm* the reason he was a war hero!"

He sat down so hard that he almost broke a chair, and made an incoherent scream of disgust. A rum and coke materialized next to his hand a moment later and I made the appropriate adjustments to his tab.

Yeah—after a while you kind of get used to stuff like that. Predestination paradox, and all that jazz.

At least Unmarried Mother wasn't as bad off as this guy who was in last month. Poor bastard. Japanese kid by the name of Akira, I think; really weird cat. Went back in time to 1912 to kill this other guy—some Count who was planning to take over the world or something like that. Anyway, he killed the Count but it turned out that the Count had commissioned a portrait from a poor, struggling painter. The deal would have put the painter on the map, but with the Count dead, the deal fell through. Of course, the painter—Hitler, of course—ended up putting all the blame for the failed deal on the Jewish art dealer who'd tried to set up the deal in the first place. How's *that* for a kick in the gonads, huh?

"Ah, guess it's my turn," said a rather plain looking guy, standing up. His accent placed him as a Brit, but I've always been pretty bad at placing the accents more precisely than that, although if I had to elaborate I would call it a standard BBC London accent. The guy looked really hum-drum; if you saw him on the street, you'd think he was a TV repairman or something. I vaguely recalled the guy's name—Gary Something-Bird. Sparrow? Hawk? Falcon? Something like that.

Anyway...

"1908 in Vienna. Hitler is coming out of the Academy of Fine Arts after being rejected for admission for the second time in two years. That's the point in his life where things really began to fall apart for him. He was going to end up broke and homeless, becoming the stereotypical starving artist. It seemed the perfect time to get him, right? So, I'm walking towards him when, out of the corner of my eye, I see three members of the Hitler Revenge Squad pop in!"

Half the crowd groaned; the other half went *'oooohhh.'*

The Hitler Revenge Squad is/will be/have been (I could never keep all those time tenses straight in my head) a legendary group of time-travelling fanatics from the 26th century, dedicated to going back in time to, well, *guess*. As you may have gathered by now, it's not exactly *that* easy to kill Hitler. Most guys with any common sense would have just given up after a few tries. Then again, if common sense was so common, it wouldn't be a trait held in such high esteem. Those yahoos have been at it at least sixty-seven separate times, by my (feeble) recollection.

They're not exactly from the deep end of the gene pool, you know what I mean?

Gary kept talking. "So my immediate reaction is, 'These guys are coming right at my direction waving big-arse machine guns.' I'm just about to back away when—bang!—in pop three members from the Neo-Neo-Neo Aryan Guard!"

Another chorus of groans and *'ooohhhs'* from the crowd.

The Neo-Neo-Neo Aryan Guard are a legendarily infamous group of Neo-Nazi fanatics from the 27th century dedicated to going back in time to stop the assassination attempts from the Hitler Revenge Squad.

Oh come on—you didn't see *that* coming?

"So," says Gary, "I'm actually caught in the middle between the two groups! I was just about to jump out of there when—bang!—in jump three members of the Time Patrol!"

Yet another round of groans and *'ooohhhs.'*

The Time Patrol is a legendary, annoying group of do-gooder fanatics from the 28th century dedicated to going back in time to 'keep history progressing as it should'. Naturally they tend to be big party-poopers. Thanks to them, people need to book tickets three centuries ahead of time and have to submit to both a background *and* foreground check whenever they go back to view the Crucifixion. Fortunately for everyone, they're kept busy just keeping up with the Hitler Revenge Squad and Neo-Neo-Neo Aryan Guard.

"So what happened?" asked someone.

"I got caught in the crossfire from nine different machine guns, that's what!" screamed Gary. "I needed to spend six god-forsaken months in a hospital in the 22nd century before I was able to walk again!" Gary sat down hard—so hard that this time the back of his chair broke–and he started to cry.

I sent him a whole bottle of rum. Only charged him *half –price*, 'cause I'm just that nice of a guy and felt sorry for him. Poor bastard.

Nobody else volunteered to tell any more Hitler stories after Gary's tale of woe—thank God—but the damage was already done. Ten minutes went by, and not a single order was placed. An hour ago, I'd had a bar full of pleasant talkative drunks happily buying booze like there was no tomorrow. Now? I had a whole bar of quiet introspective drunks staring morosely at their drinks. Forget about refills—these losers looked like they weren't even going to finish the drinks they already had before last call.

That required… drastic action.

I went to the jukebox and hit the selection for 'I'm My Own Grandpa' (the Guy Lombardo version—that dude *rocked*, man).

Then I fired up the personal time machine I had in the back office and made a few jumps just as Guy Lombardo started singing the first chorus.

First off—live bands. I picked up Jim Morrison from July 3, 1971, Jimi Hendrix from September 18, 1970, and Robert Johnson from August 16, 1938. I then jumped forward and dropped them off in a bar—*my* bar, in fact, when I'd done a jump to New York City during the Big Blackout of 1977 about 3 years ago (personal timeline, that is). I waved at myself, told my previous self to give them a few drinks so that the gang could get to know one another and that I'd be coming by when they were nice and pleasantly drunk, and then I jumped again.

Second—women. I needed some wild and crazy party gals and they had to be the type of gals who liked nerdy guys, 'cause, let's be honest; most of the time travelers that come through my door? Nerds and geeks. I picked up Mata Hari (had to break her out of prison; cool story there, but that's for another time), the complete Dallas Cowboys cheerleader squad right after the Cowboys' win of Super Bowl XXX, and then jumped to the 34th century, where I convinced Eccentrica Gallumbits (the triple breasted high priced escort whose nickname is 'The Best Bang since the Big One,' and trust me, she sure as hell *is*. Raaaarggghh) to wear a neon t-shirt flashing the slogan *Freebie Friday*, pink hot pants, and red stiletto heels, and come back with me.

Ok—so I jumped back to 1977, thanked myself for taking care of the Gang, paid him for the booze that the guys drank (hey, only fair, right?), waved at some of the regulars there and told them I'd catch them in three years and/or 260 years (as the case may be) and then jumped forward.

When I walked out of the storeroom with the Gang and girls, Guy Lombardo was just finishing off the first chorus. Nine separate time jumps, covering over 15 centuries. Total elapsed time since I left? Five point two seconds.

Am I amazing, or am I amazing?

Well—about ten seconds after I walked into the room, the Dark Brooding Depressed Crowd were no longer dark or brooding or even depressed for that matter.

Anyway—about two hours later, the libation had been flowing so freely that I had to make a quick jump forward to next Wednesday to pick up next week's delivery of beer, so that I'd have enough to last me until next week. The Musical Trio had all been sent back to their respective dates (and since they were all scheduled to die within a few hours after they returned, the damage to the timestream would be minimal; I am nothing if not meticulous) and most of the women had gone home (although one or two of them ended up at someone *else's* home) and, all in all, a fun time had been had by all.

So I was sweeping up the place and giving the glasses one last clean and was tallying up everyone's bar tab when, from somewhere in the crowd, I heard someone say, "So... anyone else tried to stop the sinking of the *Titanic*?"

I groaned.

I *hate* it when someone brings up that question.

"Well?"

A dozen hands shot up, more or less at the same time.

Well—there goes my quiet night... again...

QUEST THROUGH THE AGES
BY JL MO

He lowered himself with a grunt onto the skins in his cave. This cave would do, but he would look for a better one during the next sun. As he settled into a somewhat comfortable position, he rearranged the striped fur covering him. He had skinned it from a ferocious cat that attacked him long ago. He opened one eye. The enormous fang he'd taken from that first big kill lay within easy reach. The other men named him "Slayer" for good reason.

At the time, he had been seeking a good cave. He thought he had found one, only to startle the sharp-fanged beast that thought the same. The fight for his life had terrified him more than any other. His heart still raced with the memory of the immense claws swiping at his face. When the cat lunged with jaws gaping, exposing enormous fangs, Slayer thought death was certain. As the cat fell upon him, however, Slayer twisted. The beast's claw missed his face and istead the front legs entwined him. A lucky roll twisted Slayer on top as the two reached a ledge. The claws of the beast sliced into Slayer's arms as it fell away, crashing onto the sharp, slender rocks protruding up from the lower floor of the cave, leaving Slayer the victor.

He no longer feared the fangs of the cats as he once had. He'd learned they used the things to frighten their prey into submission. The claws are what the beast used to kill. The bite was still something to avoid, but the fear of them no longer held sway with him.

That cave did not suit Slayer's needs as well as he'd hoped, so his search continued.

That battle had been long ago, and Slayer had grown old. Now the younger men fought to replace him as clan leader. He hoped it would happen soon. He truly did not lead so much as others simply followed him on his quest for the perfect cave.

His eyes flashed open and he sucked in air. *Pain.* More pain than he had ever known crushed his chest, but it was from nothing he could see. Invisible hands reached into him and squeezed tight at his racing heart.

He gasped his last breath as blackness claimed him.

Slayer felt warm. He floated. He sought.
Then he heard them.
"What do you seek?"
"Contentment. Happiness."
"Where do you look?"
"Through the ages."
"How long have you sought?"
"This lifetime."
"Shall we show you the way?"
"No, the quest is mine."
"Then carry on to the next life."

Captain Pelagius hired Slayer to protect his boat from the predatory sea creatures that tormented cargo ships. Thanks be to the gods, only one leviathan had reared its ugly head above the surface. It was small by comparison to its kind. Slayer kept his reputation intact by slaying the beast without leaving the deck.

But he, like the rest of the crew, stood helpless before the storms.

The ship rocked hard to port. The squall showed no promise of easing as the boat tried to make way to Poros. Slayer *had* to reach the isle, and no sea monster would keep him from doing so. A griffin had stolen the love of his life, and the last rumor put her on that spit of land.

According to the whispers, the griffin belonged to a Titan who ordered it to capture the fair maiden Megara and take her to Poros. It was said this Titan occasionally visited the island to have her. Slayer did not fully believe the tale, but he'd eliminated all other rumors of her whereabouts. After years of searching, he was losing hope of ever finding his beautiful Megara.

A wave crashed against the starboard side and nearly heeled the ship. Slayer clung to the mast as the sea threatened to take him. The wave washed past and poured down the port side. The boat lunged upright again as he coughed and heaved out the saltwater which sought to drown him.

As the storm continued to lash the boat, his thoughts turned back to Megara. She had spurned him, though he still wondered why. He was as strong as a Minotaur. His father possessed wealth that would one day be his. Other women told him he was handsome enough, but none had claimed his love. Not even Megara had truly captured his affection—not until he'd watched the griffin grab her in its talons and fly into the unreachable sky. It was then he felt his heart had been ripped from his chest. He had not stopped searching for her since that fateful day. It felt like an unending quest.

A thunderous crack shook the boat and slammed Slayer to the deck. A massive wave engulfed the ship. His feet became entangled within lines attached to barrels. The wave cast the entire tangle into the darkened sea.

The heavy barrels plummeted toward the sea floor, taking Slayer with them. No matter his struggles, he remained tied fast. He looked up to the surface as a lightning bolt lit the outline of the ship he'd been thrown from. *Goodbye Megara.*

Slayer felt warm. He floated. He sought.
Then he heard them.
"What do you seek?"
"Happiness. Contentment."
"Where do you look?"
"Through the ages."
"How long have you sought?"
"This lifetime."
"Shall we show you the way?"
"No, the quest is mine."
"Then, carry on to the next life."

Skulls littered the ground at the mouth of the dragon's cave. Beyond, darkness hid all. No bird sang. No cricket chirped. No creature dared come near. Or if any did, they did so silently. Slayer, ever observant, followed their lead. He kept as still as the boulders strewn along the mountainside.

The full moon had begun its descent in the west. Soon, it would be at Slayer's back. The darkness of the cave entrance would be chased back by the soft glow for the space of one hour. The creature hated light, from sun or moon. Sunlight drove it too far back into the close confines of the cave. However, the softer moonlight would cause the fearsome beast to retreat only slightly, leaving room for him and his men to encircle the dragon. Then it could be trapped and killed quickly.

Slayer counted the skulls. How many fools had tried to battle this dragon alone? Here lay at least a dozen, in various stages of decay. The putrid odors from the rotting flesh—coupled with the naturally horrendous odor of dragons—made many of the men retch, yet Slayer had hardened his stomach to the assault on his senses.

He and the men, who had served with him for years, arrived at the dragon's lair and waited two days for it to fly out in search of food. Once it left, they laid out a net on the cave floor that was twice the creature's size, covering the thick ropes with mud and gravel. Six men stayed inside and hid along the rock wall of the dragon's lair with the gut-wrenching, blood-soaked mud smeared onto their bodies. This would hide their natural odor from the beast.

The dragon returned and retreated to the depths of its cave. Now, they waited, silent and motionless.

The moonlight had slid down the rock face of the mountainside, almost touching the ground. The time drew near. When the moonlight reached the ground, the opening would be fully lit. Slayer would stand at the mouth of the dragon's den, and shout for all he was worth. When the dragon lunged toward him, his men would ensnare the wings in that net so Slayer could drive his sword deep through its ear and into the skull.

This had been his quest, to kill dragons, since one of the beasts had dined on his own kin. When he was but a child, a dragon came to the family homestead in the middle of the night. Slayer stayed where his mother had hidden him, and had a clear view when the dragon landed and swept her up in its claws, biting her in half. It then grabbed his older brother, who had tried to rescue their mother, and squeezed the life out of him. The images still haunted Slayer's dreams to no end.

The moonlight touched the ground before the cave. Slayer ran to the entrance, making as much noise as possible along the way. He wanted the dragon to be aware he was coming, and not become too aware of the smell of men inside.

Slayer bellowed and screeched and waved his sword as he reached the mouth of the cave. He searched for the massive shadow outline that would herald the dragon. He was not made to wait long. The odor of the monster assaulted his senses. He had trained himself not to blink at the onslaught. *Swallow the urge to vomit while fighting the beast.*

The behemoth roared as it lumbered through the passageway. As it bent its neck to peer out of the cave, the men surrounding it sprang. Two in the front jumped over the lowered neck with their ends of the netting, while the two at the forelegs and the two at the hind legs climbed up and over the beast. It was entangled in a matter of heartbeats.

It tried to take a step forward and stumbled in the trap. Slayer raised his sword and aimed for the soft point of its recessed ear. As his sword was in mid-thrust, the animal twisted its neck. Slayer felt his bones crunch as he was crushed between the beast's skull and the rock wall. Blackness consumed him.

Slayer felt warm. He floated. He sought.
Then he heard them.
"What do you seek?"
"Contentment. Happiness."
"Where do you look?"
"Through the ages."
"How long have you sought?"
"This lifetime."
"Shall we show you the way?"
"No, the quest is mine."
"Then, carry on to the next life."

The fire singed the hair on his arm as he covered his eyes. The searing heat made it hard to breathe, harder to cry out. But he had to find her.

"Cynthia! Where are you?"

He had called 9-1-1 before running back into the inferno. The fire department should be in the driveway by now. The rest of his family was safe, but he hadn't found Cindy. She should have been in her room, but she wasn't. He continued his search upstairs, trying to find her in defiance of the flames.

He opened the door to the spare room. A wave of heat threw him back, crashing him against the wall. His head spun as he slid to the floor.

"Cindy," he gasped.

He thought he could hear sirens over the roar of the flames. They were faint, though. Why had it taken them so damn long? He raised himself to his hands and knees and crawled along the carpet; the smoke above was thick and suffocating.

"Cynthia. Where are you?" Tears of frustration pooled with those brought by the smoke's acrid touch. He choked on the sulfuric fumes coming from the paint he stored in the spare room.

A crash came from downstairs. He could only hope it was his fellow firemen come to rescue the rescuer.

He heard his buddy, Captain Truck, call out, "Slayer!"

"Here." His voice was weak, small. He kept crawling, looking for his daughter. They had been fighting that evening about her cutting classes—all the money she'd spent, the lies. All of it meant nothing. He had to find her. He had to find her alive.

Slayer took as deep a breath as he dared. "Cynthia! God damn it! Answer me! Where are you?"

The flames grew quiet then, as if taking a breath, themselves. In the eerie stillness, he heard the faint cry. "Daddy?"

An explosion of flames burst forth, drowning all other sound, but he'd heard her. Her frightened whisper had come from the spare room. He fell onto his belly, dragging his burned body beneath the raging fire.

"Cynthia! I'm here, baby! Daddy's here! Call to me, baby girl. I can't see you."

"Dad! I'm in the closet and I can't open the door!"

"I'm here, sweetheart. The ladder fell against the door. I'll get it. Hold on, baby. Tell me you're OK."

"I'm OK, Daddy. Please be careful!"

Slayer rose to his hands and knees and tried to coax the six-foot, searing-hot metal ladder out of the way. Rough hands grabbed his shoulders and dragged him away from the door. Lifted off of the floor by his arms and legs, he squirmed and fought those holding him.

"No! Cynthia!"

"Lieutenant Slayer! Please, stop fighting!"

"Truck," Slayer gasped. "It's Cynthia. She's in the closet. Please get her!"

The two firemen set him down in the hall and went back into the room. The Captain took off his helmet and mask and leaned close to Slayer's face.

"You ain't slaying this one, Lieutenant Slayer. This fire almost got you and your girl," Truck shouted over the flames. "We're gonna get you both out of here!"

As the Captain spoke the words, the two firemen lifted Slayer's seventeen-year-old daughter out of the closet.

"Cynthia!" Slayer sobbed. She clung to the neck of one fireman as the three rushed past him and disappeared into the smoke down the hall. Her hand reaching out to him was the last he saw of his daughter. His quest to save her was done. Relief rushed through him as Captain Truck lifted him from the floor.

A crack of timber above Slayer and Truck's head was the last thing he heard.

Slayer felt tired. In his exhaustion, he floated.

Then he heard them.

"What do you seek?"

"The end of my quest."

"Where do you look?"

"Through the ages."

"How long have you sought?"

"Too many lifetimes."

"Shall we show you the way?"

"Yes, please."

"Follow us, brave one. Your quest is done."

POETIC JUSTICE
BY EDMUND WELLS

It was another quiet Friday evening in Olney, Illinois, with only a Pocket Poetry reading at the Elm Street Starbucks to look forward to at 9:00. The sofa creaked beneath Oliver in a complaining sort of whine. This week, the ancient Japanese Haiku.
He frowned at the scrawl on his note pad.

Orion cries out,
   The Pen skewering his eye—
My Lady flies free!

Oliver crumpled the poem and tossed it onto a growing pile of paper-ball failures. No one would understand it anyway, least of all some neo-hippies revved up on mochachino. The structure was easy to work with, but blank verse was his preference, as immortalized by his man, Bill.
A passing glance at his cell phone.
Maybe he should just grade papers until the call came. *If* it came. Some weekends passed without incident, and those were the worst. His powers were being wasted, just sitting here, untold crimes going unseen and therefore unpunished. But he needed to be ready. Let the major super heroes pick up the slack for his absenteeism. They got all the credit, anyway. The minor heroes still had regular lives to lead, rents to pay... hopes to keep alive. Oliver knew his priorities.
He pressed the stereo remote; sweet violins twirled through the air. *Ah, Mozart.*
With a sigh, he plucked the first essay from the pile. *Which of Shakespeare's villains was the most villainous—Richard III, MacBeth or Iago? Compare and contrast.* A smile quirked his lips. They should *all* be fitted for a suit of flame, although Lord MacBeth allowed himself to be poisoned by Lady MacBeth's dark ambitions rather than his own.
The phone rang.
He leaped up and grabbed it. "Prithee, speak."

"McDonnell Planetarium, St. Louis." A woman's whisper. Sultry. "Tomorrow night."

His heart leaped like a stallion. "How farest thou, my love? Hast thou yet 'scaped?"

A pregnant pause, her breathing quick, shallow. A vision of Cassie's long red curls falling about her divine face, her coral lips trembling, nearby roses fist-fighting to smell as sweet as she. "Not all will survive, this time."

Oliver blinked, heat rising to his cheeks. Her flair for prophecy was well documented, but was often misleading. And he'd struggled for so long to free her... "Poetic Justice cannot die, sweet Cassandra, and neither shalt thee. That leavest only Bernard, that fat—"

"I must go. Be careful."

The line went dead. She could never risk talking long.

Hands trembling, Oliver ran a Google search. The James S. McDonnell planetarium was part of the St. Louis Science Center, which included a multi-level science museum, an IMAX Theatre, and a *Star Trek* Exhibit with a full-size bridge from the USS *Enterprise*. How... mature.

So Bernard would be there, eh? Plotting his next deviltry... but what? He was a Trekkie, of course—weren't all science nerds? But as an astronomy teacher, the lout would naturally be drawn to the planetarium, as Cassie had indicated.

He clicked a link.

The planetarium advertised a laser light show, this Saturday, featuring the music of the Grateful Dead. *Zounds!* A pity it wasn't Pink Floyd. The ad touted a Zeiss Mark IX star projector, one of only a handful in the world, with a grant from *blah-blah-blah*. Much ado about nothing. First showing at 9:00 p.m.

Humming, he poured himself a glass of cognac. He would finish grading the essays tonight, pack a bag, and head off to deal with Bernard—the self-styled *Orion the Hunter*—tomorrow.

* * *

It was less than a three-hour drive from Olney to St. Louis. Oliver knew this from his visits to the small city's annual Shakespeare Festival, where he'd sometimes enacted minor roles. His beloved white VW Beetle thrummed beneath him, charging along Route 50, as eager as he for vengeance. He played a little Wagner to heighten his mood.

The miles passed and his mind drifted, lulled by the fleeting scenery as dusk descended around him. *Five years*. It was hard to believe it had been that long since he and Bernard had eaten those irradiated espresso cookies, changing each of their lives forever. Back then, they'd both been dating Chrissie, and despite competing strenuously for her affection, somehow each had gotten into the same batch of cookies.

Being the bully that physics teachers often were, Bernard assumed the role of the anti-hero *Orion* and kidnapped Chrissie, re-named her Cassandra for the mythological prophetess, and made her his captive. Now trapped with that astronomical ass in his secret hideout, she was afraid for her life to attempt escape.

And so his nemesis was born.

As extraordinary as Cassie was, she was no heroine. Her main attributes were her brains, her foresight, and her astounding beauty— and not necessarily in that order. Her career as an Art History and French teacher were now behind her, as was her more profitable profession as a nude model for artists in and around Chicago. She also happened to be a fantastic baker—with one notable exception.

In Oliver's guise as *Poetic Justice*, he had nearly rescued Cassie a dozen times—at the Lowell Observatory in Flagstaff, where Orion made off with a telescope; at a lab in Rochester, where he stole a laser; at a Cal-Tech research library, which Orion burned to the ground; a private auction in Dallas, where he stole the *Polar Star Diamond*; and even on the Cyclone at Coney Island, where he'd tossed flash-bang grenades at patrons, just for laughs.

The man was mad, north by northwest, and in every other direction on the compass.

On most of these occasions, the intensity of his and Orion's struggles over Cassie resulted in unfortunate injuries to her divine body—concussions, broken arms and legs, twisted ankles, burns, and so on—and more than once she'd nearly been killed.

Not all will survive, this time, Cassie had warned. He'd need to take special care to ensure that only Orion was harmed this time. Permanently, if necessary.

At 7:50 p.m., with over an hour to spare, he took the second St. Louis exit and drove to the Scottish Arms, a small restaurant and pub within a mile of the science center. Not the fanciest of places, but on a teacher's salary one had to be frugal. He and other Shakespearean actors liked to come here after a performance for some imported whisky, cock-a-leekie pie, and a little impromptu *MacBeth*.

The pub's owner, a native Scotsman named Scot, stood behind the bar, tidying up. He offered a gap-toothed grin. "Evenin', mi' lord," quoth he, inclining his head. "Islay whisky?"

Oliver nodded, settling onto a stool. "This castle hath a pleasant seat; the air nimbly and sweetly recommends itself unto our gentle senses."

Scot sniffed the air and hoisted a bristly eyebrow. "The cleaning wench does her part, aye." He poured out a drink. "Is the Bard back in town, then?"

"Nay, sweet Scotsman." He drained his glass; the smoky malt flavor warmed his throat. "A play o' laser lights, if truth be told. Held at yon starry planetarium—a different sort of Globe Theatre, one might say." He chuckled.

"I dinnae ken such displays were o' interest to ye."

"Thou thinkest aright, worthy thane." Oliver motioned for a refill. "'Tis business alone brings me forth this portentous night. And... a fried Mars bar, mayhap." Sweets were his greatest weakness. Even Superman had his kryptonite.

As Scot retreated to the kitchens, ablaze with the bright fires o' Scotland, a conversation reached Oliver's ears. Three young men at a nearby table debated over what the opening Grateful Dead tune would be at the laser show. As if one drug-induced jam-fest were any different than another. He emptied his glass, his duty clear.

Oliver stood and, moving with a bit of a whisky-swagger, approached their table. "Friends, non-Romans, countrymen. Lend me your ears."

Three pairs of eyes scowled up at him, like witches round a cauldron of beer.

"We're using them," one quipped.

Philistines. "Toil and trouble await at yon Dead Fest," Oliver continued. "Best stay clear and smoke your ill-gotten herbs elsewhere."

A bearded youth whose t-shirt depicted a skull in a top hat spoke first. "You a cop?"

No, cops are paid better. "Not precisely. I'm an English teacher."

The trio exchanged quizzical glances. "Have a seat, dude." A chubby fellow whose shirt showed a skeleton with red roses in its hair motioned to an empty chair. "We planned for this trip a while. What sort of trouble?"

Sighing, Oliver took the proffered seat. A plump, tawny-haired waitress reached over his shoulder and set down a plate cradling his fried candy bar, alongside another glass of whisky.

"I thank thee verily, O lusty wench." He slapped her on the rump.

The three youths looked on as Oliver attacked his snack with a fork and knife. "When sorrows come," he said, chewing, "they come not as single spies, but in battalions." He glanced up. "*Hamlet*, act 4, scene 5."

"So, an army is going to attack the planetarium?"

Oliver swallowed his final delicious morsel. "Nay, fool. Not an army, an *Orion*. Which is worse, but also marches on its stomach." He chuckled.

The brood of male witches blinked. "Dude," one said, seizing Oliver's whisky glass. "You've had too much to drink, methinks."

"And you got some chocolate on your ruffles."

A glance down revealed this to be true. He licked the corner of his napkin and rubbed the smudge furiously. "Out, damned spot. Out I say!"

One of them slid his whisky glass back to him. "Then again, maybe you need more of this."

Oliver took the glass and finished it off.

"You should hang with us," said the one in the top hat.

"Yeah, we'll skip the laser show, okay? Just chill out."

A strange lassitude spread over Oliver, his muscles loosening. "You gentlemen of Verona stay here," he said, his tongue thick. His vision blurred; his eyes felt as heavy as coffin lids. "I must reckon with that rogue, Orion, whose boorish, er, fatness imperils my sweet lady." He tried to stand, but his legs had turned into rubber chickens; he collapsed.

Three smiling faces leered down at him. "I think you'll hang with us."

Oliver's eyes slammed shut. *One may smile and smile and be a villain...*

* * *

Oliver floated on a cloud. The angelic countenance of Cassandra gazed down upon him, a beatific goddess, her skin as fair as sunlight, blue eyes like stars glimmering from the heaven of her crimson curls. All around him, the voices of cherubs ebbed and flowed, like violins weaving a tapestry of light through a heavenly mist.

"...heavier than he freaking looks ...what's with all the Shakespeare quotes? ...don't forget your gas mask ...projector is worth three point five mil? ...dude, drive faster..."

At long last, his feather's flight came to rest and the sweet voices faded into silence.

He awoke to darkness, a cloth across his face. The distant thunder of music vibrated the walls. The laser show was near, it seemed, and so would be his nemesis. He reached to remove the offending fabric and learned his hands were cuffed behind him to a metal chair. His mind still whirled in a pleasurable haze, but less pleasant thoughts were breaking through. The thrice-headed swine had drugged his whisky. His teeth clenched.

Those Dead Heads were dead.

Thank the gods the fools hadn't gagged him. "Rings of steel clasped o'er my wrists; Loose thy hold and turn to mist." And lo, the handcuffs faded. Being a minor hero, as well as an English teacher, offered certain advantages over being a cop... notwithstanding the free coffee.

He tore off the blindfold. By virtue of a band of light seeping under a door, Oliver saw he was inside a utility closet: shelves of cleaning chemicals, paper products, tools, fuses and the like, alongside mops, brooms, and other janitorial implements of war.

And now, behold the trappings of *Poetic Justice*!

"Come cloak, night's veil, fend me from harm; Come sword, bright blade, strengthen mine arm." In a ballet of poetry, his clothes transformed to a mantle of shadow, while at his side appeared a slender sword—one he'd dubbed *The Pen*.

He had to smile. Since every writer worth his salt knew that "the pen" was mightier than the sword, his blade was, ipso facto, mightier than itself, hence an oxymoron only the literate would appreciate. Let the minions of the hard sciences tremble!

"Come what may, time and the hour run through the roughest day."

Oliver turned the handle and drew the door slowly inward. No one stood guard. Clearly, his foes bore little respect for the resourcefulness of the liberal artist. As he crept from the hidden alcove, the sound of the Dead grew louder, extolling the sundry virtues of truck drivers.

The room opened up, widening into what appeared to be the museum's lobby, devoid of patrons or workers at this late hour. To his left, a giant rubberized T-Rex scowled at him. Nearby, a triceratops looked on with stoic indifference. An "Energy Ball Machine" loomed in another corner, its myriad metal rails running off to all corners of the building. High overhead, an impressive model of the solar system shone in the darkness, the planets circling a yellow sun in quiet splendor.

All very nice, but as nothing compared to the power of a heroic couplet, a razor wit, or a well-crafted hyperbole.

A neon arrow marked "Planetarium" split the darkness.

Cloaked in shadow, Oliver followed the kindly arrow's lead and soon came upon a policeman, slouching near a set of double doors. His head bobbed to the rhythm of the pulsing music, threatening to dislodge his hat, which already sat somewhat askew.

While Oliver's duties as a hero were rather loftier than those of a common policeman, they both worked for the public good, and he was loathe to harm a man or woman in blue.

In the darkness, the policeman lit a doobie... proving he was no policeman. Or, at the very least, not one on duty.

Oliver crept closer, keeping to the pseudo-cop's peripheral vision, and leaped out. "You, sir, are so slow-witted," Oliver shouted, "that merely *thinking* about continental drift exhausts you."

The counterfeit cop blinked once, twice, scratching his head, and then collapsed. Few appreciated the power of the hyperbole. Oliver searched the young man and removed a gas mask hanging from his belt, and twenty dollars from his wallet. He also located a hand gun and emptied its chambers of cartridges.

Here Oliver faced a problem. If he donned the gas mask, presumably to avoid some noxious vapor Orion intended to expel from lord-knows-where, he'd be unable to articulate his verses, which were his greatest power. Without the mask, he might be rendered senseless, or worse. Unlike Orion, who had somehow developed an immunity to poisons following his anti-heroic transformation, Poetic Justice remained vulnerable to the thousand natural shocks that flesh was heir to.

It seemed he had little choice.

He strapped the mask on and opened the door, one hand clutching *The Pen*.

A wall of noise assaulted him. Rainbow lights split the smoke-filled air in a frenzy of spinning lances. The domed sky above was illuminated by a thousand dancing bears of every color, all of them smiling. Closer to the ground, a cloud of neon-green gas swirled and slithered, like an evil mist from some cheap science fiction movie. Even amidst the seething psychedelic drama, something was amiss. The crowd sat in utter silence, motionless, a sea of overweight, middle-aged hippies staring with slack jaws into the flickering madness of the bear-infested sky.

Not entirely unusual for Dead Heads, but still odd *en masse*.

At the center of the domed theatre, four shapes scurried about a spherical machine, perhaps seven feet in diameter, which rose up on four slender legs. The surface of the contraption was covered in dozens of multi-sized lenses, making clear it served as the planetarium's star projector. The laser machine itself was a mere black box, flickering away in another corner.

Three of the toiling men wore gas masks—the duplicitous Dead Heads from the Scottish Arms, no doubt—each applying tools to dismantle the projector's legs. A fourth figure towered over the others, pointing here and there, not deigning to wear a mask.

Orion.

He wore light leather armor, a short hunter's cape, and leather sandals with straps that crisscrossed his bulbous calves. A longbow rose above one shoulder, while a short sword hung at his hip. If the great Roman gladiator, Spartacus, had lived comfortably into his fifties, spent a few decades on a couch subsisting on beer and stuffed-crust pizza, and had otherwise given up on grooming, you'd have a close approximation to what Bernard looked like. It wasn't pretty.

Due to his impressive paunch, Orion could hardly swing his sword, but was a fair shot with the bow. Of greatest concern was his gravity belt, which heroically circled the man's mighty midsection. It was a contraption he'd built, its power focused through three star-like gemstones embedded in the belt.

Oliver wondered if perhaps Cassandra had been left at home for this caper, when she appeared from around a corner, like a shaft of sunlight breaking through weed-scented storm clouds. The red-haired beauty strolled backwards, spraying the aisles with green gas from a tank strapped to her back. Her attire was tailored to the audience: clear platform shoes, tie-dyed bandana, dancing-bear tube top, and curve-hugging bell-bottoms. The only item out of place was her gas mask.

Had they not been catatonic, the hippies would have applauded her outfit.

Oliver needed to get her attention without alerting the others to his own presence. He removed the mask. "Divine Cassandra, hear my plea; Stroll thy buttocks nearer to me." Okay, so that one needed some work, but it had the benefit of being a heroic couplet.

As if uncertain of what she'd heard, Cassie's shoulders slowly swung about, and their eyes met. He replaced his mask. Crouching in the doorway, he waved an arm, urging her toward him. *Come live with me and be my love, and we will all the pleasures prove...*

She cast a furtive glance toward Orion, prompting Oliver to do the same.

The star projector now hovered in the green-misted air, two beams reaching from Orion's belt like arms of light. His three lackeys stood by, dancing and congratulating each other. Oliver was forced to think of Luke Skywalker's lifting of objects while training to be a Jedi... not that he'd ever seen that silly movie. Just clips.

Cassandra began backing toward Oliver, continuing to spray mist in her wake. Damn if her cheeks weren't the very definition of callipygian... He'd have to compose a sonnet.

When she was within a dozen feet of the door, a cry of alarm went up. Eyes wide, she shrugged off the gas tank and bolted. Oliver extended an arm and clasped her pretty hand just as a beam struck her; she collapsed to the ground like a ton of bricks—dainty ones, of course.

No! Oliver bent down to lift her, but she was far too heavy, held in the crushing grip of Orion's gravity beam—damn him! A second beam stabbed into Oliver, negated by the charms imbuing his cloak. It was the only defense he'd been able to devise, though it was less effective against other modes of attack, such as Orion's arrows.

He ran, heading for the cover of the information desk.

He was struggling with a verse for something that rhymed with triceratops, when a roar shook the air—louder even than Jerry Garcia's echoing admonitions to Casey Jones, that notorious train conductor and cocaine dealer.

A sizzle of energy struck Oliver in the back. This time, rather than dissipate harmlessly, he flew upward, gaining speed as he hurtled toward an ever-growing solar system. The bastard had used an *anti-*gravity beam! If he didn't slow down, he'd go splat on the ceiling, four stories up, and then double splat when gravity returned to normal.

Oliver needed a quick verse, but was drawing a blank. Heart pounding, he blurted the only words he could recall that had any relevance to flying:

"Fair is foul, and foul is fair; hover through the filthy air."

The witches' chant from *MacBeth* seemed to do the trick; his ascent slowed. Narrowly avoiding a collision with Mars, Oliver grabbed hold of rafters near the ceiling and held on for dear life. A few moments later, the pull of Orion's anti-gravity relented and normal gravity re-asserted itself.

Gravity sucks.

Far below, Oliver could see that Orion had once again asserted control over the star projector, which hovered before him like some alien robot prisoner. Trailing behind, Cassandra floated like an angelic balloon, bound in a cocoon of light. Orion's three lackeys led the procession; two opened the service exit doors while the third entered a box truck parked outside.

Orion was going to march right under him.

Moving as fast as he dared, still buoyant from his "hover" verse but taking no chances, Oliver climbed along the rafters to the center of the solar system. *The Pen* rang as it flew from its sheath.

"Orion foul, Cassandra fair; Strike down my foe, her life please spare."

A slash parted the central cable, dropping sun, earth and all the planets. The gravity cocoon surrounding Cassie would shield her from harm—or so he prayed.

A tremendous crash echoed through the open-air lobby, like a garbage truck dropped off the Empire State Building. A cloud of dust rose up, mingling with tendrils of green mist, and the squealing contraption came to rest, quivering like a giant swatted spider.

The two hapless lackeys picked themselves up, coughing. They stumbled into the idling box truck, which screeched off before the real police could arrive.

Cassie's words of prophecy came to him unbidden. *Not all will survive, this time.*

Through dry lips, Oliver repeated the *MacBeth* witches' chant and floated to the ground. Heart in his throat, he crept toward the astronomical wreckage, afraid to find what fate had delivered by his hand.

Searching, he encountered a pair delicate feet clad in see-through platform shoes, extending from behind a smooth, ivory-colored orb—Venus. *Oh, please gods, no*. He circled around to see the planetary body pressed up against Cassandra's rosy cheek. A trickle of blood ran from one tiny nostril. Stifling a cry, he reached under her arms and dragged her free.

She groaned.

"Cassie, my love! Art thou all right?"

She lifted herself up to her elbows. "What... what happened?" She looked around. "Is he dead?"

"I don't know yet."

Oliver lifted Cassie under one arm, helping her to her feet. "I'm okay," she said, rubbing her head. "We need to be certain about Bernard." An eager gleam seemed to alight behind her blue eyes.

Walking arm in arm, the pair circled the celestial detritus, stepping over bent metal bars, working their way toward the center. The janitor was going to be pissed. They rounded Mercury, and there they found him, Orion the Hunter, his rotund form buried beneath the yellow curvature of the sun. *Splat.*

At long last, death had found him—and nothing in his life became him like the leaving it.

Oliver paused a moment to consider the poetic justice of Orion, one of the brightest constellations in the night sky, meeting his end by being crushed by a star—and a false one at that. The irony of it was not displeasing, to say the least.

* * *

Later that night, after verifying that the crowd of catatonic Dead Heads had recovered without any permanent damage—at least no more than their usual habits inflicted—Oliver drove Cassie to Bernard's secret hideout to retrieve her things. It turned out to be an underground lair, complete with an observatory, game room, movie theatre, and a dome much like a planetarium, where the sociopathic astronomer would have installed the stolen Zeiss star projector.

It seemed like a lot of effort when the planetarium's admission price was only $5.00.

Oliver sat on a sofa in Bernie's living room, watching television, while Cassie showered and changed into something less groovy.

An Agatha Christie movie mystery was in progress.

His stomach growled. It had been a long time since he'd eaten, and a fried Mars bar was only so nutritious. He poked around inside Bernie's ex-refrigerator. Beer, beer, mustard, pickles, more beer, catsup, an empty pizza box, and leftover potato salad. Not much to choose from.

Tucked away at the back of the fridge, he noticed a white box wrapped in blue ribbon. Now, this looked promising... He untied the ribbon to find a dozen tarts!

Huzzah! A little victory celebration was overdue. Orion the Hunter was no more, he had ceased to be... and the world was now a safer, less malodorous place. He'd rescued the beautiful damsel, Cassandra, from the ogre's greasy fingers. She was now Oliver's to cherish and protect, and take to *Victoria's Secret*. If that wasn't worth celebrating, what was?

Cassie was certainly taking her sweet time changing. *Time and tide wait for no man*, or so quoth Chaucer. That sentiment applied doubly to women.

Humming a jaunty tune, he took the tarts and a bottle of Heineken to Bernie's ex-sofa. *Mmm... delicious!* That tart of a wench certainly knew how to bake tarts! Though the almonds were a tad bitter. No matter. He devoured a couple more, chasing them down with beer.

He eyed the ongoing television drama, trying to recall if he'd seen it before. A man at a dinner party raised a toast to his guests, drank some champagne and collapsed, dead as a doorknob. Yes... he'd read this novel, he was certain. What was it called?

"To you, Bernard." He raised his bottle. "I hope it hurt." His heart raced, a feeling of light-headed joy washing over him.

Cassandra would probably go back to teaching. Or better yet, she could join him in his quest against evil as an associate heroine. With her powers of foresight, they'd make an excellent duo, stopping crimes before they began. And at long last, they could be married.

His breathing grew more rapid, and he could feel a headache coming on. He needed to calm down; he was becoming giddy with excitement.

Cassandra entered the living room, her body wrapped in a towel. A beautiful raven-haired woman followed, holding Cassie's hand, her voluptuous body barely concealed in a short silken kimono. She cast a smile at Oliver, her bright green eyes impish.

"Oh, I see you've already found our little gift." Cassandra kissed Oliver on the cheek. "This is Morgana, as I like to call her. She's also an artist. And better with herbs than I am. She made the tarts."

What? Where did she come from? His muscles felt listless, his breathing labored.

"We wanted to thank you for getting rid of Bernie, though it took longer than expected. He was a tough nut to crack. Just our luck he'd be immune to poison, eh?" She winked, tilting her head. "The hideout is a little stuffy, but it has a lovely open-air grotto where the light is just perfect for painting or photography, or just making love."

Morgana leaned toward Cassandra and kissed her on the ear.

Trembling, Oliver tried to stand, but his legs wouldn't support him. He strained to find the air. "Cass... help... me."

There was no pity in her eyes. "I don't think so, Oliver. There'll be no more idiotic men fighting over me day and night, hurting me, dressing me like a whore, or dictating how I can live my life. Apart from the smell, you were little different than he was. I only wish the espresso cookies had killed you both as intended, rather than turning you into second-rate super jerks." The pair sat on a love seat, holding hands, watching him. "Goodbye, Oliver."

Sparkling Cyanide... that was the movie. A laugh escaped him in a hoarse croak.

So, he'd killed Bernie to free Cassandra—an act encouraged by her—only to then be poisoned by Cassandra so she could be free of Oliver as well. Furthermore, he was dying in his enemy's *living* room, having eaten poisoned tarts in celebration of his enemy's death, baked by his girlfriend's girlfriend, while a murder mystery played in the background. Cyanide tasted like bitter almonds, as Agatha Christie's lesson came to him, not nearly in the nick of time.

The delicious irony of it all was killing him.

The room spun, his eyesight falling to dusk. His mind raced alongside his fluttering heart. Why would Cassie do this? He loved her with every fiber of his being, had devoted his life over the past five years to rescuing her... and *this* was his reward? Murder most foul?

Love was truly blind.

Anger flared in him, shoving sadness and regret aside.

From Hell's heart, I stab at thee...

Through cracked lips, his final words flew like icy daggers. "Cassandra, dear, apart we'll never be; our spirits joined through all eternity."

Her scream filled his ears, and everything faded to black.

WIPEOUT
BY A. C. HALL

"You're not even going to let me peek?" Max asked through the door.

He dropped to his belly on the floor and tried to see into the bedroom. All he could make out were shadows, but the smell left no doubt as to what his roommate was doing.

"When it's done, you'll know it," Reginald said from inside the locked room. "You know how you'll know?"

Max sighed and rolled his eyes.

"Because I'll tell you," Reginald said. "Now stop trying to look under the door and go get us some food."

Accepting defeat, Max got up and brushed himself off. The one bedroom apartment was tiny, but Max prided himself on keeping it clean. He moved to the couch and started putting on his disguise. The pieces were well worn, from the tattered blue cape to the ripped wide brim hat and the cracked demon mask, but it had served him well over the years. He was just about to strap on the mask when someone knocked on the door.

He moved to the door cautiously. Less than a handful of people knew they lived here, and only a couple of those people ever came by.

"Who's there?" Max asked, trying to disguise his voice.

"Lemme in, I'm gonna sweat to death in this thing."

Max smiled and opened the door. No matter what kind of day he was having, seeing his cousin in her full body chicken costume always put a smile on his face. It was dirty from years of use, and the sewn on eyes were long gone, giving the chicken head an odd appearance.

He stepped aside as she came in. Max leaned out into the hallway to make sure she hadn't been followed. He made sure to lock all three locks on the door, then turned to greet his cousin. She had the chicken head off and was wiping the sweat from her face. Even wet with perspiration, her bright red hair was still the first thing he noticed.

"What, do I look awful or something?" she snapped.

For some reason, Beth had been on edge the last few times she came over. Max put his hand over his heart and smiled. "Hand to God, you're a sweat soaked beauty," he said.

Beth punched him in the arm, but he barely felt it due to her oversized chicken gloves. His comment did the trick, however, and she was smiling now. "You headed out?" she asked.

He nodded. "Food run. We haven't eaten in a few days."

"Is it done?" Beth asked, motioning towards the bedroom.

"Not sure, but he's really close. We don't have much money, so if he's sending me on a food run then I think he's just about ready to celebrate," Max said. He went into the kitchen and pulled a small bag out of the cabinet. He tucked it into his shirt, then turned to face Beth. "You okay alone with him for a bit?" he asked.

She gave him a dirty look. "I'm not a kid anymore, Max."

It was hard for him to admit, but she was right. He'd been looking after her since she was twelve and he was sixteen, but now she was twenty two.

"I know, but don't forget who he is," Max said.

"I've been around peddlers before."

"He's not a peddler, he's *the* peddler, one of the originals," Max reminded her.

Beth crossed her arms. Even though she was upset, it was hard to take her seriously while she was still in her chicken suit.

"You trust him, you told me you do," Beth said.

"I know I said that, and I meant it, but that doesn't mean he's a saint. Don't forget what this guy and the originals did to the world."

This wasn't a new argument, and he could tell Beth was getting upset.

"The world wasn't innocent in that, you know," she seethed. "And besides, he's changed. Reggie's trying to fix the world now."

Max sighed. He didn't disagree with her, so he wasn't even sure why he was picking a fight about it.

"I just want you to stay alert, even around people you trust. One slip up and that's it," Max said.

Anytime he parented her, she couldn't stay mad at him. She uncrossed her arms and came up to him. She put her chicken gloved hand on his shoulder and said, "I'll be fine. Just go get the food."

Before Max could follow her instruction, she turned her back to him and pointed. "But unzip me first. I gotta get out of this fricken chicken."

Max unzipped the chicken suit for her, then picked up his demon mask and put it on. She called out to him as he reached the door. "How long will you be gone?"

Max shrugged. "Thirty, forty-five, something like that."

Beth nodded and waved.

"Lock up behind me," Max said as he left.

He waited outside until he heard the door lock, then took off down the hallway. His pace was always quick inside the apartment building. Becoming too familiar to the people in the area was a death sentence. The less time he spent out in the open, the better.

Max avoided the main stairs, instead going all the way down to the service steps at the far end of the hall. He rushed down them, knowing that a run-in with the wrong person in such an enclosed space could be the death of him.

When he reached the bottom he shoved the heavy steel door open, emerging on the side of the building. He took a deep breath of the fresh air and relaxed slightly. Now there was open space to run if he needed to, and that always made him feel better.

Max made sure his costume was still in place, concealing any notable traits about him. Satisfied that it was, he moved around to the front of the building.

"Oh no," Max mumbled.

A pretty young woman was dancing on the sidewalk in front of the building. She was one of their neighbors, Jennifer, and her disguise of choice was a hockey mask with glitter all over it. But there was no disguise anymore. She was completely nude, and dancing in place as fast as she could. Max moved towards her quickly.

Her eyes shot over to him as he approached, but she didn't stop dancing. A maniacal smile was stuck on her face and she was covered in sweat. He could tell that she'd been out there dancing for a while.

"Jennifer, who'd you trust?" Max asked quietly. "Didn't you listen when I told you to stop telling people who you are?"

It was crushing to see her in this position, but not surprising. The third time they'd met, she had revealed her face to Max. He tried to warn her about doing that, but it was just who she was. Jennifer was warm and beautiful and trusting. Now she would be dead.

"Who got you?" Max asked.

He knew she couldn't answer him, so he scanned the streets, trying to see if whoever had cursed her was openly watching. People didn't come out onto the streets unless they had to, and the few people he saw looked to be minding their own business. A few younger looking men in kabuki masks were gawking from across the street, but there was nothing sinister about them.

"Show's over!" Max yelled. "Scram!"

The two of them pointed and laughed, but when he started to come towards them they ran. Max returned to Jennifer, frowning as he stared into her frightened eyes. She couldn't speak, but her stare screamed for help.

Max put his hand on her shoulder and pushed. It was like pushing on the side of a building. Whoever had cursed her had specified that she couldn't move from this spot. He shook his head, then pulled off his cape and draped it over her. At least she could die with a little bit of dignity.

"I'm sorry," Max said.

He turned and walked away, knowing that if he hung around too long whoever cursed her might see him. He'd spent most of his life trying to avoid being noticed, and his instincts kept him from changing that now.

Max tried not to picture her dancing herself to death as he walked to the store, but he couldn't help it. It joined a thousand equally horrific pictures in his mind of people being cursed. This always led him back to the first memory, the first two people he'd watched die from a curse. His parents.

He shuddered, not wanting to relive the memory yet again. Yells from up ahead grabbed his attention, and he prepared himself to run.

A heavyset man came sprinting out of the front of a building. He was yelling and screaming. When he reached the street, he stumbled. His feet were slowly melting, turning into a thick ooze. The man froze in place, knowing that if he kept trying to run he'd fall. His calves and knees were starting to melt now too.

"Help me!" he screamed. "You, in the demon mask, help me!"

Max froze. He didn't like being pointed out like that, but he also didn't like watching people die. A pool of thick ooze was spreading out below the man as he melted. He was sinking lower and lower as his upper body started to melt.

"HELP ME!" the man screamed.

Max adjusted his hat and walked away. There was no helping that man; not now. He tried to block out the screams as he turned the corner, but they continued to follow him for another minute. Mercifully, they ended, and he was pretty sure it was only because the man had fully melted. It was a nasty curse, one that a local peddler was fond of putting on people. Max had seen it six times before. He could think of much more humane ways to curse people, but those who paid this particular peddler always seemed to end up getting that human melt curse. Maybe it was the only version the peddler knew, but Max had never heard of a peddler that only sold one type of curse.

He reached the store, but before going in he peered through the window. It was a small place, and he didn't like the thought of being in there with too many people. Not enough exits, not enough room to run, and too big of a chance someone could get his mask off and find out who he was.

There was only one other person inside, so Max opened the door and stepped in. The shelves were almost completely bare, with only the occasional product present. Most of the food was dirty and old, but he picked the freshest stuff he could find. It wasn't much, but it was a feast compared to how they'd been eating lately.

Max took his selections to the counter. A man in a Ronald Reagan mask was working the register. He looked through the items Max had, then held out his hand. Max got his bag of currency out of his shirt and opened it up. He handed the man a ten dollar bill, but Reagan grunted and dropped it onto the counter. Max was afraid that was going to be the case. This had been one of the last stores around that was still taking paper money, something he and Reginald had plenty of. Now, it appeared he was going to have to pay with something else.

Max poured the contents of his bag out onto the counter. Out came animal bones, a preserved bat brain, a woven cross, a bloody nail, and a pile of cash. Reagan grabbed two animal bones, the cross, and the bloody nail. Max frowned. That left them with nothing to pay their rent.

"That's too much," Max said.

"All sales final, take your items and go," the man barked.

Without another word, Max gathered up his stuff and left. He was happy to have food, but now dealing with the landlord was a new worry. He'd only had to face down the man once, and it was something he never wanted to repeat. Plus, it was dangerous for anyone to know Reginald was staying in that apartment, so he'd have to find a way to pay the landlord and prevent him from coming by.

On the way back home, he tried not to look at the grotesque pool of melted human goo in the street. He also circled around his apartment building, knowing that having to see Jennifer again would simply be too much. He didn't know who he hated more, the person who had hired the peddler to curse her like that, or the peddler that had actually done it.

He went up the service stairs, taking them two at a time, not slowing down until he emerged onto his floor. Max hurried to his door, unlocking it as fast as he could, then rushing inside.

Something was wrong. Beth wasn't in the living room, and her chicken suit was lying on the floor haphazardly. She always took care to fold it up. Sounds of a scuffle came from the bedroom. Max tossed the food onto the counter and ran to the bedroom, flinging the door open.

"Oh no!" Max yelled.

He tried to cover his eyes, but he'd already seen something he could never unsee. Beth squealed and covered her naked body with a sheet, while Reginald just stared at him, making no move to cover his own nakedness.

"Get out, Max!" Beth yelled.

"You get out!" he yelled, still covering his eyes. "You can't do that with him!"

"You said you'd be gone thirty minutes," she shot back.

Max uncovered his eyes for a moment, only to be treated to a full frontal of Reginald, who was standing beside the bed now. He recovered his eyes, using both hands this time.

"So I'm the bad guy because I didn't stay gone long enough?"

Reginald crossed the room, then slammed the door shut in Max's face. "Come back later," he said forcefully.

Max was seething. Of all the people for his cousin to do that with, why did it have to be Reginald?

"I hate to be the guy that just keeps talking while people are trying to... get busy, or whatever, but don't you think you have more important things to be doing, Reginald?"

"Hey!" Beth complained from the bedroom.

"I'm done," Reginald announced. "We're celebrating."

It took a second for the words to sink in. Max blinked several times, trying to process what this meant. "You're done? Like, really done?"

"Yes, it's finished, it's on the table, go admire it for the next twenty minutes..."

"Forty minutes," Beth interrupted.

"Admire it for forty minutes. Then we'll talk!" Reginald finished.

Max looked over at the table. A single small green vial was there.

"One dose? You said you were gonna have enough doses for everyone," Max said.

"The rest are in here—I'll show you later! Now, please, please please get away from the door!" Reginald bellowed.

Max moved over to the table, suddenly far less concerned with the sordid business going on in the bedroom. He gingerly picked up the vial. It was hard to believe something so big could fit in a container so small.

An idea sprang into his mind. It was something so inspired that he acted upon it immediately. Max grabbed the vial, checked that his mask was still securely in place, then raced out of the apartment.

This time he took the main stairs, and was out the front door of the building in thirty seconds. Jennifer was still there, dancing. The cape he'd put around her was on the ground, exposing her to the street again. Her muscles were straining and she looked like she was about to collapse.

Max pulled out the vial and popped the lid off. He put it against her lips.

"Drink this," he said.

He poured it into her mouth, and a few moments later she stopped dancing. She fell forward onto him, and Max wrapped his arms around her to hold her up.

"How?" she wheezed, barely able to speak. "Curses are unbreakable."

Max smiled. Reginald had done it! "Not anymore," he said. "Things are going to be different now."

Feeling eyes on them, Max quickly retrieved the cape and draped it over Jennifer. He looked around, seeing a few too many people watching.

"Let's get you inside," Max said.

He led her back into the building, supporting her as best he could as they went up the stairs.

"The person who cursed you, do they know where you live?"

Jennifer nodded. "Ex-boyfriend," she wheezed. "He wanted me to do a striptease for his friends and I refused."

Max gritted his teeth. People's petty use of curses had ruined the world. He wanted to get his hands on this ex-boyfriend, but more than that he wanted to get out of sight. If the ex knew where Jennifer lived, he couldn't take her back there.

He brought her to his apartment and led her to the couch. She collapsed onto it and he ran to the kitchen to get her some water. The bedroom door opened, and Reginald and Beth came out.

"Uh, Max?" Beth said as she saw Jennifer on the couch.

"Get some bandages for her feet," Max said.

Beth went to the bathroom to get bandages while Max brought the glass of water to Jennifer. She drank deeply, gulping it all down within seconds.

"What'd you do?" Reginald asked.

His voice was quiet and dark. Max had only seen him angry a couple of times over the years, and it was always a terrifying occasion.

"She was cursed, her jerk ex-boyfriend had her down there dancing herself to death, what was I supposed to do?"

Beth returned with the bandages and started tending to Jennifer's sore feet.

"You gave her the cure?!" Reginald roared.

Max couldn't understand why he was reacting this way. "That's what it's for, to help people," he said.

"You took my vial without asking me!" Reginald yelled.

"I'm sorry if you were too busy boinking my cousin for me to ask your permission."

Beth stopped what she was doing and looked up at Max. "Boinking? Really, Max?"

Reginald rushed across the room. Max recoiled. Reginald slapped the demon mask off of his face, then shoved him against the wall.

"That vial wasn't yours to take. You had no right!" Reginald yelled.

Now Max was getting angry too. He shoved Reginald back.

"Some tool wants to use her to tantalize his friends, and when she refuses he puts her on display and makes her dance herself to death. You've done more heinous curses than that and you know it, so don't tell me I have no right to help her. You don't have the right to stop me from helping her."

Reginald relaxed a bit, so Max continued.

"You've spent over half a decade on this cure because you want to fix the world and atone for the mistakes you made, the curses you put on people. I thought you'd be proud of me for saving her."

Reginald sighed and shook his head. "It's not that I'm not proud of you, Max. You're a good man, and without you the cure wouldn't have been possible, but..." He stopped mid sentence, cocking his head towards the door.

"Is everything..." Max started.

Reginald silenced him with a look, then returned his focus to the door. Max couldn't hear anything yet, but he'd learned to trust Reginald's hearing.

After another moment passed, Reginald turned his attention to Jennifer. She was breathing more normally now and had a blanket covering her. Beth was just finishing up the bandages on her feet.

"Your ex-boyfriend, who were his friends?" Reginald asked.

She shrugged. "I never met them, he broke it off when I refused to strip at some party they were throwing."

Reginald came around the couch and knelt in front of her. "I need a name, something, anything he might've told you."

"They had dumb nicknames. Frankie Fingers, Quick Nick, stuff like that."

Reginald threw his arms up in the air.

Max rushed around the couch to face Jennifer. "Your ex's friends were the Curse Academy?"

She nodded. "Yeah, I think I remember him calling them that once. Is that bad?"

Reginald stood up and laughed a humorless laugh. He appeared to be on the edge of a full breakdown. "Oh, it's bad. It's really freaking bad!"

Max looked at him. "I didn't..."

Reginald cut him off. "You didn't what? You didn't think? You didn't know? What *didn't* makes this situation any better? What do you have to say that will stop the men who are knocking on doors out there from coming in here and killing us off in the worst of ways?"

Max could hear it now too. They were coming down the hall slowly, knocking on each door and looking for Jennifer and the man in the demon mask who had saved her.

"So, his friends are really bad?" Jennifer asked.

Reginald laughed again. He shook his head, then wiped his face, barely holding it together.

"These aren't just regular curse fetishists and peddlers. Nobody has to pay them to throw a curse on someone. They do it for laughs, the more inhumane the better," Max said.

"I knew most of their fathers, some of them were peddlers like me, in the beginning," Reginald said. "But most of their daddies are dead now, and the kids are more twisted and wild than their parents ever dreamed of being." He took a deep breath. "And if somebody found a way to break curses, no one is gonna want to shut that down more than the Curse Academy."

The weight of what this meant was heavy in the air. For a long moment no one said anything.

"So we gather up the other vials of the cure and we run," Max said. "We can hide at Beth's until the heat from the Curse Academy dies down."

Reginald shook his head. "It's not that easy. You don't quite understand what's happening here."

Before he could elaborate, someone knocked on the door. They all turned to stare at it, no one saying a word or even breathing.
Reginald walked slowly towards his bedroom. "Stall them, Max," he said, then pointed to the girls. "You two, get ready to move."

Max moved towards the door.

"Open up," a gruff voice said from outside.

"You're gonna have to give me a minute," Max said. "This lock sticks. Let me find the pliers."

The person outside banged harder. "Hurry it up."

Max moved away from the door. He picked up his demon mask, then the chicken suit head. He handed it to Beth.

"No time for the whole suit, but at least cover your face," he said.

She nodded and took it.

"What about me?" Jennifer asked.

Max looked at his demon mask. He'd never been out of the apartment without it, but he couldn't shake the horror of watching Jennifer dance herself to death. He didn't wish that on her again, but if they saw him then they'd know his identity and he'd be vulnerable to getting cursed.

"You don't need anything," Reginald said as he emerged from the bedroom. He was dragging three trash bags, each one stuffed to the point that it was a struggle to move them.

"If they see her face…" Max started.

"They already know her face, so that doesn't matter," Reginald interrupted. "But what she drank didn't just cure her curse, it made her immune to them forever."

Max's eyebrows went up. "Huh? That's not what you said it was going to do. You didn't even tell me that was possible." Now he was growing more curious about the trashbags. Whatever they were filled with, it wasn't more vials of the cure.

"What's in the bags?" Max asked.

The man outside banged harder now.

"Just take one and let's move," Reginald said.

They all started for the door. Reginald threw it open. The man outside was skinny and old, and his eyes went wide when he saw them.

"Got ya!" he cackled.

His eyes blazed a bright orange and his skin started to crackle.

"Get down!" Reginald yelled.

They all dove back into the apartment as the man outside exploded into flames. Max kicked the door closed, but soon it was engulfed in flames and falling apart.

"Fire escape!" Reginald yelled.

They made their way to the window and climbed out. As soon as they emerged they saw a group of men with guns on the ground below.

"Up," Reginald said.

They started up the fire escape, taking it ten stories to the roof. The decrepit metal fire escape groaned and swayed under them as they rushed up it. The burning man was following close behind.

When they reached the roof, Reginald pointed to the fire escape. "Think we can break it off?" he asked.

Max examined the metal ladder where it connected to the roof. The brick was cracked and worn, and some of the screws were missing. He nodded. Reginald joined him as they started shoving on it and wrenching it back and forth. It groaned and creaked, then it bent. Screws were torn loose, brick shattered, and the fire escape started to fall.

The burning man screamed as he plummeted fifteen stories to the alley below. A few other goons had started climbing up behind him, and they too screamed as they fell.

"Roof access door," Reginald said, pointing.

It was on the far side of the roof, and Max started running for it.

There wasn't much he felt good at in life, but running fast was something he'd always been able to do. He raced for the door, but just as he neared, it opened. A muscular man with a bushy mustache sneered at him.

Max didn't slow down. He lowered his shoulder and plowed into the man. They both went flying into the stairwell, and suddenly Max didn't know up from down. All he knew was spinning and bouncing and falling and flipping and pain. They came to a stop at the bottom of a small staircase.

Max tried to move his fingers and his toes, afraid he might be paralyzed. His back was in agony, but his wrist was on fire. The mustached man was in worse shape. His legs were shattered, folded up underneath him at a grotesque angle. But there was a smile on his face. He was gripping Max's wrist.

"Gotcha'," the man said.

Even though his body was still in agony, Max got to his knees. He pulled his wrist away from the man, but paused as he saw why it was burning. His skin was turning to gold where the man had touched him. It was slowly spreading up his arm.

Max got to his feet and limped up the stairs. His mask had fallen off and there was no sign of it. Even though he wanted to look for it, he could hear more men coming from below. He came back onto the roof and slammed the door closed behind him.

Jennifer was there with a bent metal pole. She jammed it under the doorknob, bracing the door shut, then turned to Max. "Are you okay?" she asked.

He instinctively hid his hand behind his back and nodded. She helped him to the middle of the roof where Reginald was unloading the trash bags in a hurry. It was the biggest mishmash of spell components Max had ever seen. It was also some of the rarest things he'd ever seen. The arm of a mummy, ten preserved human brains, an entire spinal cord, and a myriad of stuff he didn't recognize.

"This is what you've really been working on the entire time," Max said.

Reginald didn't stop working to set it all up as he answered. "This and the vial, yes."

"All this stuff, where did it come from?" Max asked.

"I don't sleep much," Reginald said. "You never heard me come and go in the middle of the night?"

Max shrugged.

"I guess not." Reginald said, slightly surprised.

"What's that?" Beth asked, catching sight of Max's arm. It had been exposed when he shrugged. He tried to conceal it again behind his back, but his cousin wouldn't let him hide. Coming toward him, she persisted. "What happened?"

There was no use in lying, so he showed her. His arm was heavy now, solid gold up to the elbow.

"Max, no," Beth cried.

"It's okay," Max said.

"It's not okay," she argued. "Reginald, do something."

He kept setting up his spell components, pouring a vial of blood over a severed goat head.

"The Midas touch, it's a clever curse," Reginald said. "Curse one person, and they can hurt others even without seeing their face."

"Cure him," Beth begged.

"Just be quiet, it's going to be fine soon," Reginald told her.

Someone was banging on the roof access door. The brace was holding for now, but it wouldn't be long before their pursuers broke through.

"You were a good friend to me when I didn't deserve it Max, and I want you to know how much that meant," Reginald said as he worked furiously. "And Beth, thank you for today. I've always admired your tenderness and your humor and the woman you grew into. Thank you for sharing that tenderness with me."

Beth stared down at him. "Why are you talking that way? You just said everything is going to be fine soon."

He was lighting a doll on fire and didn't look up at her. "It is," he said simply.

He pushed the burning doll up into the goat head, then motioned to Jennifer. "Come here."

She looked frightened, especially now that she knew he was a big time peddler, but she did as he ordered.

"Things are going to be different for you than for the others," Reginald said.

"I don't understand," she said.

"I know, but you will, and I hope that when you do understand you do the right thing."

He said one more thing to her, but Max and Beth couldn't hear what it was. Jennifer looked pale as she listened, but she slowly nodded.

"I'm so sorry," she said. "If I'd known it was for you..."

"It's for the best it worked out this way," Reginald said. "It's okay."

The banging on the roof door intensified. The metal brace was starting to bend. Max looked worriedly at it, trying to ignore the burning sensation running past his shoulder and up his neck. He heard a crackling noise, and when he returned his attention to Reginald he saw blue smoke rising from the pile of components.

"What unlucky person is getting hit by that curse?" Max asked.

Reginald gave him a grim smile. "Every person. Every last one of them." He waved at Max sadly. "Starting with you."

The pile of spell components exploded. A cloud of blue smoke assaulted Max, sending him to the ground. Beth ran to his side.

"What did you do to him?" she screamed.

Jennifer came over too. She put her hand on Beth's shoulder. "It's okay. He's about to be safe forever. So are you. So is everyone."

Beth looked at her. "What do you mean?"

"This was Reginald's plan all along. It's a curse, the biggest ever made, and it spreads like a disease from person to person."

Beth shook her head. "I don't understand, what does it do?"

"It wipes out every trace that curses ever existed. Memories, records, everything. Cured and abolished, forevermore."

The gold was already fading from Max's skin. Blue smoke was pouring out of his eyes.

"What good will that do?" Beth asked. "The peddlers will just…"

"Cease to exist," Jennifer interrupted.

Beth turned around. Reginald was gone.

"The vial was for him. It would've made him immune to curses, including this one," Jennifer said quietly. "He would've survived it, the only peddler left on Earth." She squeezed Beth's shoulder. "I'm sorry, Beth, Max didn't know when he gave it to me."

Beth was crying now. She didn't see the blue smoke coming out of Max and floating towards her.

"But if it won't work on you, then you'll know what happened," Beth said.

The smoke went into the earholes on her chicken head costume. She fell onto the ground and started to convulse. Jennifer watched, tears filling her eyes.

"I'll know, but you won't," she said. "I'll remember…"

Jennifer turned towards the roof access door as it burst open.

"…but I'll never tell."

Three men came rushing towards them. When they got near, the blue smoke entered into them. They dropped to the ground. Jennifer just stood and watched.

"Jennifer? What's going on?" Max asked.

He swayed as he got to his feet. She put her arm around him to steady him. "Nothing much," she said. "Let's get Beth up and get out of here."

Max's eyes were glassy. Reginald told her people would be confused for a while, but that it would pass. The important thing was to spread the curse around to as many people as possible.

Jennifer and Max helped Beth up, then they started towards the door. Max pointed down at the men on the roof who were just now recovering.

"They'll be fine," Jennifer said. "Let's get downstairs, get on some clean clothes, and then go for a walk through the city." Once they got the neighborhood infected, it would spread quickly.

Max looked over at Beth and pointed. "Why are you wearing a chicken head?" he asked.

Beth pulled it off and stared at it. She frowned as she studied it, then tossed it behind her.

"I have no idea."

Hooked on Questing
by Gerald Costlow

The wizard Bertram heard the howls of the werewolf pack coming closer as he limped into the dark alley. The beasts couldn't be more than a block away. That doppelganger he'd conjured and sent running in the other direction hadn't fooled them at all, not with the lingering trail of blood from his chewed-up leg for them to track. He figured the alpha leader would be on him in less than a minute and he was too exhausted to win another battle.

A minute was all he needed—that and a doorway. Even a brick wall would do in a pinch. He thrust his staff out. *"Sanctuary!"* he intoned. The wall before him shimmered and a solid wooden door appeared, light and sound spilling out around the edges. Bertram grabbed the latch, yanked the door open, and stepped through just as a snarling, furry demon bounded into the alley.

The noisy tavern fell silent as Bertram slammed the door shut behind him and limped into the extra-dimensional tavern called Sanctuary, using his wizard's staff as a cane to spare his injured leg. He ignored the curious faces and made straight for his reserved corner booth, sighing with relief as he slid onto the cool, vinyl padding. His leg throbbed even with his weight off it and he checked the bandage under his torn trousers. There was fresh blood seeping through, so his healing spells weren't up to the task. No surprise there. A werewolf bite was resistant to ordinary magic.

The noise level of the tavern picked up where it left off, as the other drinkers decided Bertram probably wasn't in the mood for company and went back to minding their own business. He looked across the room and caught the bartender's eye. Old Chiron the centaur was on duty tonight. Chiron pointed to the top shelf and Bertram nodded. The centaur clopped out from behind the bar, bringing over a shotglass and a couple of bottles from the wizard's private stash.

"This is the last of the Healing Elixir," Chiron said as he filled the glass from the smaller bottle. "You keep getting yourself chewed up like this, you need to buy more. I gotta warn you: the guardians of the Spring of Eternal Youth have doubled their prices again. They say there's been another drought. Supply and demand, you know."

Bertram's hand shook as he scooped up the glass and downed the elixir in one gulp, closing his eyes and leaning back while it took effect. It tasted like pond water but the familiar icy effects of the magical fluid soon spread from his guts to every part of his body, erasing all the aches and pains he'd accumulated on this last quest. Eventually, even his toenails tingled.

Oh yeah, that's the good stuff. Bertram sat up straight, reached for the other bottle, and poured himself a chaser of bourbon, then pulled his pants leg up to examine where the werewolf's teeth had torn into his calf. He peeled a large scab off. The wound had healed without even leaving a scar, as expected.

"Can't blame them," he replied while peeling the bandage off his leg. "I'd be dead or crippled a thousand times over without the elixir. I'll pay whatever they ask." He pulled an ornate medallion on a chain out of his pocket and handed it to Chiron. "Put this in the safe, would you? It keeps a person from changing into a werewolf every full moon. Once my client comes to collect it and pays my fee, I'll have enough for more elixir. Don't worry about me."

"Bert, have you ever heard the term *junkie* used in any of the realms you've explored?" The bartender stood with arms crossed across his broad chest, the bit of face that wasn't hidden by his long, grey beard scowling down at his friend.

"I've heard of junk yards," Bertram said. "Is a *junkie* someone who picks through other people's trash?" Bertram poured another shot of bourbon. Fortunately, the world of *Kentucky* this particular elixir came from remained unaware of how much a bottle of quality sipping whiskey was worth across a dozen thirsty realities.

Chiron shook his head. "Never mind. Don't get too comfortable. The Boss says you have a new quest and you need to see the client soon as you get back."

"Oh, no! I'm off the clock for now. I'm going upstairs to my room for a shower and a change of clothes, and then I'm going to find a woman and pretend I actually have a life of my own for one night, at least. Nothing Dion can say is going to change that." Bertram started to slide out of the booth. "Tell the client to come back in a few days."

The centaur shook his head again. "She's already been here a week and nobody else will accept her quest. We finally rented her a room upstairs until you got back. The Boss says he'll erase your debt if you're successful and if you have any questions, come see him about it. It's a friend of his from the old country named Apate." The centaur stomped a front hoof, a sign that Chiron was getting tired of arguing with this obstinate mortal.

Bertram slid back into the booth. As long as he owed Dionysus, that god pretty much owned him. Dionysus might have been the god of drunken revelry to the ancient Greeks, but retirement, joining an AA group, and opening a magical tavern connected to all the realms had brought out a shrewd businessman who never failed to collect a debt. This was too good an opportunity to pass up. *Too good. Must be a catch.* He started to reach for the bottle of bourbon again while trying to make up his mind, but the centaur scooped up the bottles and glass and turned to clomp away.

This revealed a lovely young woman standing behind the centaur, hidden until now and patiently waiting her turn. So this would be Dion's friend with the quest. She looked like something off of a Greek vase, from the simple white sleeveless dress that came to her knees and cinched with an ornate girdle to the matching white sandals strapped to her pretty feet. She had the same dusky skin and wavy, deep black hair as Dion. There might've even been a family resemblance. If not brother and sister, they were at least cousins.

But then, all those Greek gods were related. *A friend of Dionysus from the old country?* A goddess, in other words. Divine egos were always tricky to handle, so it was no wonder the other questors for hire didn't want anything to do with her. He motioned for her to sit at the booth while racking his memory.

Apate...Apate...nope, doesn't ring a bell. Those damned Greeks had a hundred obscure gods and goddesses. Who can keep track of them all? She wasn't one of the important ones, obviously.

She smiled at him but remained silent, and he had to make a conscious effort to look her in the eyes. Apparently, Greek goddesses didn't wear bras, and the thin white dress that cradled her breasts above the girdle made sure he knew that. Bertram's heart beat faster. The Healing Elixir also acted as an aphrodisiac, so he was glad for the table that hid his lap and hoped he wouldn't have to stand up for a while.

"You must have been listening in," he told her. "I might not have made a good first impression. I'm a powerful wizard and if I agree to your quest. I'll use all my power to complete it. I've never failed a client."

The goddess nodded, eyes sparkling, but still didn't say anything. It was starting to get on his nerves. "Please don't be insulted," he finally said, "but I don't recognize your name. Are you the Goddess of Silence?"

"I don't like to talk much," she finally replied. "I'm the Goddess of Truth. Everything I say must be the complete truth."

Seems harmless enough. "So what's this big, important quest of yours?"

Instead of answering, she pulled a folded piece of paper out of her cleavage and handed it to him. It was a page torn from a book with an illustration on it. He didn't even need to read the title to recognize the drawing.

"Pandora's Box? It's been lost for thousands of years and everyone knows it's empty now. That's what you want?"

She seemed to think about that question for a minute. "I don't *want* the box," she replied. "I *need* it."

"I'd need some clue where to start looking."

She reached out and turned over the page. There was a detailed map on the other side. He examined the page closely. "Ancient Thebes, and a maze, and I'll bet that little bull sign means a Minotaur. Tricky, but I can handle it. I'll get a good night's sleep and tackle it in the morning." He slid out of the booth and took her hand to help her up. "Anything else you can tell me about what I'll be facing?"

She shrugged her shoulders. "The trip into the heart of the maze to get the box will be very, very dangerous. The trip back out will be very, very easy."

"Huh. Thanks for the warning." He was about to make his excuses and head for a hot shower and cold bed, but hesitated and continued to hold her hand. Most of these Greek gods and goddesses had quite a reputation for being... he supposed *lusty* would best describe it. This one certainly gave off the right vibes. Bertram decided it wouldn't hurt to ask.

"You, um... You wouldn't happen to be in the mood to... spend some time getting to know me better... would you?" He looked down at his bloody, ripped pants. "After I clean up a bit, of course. I could come by your room later with a bottle of wine."

She cocked her head and smiled as only a perfect goddess could smile. "I couldn't allow that," she replied. "I would be highly disappointed if you came to my room tonight." Then she pulled her hand away, turned, and walked off, her swinging hips clearing a path through the crowded tavern.

Just my luck. She's one of the few chaste gods in the entire pantheon.

He started for the stairs to his own room when Chiron waved him over. "So, you're all right with this?" he asked. "You know what she is and what she wants?"

"Yeah, she told me," Bertram said. "I've dealt with worse. As for Pandora's Box—well, I guess she's got as much right to it as any of those Greek gods. Now, if you'll excuse me, I need a *cold* shower and a good night's sleep."

* * *

The following morning, Bertram picked through his arsenal of tools and supplies, magical and mundane both, trying to select everything he might need for this particular quest. His trusty staff always went with him, but anything else was optional, and a matter of weight versus utility and the right tool for a job.

For a quick smash and grab like this quest, he decided on a vest covered in pockets instead of a backpack. The license on his wall proclaimed him a wizard in good standing, but he didn't even own a robe and thought peaked hats were just silly. He ended up in comfortable jeans, a light shirt because of the hot Thebes climate, and stout hiking boots to complete the outfit.

The morning shift had finished cleaning up the tavern when Bertram finally stumbled downstairs and headed for the continental breakfast provided for overnight guests. The buzz from the healing elixir was long gone, so he settled for coffee to clear his head.

Apate was already sitting in his booth and nibbling on a piece of buttered toast. He supposed even a goddess had to watch her weight. Bertram pulled out the page with the map she'd given him, giving it another careful look in case he lost it and had to trust his memory.

"This shouldn't take long," he told her, "but those can be famous last words. There's never a guarantee. If I'm not back by tomorrow morning, don't bother waiting around. Leave instructions with Chiron on how I can notify you when or if I return."

She nodded, started to say something several times, then came over to grab him by the vest and plant an unexpected kiss on his lips. "I'm glad you didn't come to my room last night," Apate said as she stepped back.

If the goddess wanted to confuse Bertram, she'd succeeded. He decided to concentrate on the job in front of him instead of standing there pondering the mysteries of women. He walked over to the tavern door, gripped his staff tightly, took hold of the door latch, closed his eyes, and willed himself into the world of the map where Pandora's Box awaited. Then he opened the magical tavern door and stepped through... and just like that, he was there.

The first thing Bertram did was quickly scan for threats or people looking his way and likely to start screaming about a stranger. He was alone in a town that seemed in ruins and abandoned. The magical doorway had appeared on the crumbling wall directly across from an arched stone entryway on the side of a hill, topped with the same carving of a bull from the map. He hadn't expected to arrive any closer because the doorways wouldn't work below ground. It was hot, the sun was beating down out of a cloudless sky, and not even a bird could be seen. He sighed with relief as he walked across the short distance to the maze. This was a promising start.

Traversing a dark, underground maze of tunnels wasn't particularly worrying or new to Bertram. Half the magical doodads that he'd been hired to quest for were found in places like this. He lit up the end of his staff with a whispered word. Then he pulled a can of spray paint out, popped the lid off, and started shaking it as he began walking the maze. Every time he came to an intersection, he painted an arrow on the wall pointing to the way out.

The longer Bertram went without encountering anything more dangerous than another dark tunnel, the more nervous he became. He finally came to the conclusion that the Goddess of Truth was simply unaware that things had changed since the old days when she'd last been here. Time takes its toll.

It took him half a day of careful exploring before he finally made it to the center of the maze. Only then did he notice signs of life, as he saw a glow coming from around a corner to the central chamber and heard noises. It sounded like splashing accompanied by singing, if a cow could sing. The sounds cut off as he got closer, so he bet the creature had noticed him coming. Bertram decided to simply confront whatever was in there openly, painted one final arrow on the wall, dropped the now-empty can, and stepped into the room.

It was a large, cluttered room built to scale for a giant—Bertram could see that right away. Several tall oil lamps provided adequate light. The oversized furniture made him feel like a child again. There was a large desk that easily came to his chest, with a large chair behind it and a very large bed in one corner. The Minotaur still managed to dominate the room. It was exactly as Bertram imagined: a huge, naked, muscular human body topped by a bull's head and with lethal horns sticking out on either side of its head. The creature was on the far side of the room next to the biggest bronze bathtub Bertram had ever seen, standing in a puddle of water while drying an ear out with the corner of a towel.

"It never fails," the Minotaur said in a rumbling voice. "First bath I take in years and some hero pops in to interrupt me. Who the hell decided *kill the Minotaur* should be on everyone's heroic task list, that's what I'd like to know." The creature tied the towel around its waist, thankfully hiding another oversized part of its anatomy inherited from its father, and walked over to a table. It picked up a vase half as tall as Bertram and filled a large goblet with about a gallon of wine, then sat down in the chair, leaning back and putting its big feet on the desk. It motioned to a stool on the other side.

"Take a load off. Nice to have company for a change."

Bertram had never met such a chatty monster, or one that acted so civilized. Nothing about this quest made sense. Maybe he could talk instead of battle his way through this. He perched on the stool, but kept his guard up and staff ready.

"So what's your story?" the Minotaur asked, taking a slurp of wine. "Out to impress a girl, are you? You don't even wear a sword. Planning on beating me to death with that little stick?"

"Uh…the name's Bertram. I'm a wizard. I'm not here to kill you. The Goddess Apate sent me here to get Pandora's Box. Do you have a problem with that?"

"Apate? Boy, I haven't heard that name spoken in a long time. Rumor is, she's a goddess likes to have fun. So she wants her box back? I just wish she could come here to collect it herself. The big boys declared this place off limits to all the gods a long time ago, so everyone started stashing all the crap here that they wanted to keep out of divine hands."

"*Her* box? Why would the Goddess of Truth claim something that contained the evils of the world?"

The creature snorted and wine shot out of its nose. "Goddess of *Truth*?" it said. "Of course she has to say that, but you believed her? So you don't—" The Minotaur threw its head back and started bellowing with laughter.

Bertram knew when the joke was on him and didn't like it one bit. He'd never considered himself stupid, and surviving many years of dangerous questing had proven his intelligence the hard way. His pride on the line, he set his mind to figuring out the joke.

All right, so it's her box. The box contained all the evils of the world, and after Pandora released them the Greeks turned those evils into gods of their own. The box contained greed and blame and revenge and deceit and violence and...oh, crap.

"Deceit," Bertram said. "Apate is the goddess of deceit, not truth. She lies. I bet she's not allowed to do anything *but* lie. You have to take the opposite of what she says. *I'm the Goddess of Truth* means she's the Goddess of Lies. So when she told me..." Bertram felt himself blush deeply. *I would be highly disappointed if you came to my room tonight, she'd said.*

He didn't say the last out loud but the Minotaur must have figured it out from the blush because it brought another bout of laughter. Finally the creature wiped the snot from its nose, stood, and walked over to a shelf. It took down a small bronze box, blew some dust off it, and brought it over.

"Here, you earned this," the Minotaur said, handing it over. Bertram held it up to the lamplight, finding it hard to believe this was the famous Pandora's Box. It was smaller than a cigar box. He supposed the evils of the world didn't take up a lot of room when they were squeezed down to their very essence. He slid the box into a vest pocket while the Minotaur put a huge, friendly hand on his shoulder.

"Oh, I should probably mention," the creature said. "You're not getting out of here alive."

The friendly hand on his shoulder squeezed and Bertram screamed as bone crunched. The creature used that grip to sling him across the room and he slammed into the side of the huge bed, causing another wave of overpowering pain from his shoulder. Somehow, he'd managed to hang onto the staff, but before he could get to his knees the Minotaur was on him again and jerked it out of his hand.

"Heroes are the only people who visit anymore," the creature remarked as it reached down and removed its towel. "Too bad none of the heroes are ever women, but a Minotaur's got needs so I can't be choosy." The creature looked closely at the carvings on the staff. "Don't know what a wizard is. I suspect it's another name for hero."

"Flash," Bertram whispered, and the staff went off like a strobe light in the Minotaur's eyes. It bellowed again, this time in pain instead of laughter, and threw the staff away to rub its eyes. "Attack," Bertram whispered then, and the staff flew back to start whacking the creature around the head on its own as the Minotaur stumbled around the room, blinded and swinging those big fists at an attacker that wasn't there.

This was only giving him time to catch his breath. The staff was raining blows that had recently kept a werewolf pack at bay while he dealt with the cub that was chewing on his leg, but this was only annoying the powerful giant. Bertram concentrated and muttered a spell that numbed his shoulder, dangerous because it didn't heal the broken bones inside and those could end up slicing an artery. Not as dangerous as staying here, though. He scrambled to his feet and ran for the exit, holding his bad arm against his chest. He stuck his good arm out and recalled the staff as he ran past. He needed it for light.

This allowed the Minotaur to stop and sniff the air. "I can't see," the creature said, "but I can smell and hear you, little hero. I don't need light to find my way through the maze. I wonder –"

Bertram never found out what the creature was wondering because he was already past the first turn and on his way out of the maze. *Very, very dangerous to get in; very, very easy to get out,* the Goddess of Lies had said. He should have remembered that instead of worrying about a missed opportunity in her bedroom.

The race out was a matter of running from one painted arrow to another. He didn't have time to set an ambush or do anything other than use the thought of what awaited him in the creature's bedroom to spur him on. When Bertram did finally have to stop and rest, he realized there was no way he could keep up this pace with his injury. All he'd done was open up a few minute's lead. He'd have to deal with the Minotaur instead of outrun it.

Suits me just fine. I've been doing too much running from trouble lately. This creature deserved to be taken down a peg or two, and he was just the wizard to do it.

He propped his staff against a wall, took a piece of chalk out of his pocket with his remaining good arm, then dropped to one knee and started drawing on the flat stone floor. The tunnel had narrowed to only about four feet wide at this point, so it didn't take long to create a simple pattern of mystic runes surrounded by an unbroken circle that stretched from wall to wall.

He'd just finished when he finally heard the creature approaching. Bertram grabbed his staff, walked another ten paces or so down the tunnel, and stood with feet planted. He began softly chanting ancient words and the light from the staff brightened.

The Minotaur stomped into view, its huge body filling the tunnel. It stopped and squinted at Bertram. "Trying to blind me again?" it said. "Won't work. I can follow the stink of your sweat with my eyes closed. You might as well get it over with. You and me got a date tonight." The Minotaur was still naked and gave a thrust of its hips to illustrate.

Bertram finished the spell and relaxed. "No thanks, big guy. I already have a date tonight with a goddess."

The creature only grinned and stepped forward, closer to the circle, then hesitated and gave another long sniff. "I smell magic. I figured out a *wizard* must be like a Priest. Those guys were always full of magic tricks. What are you up to?"

"I'll give you one chance to turn around and leave, or you'll find out the hard way." The monster had stepped far enough into the light that Bertram could see his spell working. It was Bertram's turn to grin. The impressive horns that stuck out on either side of the Minotaur's head were growing longer. The powerful creature hadn't even noticed the extra weight.

The Minotaur looked at the chalked floor. "So this is your big trick? I've seen these before. Circles are traps." It stretched a leg out and stepped over the drawing. "So much for your magic. What you going to do now, smart boy?"

"I already did it," he replied. "I placed a growth spell on your horns when you arrived. The circle is there to distract you while it worked."

The ends of the horns finally reached the tunnel walls and continued to grow, locking the Minotaur's head in place. The creature bellowed, grabbed the horns, and tried to twist himself free, but only succeeded in jamming the points deeper into the stone. When it was obvious the monster was securely caught, Bertram stamped his staff to stop the spell. He could have allowed the horns to grow until they crushed the skull between them like a vise, but he generally preferred not to kill unless absolutely necessary.

He waited for the bellowing and thrashing to stop. The creature finally hung there with fearful eyes and foaming mouth. "Kill me now," it pleaded. "Give me the mercy of a quick death."

"Oh, stop that," Bertram said. "The spell will wear off in a day and your horns will shrink back to their original size. Let this be a lesson. If you're *that* horny, find yourself a nice cow and take *her* out on a date. Heh...*horny*, get it?"

Bertram turned and continued following his arrows while the Minotaur bellowed what were probably dire curses and threats at him in another language.

When he finally exited the maze, he was staring directly into the setting sun, and it blinded him as completely as the Minotaur had been earlier. Bertram tripped on a stone, staggered, and almost fell, using his staff as a crutch to keep going. This situation was getting to be all too familiar.

He made it to the wall of the building across the dusty clearing, yelled *"Sanctuary!"* and saw the cracked plaster turn into the familiar portal. He stepped into the cool tavern and leaned against the inside of the door while the room stopped spinning. The numbness spell was beginning to wear off. He needed to sit down before he passed out.

It wasn't until he'd slid into his booth with a deep sigh that he realized there was someone already sitting on the other side of the table. It was Dion. Apate might have stuck with the classic look, but Dionysus had long since moved to an expensively tailored business suit. Bertram thought the god resembled a young Dean Martin. Dionysus even preferred to be called by the shortened "Dion". This was a god who tried to keep up with the times.

Right now, Dion was sipping on a cup of coffee and taking his time checking Bertram over. "You look like crap, Bert," he finally said. "You've only been gone twelve hours. It usually takes you a whole week to get this banged up."

"Thank you, Captain Obvious," Bertram replied. Just because this was an immortal being as well as his sometimes employer didn't mean Dion got special treatment from him. To his credit, the old god tolerated this irreverent attitude without comment. "Is Apate around?" he asked. "I have something for her, which means I don't owe you anything as of tonight." He pulled the box out and slid it across the table.

"She's in her room. My cousin had a bit too much to drink and retired early." Dion gave the box a brief examination and put it back down. "I notice you keep looking over at the bar and from the way you're holding that shoulder, your collar bone is shattered. Chiron told me this morning you're out of Healing Elixir. I can either help you get to a hospital, or…" Dion pulled a flask out of his pocket and set it on the table next to the box. "You can arrange to get it from me. It's expensive, but your credit is good."

It meant once again being in the god's debt, but at this point Bertram would have sold his soul to get rid of the crippling pain. He started to reach for the flask, but Dion grabbed his wrist in an unbreakable grip.

"Not so fast," Dion said. "Chiron also told me, as your friend, that he was concerned you might be addicted to this stuff. He means a lot to me, so I agreed to help. Here's what I'm offering—I keep you supplied with Healing Elixir, but you stop the questing. From now on, you work behind the bar and the closest you get to risking your life is ejecting drunks at closing time. I'll pay top wages and benefits. Deal?"

Bertram looked over at Chiron, but the centaur was pretending to clean already clean glasses and refused to catch his eye. He looked back at the flask of elixir. He wanted it so bad, it made his mouth water. Did he really need to risk his life questing for other people?

He never doubted his answer. "No deal. Guess I'll have to heal the hard way. I'd appreciate some help getting to a hospital. I figure you owe me that much."

Dion laughed and pressed the flask into Bertram's hand. "I knew you'd say that. I tried telling Chiron—it's not the elixir you crave, it's the quest. You're addicted to the danger, just like every hero I've ever met. Here, this one is on me, with no strings attached."

He stood and brushed the wrinkles out of his expensive pants while Bertram unscrewed the cap and took a big gulp of the elixir. "Get yourself healed before you go upstairs," Dion said. "I'd hate for you to disappoint my cousin again. I believe she's determined to thank you properly this time for getting the box. She's in room twelve."

Bertram took the stairs two at a time and knocked on her door, tingling from head to toe with the magic effects of the Healing Elixir. Apate opened the door, saw the box he held in his hand, and squealed. She wrapped her arms around him, gave him a kiss on the cheek, then grabbed the box and clutched it to her chest. When he started to say something, she held a hand up, turned her back to him and did something with the box. Near as he could see, she opened the box, held it up to her mouth, and whispered into it for a minute before closing it back up. When she turned around there was a huge expression of relief on her face.

"Finally!" she said. "I can talk normally. Tell me you've figured out I'm the Goddess of Lies."

"Yessss…" He'd come prepared for her opposite-speak, and she'd thrown another curve his way. He needed to know what this meant for any plans tonight. "I figured out that when you said you *didn't* want me to come to your room, it meant you *did* want me. So how are you–"

"Pandora's Box." She held it up. "I can store my lies in it. They leak back out after an hour and I'm forced to lie again every time I open my mouth, but in the meantime I can hold a normal conversation." She put the box down, came over and put her arms around him. "Now shut the door, get those clothes off, and let's make wild, passionate love. I've wanted you ever since I first saw you limping through the tavern door, and that's no lie. Some of you mortals are better lovers than even the gods."

* * *

Bertram woke up to an empty bedroom the next morning. Since Apate's divine toothbrush was missing from the bathroom, he figured she'd moved on.

He spent the day catching up on gossip with the other regulars in the tavern and making a short trip to a market to replenish supplies. That evening, he sat at his booth nursing a beer and brooding.

Chiron came on duty and waved to him before checking the cash register. Bertram tried to ignore him, but soon enough the clopping announced his old friend's arrival. He looked up to see Chiron's familiar scowl above arms folded across the vast chest.

"The Boss told me about the deal with the box and that you spent the night with his cousin," Chiron said. "Thought you'd be in a better mood. You mad at me for getting the Boss on your case?"

Bertram waved a hand. "Nah. Hell, you've got a point. Lately, seems like every quest I take on, I get banged up. Maybe I'm starting to look for excuses to get hurt so I'll have a reason to hit the elixir. It's that, or I'm slowing down. Tell me the truth, Chiron—am I getting old?"

Chiron threw his head back and laughed. Finally, he wiped his eyes with the edge of his bar apron. "My friend," he said, "every single questor in this place refused Apate once they found out they'd have to face a Minotaur. They all told her that only you were foolish enough to enter that maze and skilled enough to come back out again." Chiron took the empty mug from the table. "Everyone here knows you're the best in the business. I'll get you a free refill, if you first tell me what's really bothering you."

Bertram looked around to make sure nobody else could hear, then spoke softly. "It's silly, but... Dion told you how Pandora's Box lets Apate tell the truth for an hour if she whispers into it, right?" Chiron nodded. "Well, late last night we were... relaxing in bed, and I asked her if I was one of those mortals who were *better lovers than the gods* that she'd talked about. She patted me on the arm and told me I was a great lover, then went to sleep."

"Congratulations. So?"

"It was only later that I realized it had been way over an hour since she'd last whispered into that damned box. She was lying."

Being a good friend, Chiron managed not to laugh this time. He clopped away to get the well-deserved refill. Bertram sighed again, wishing Apate had stayed for another day so he could try to improve her opinion of him.

"*Ahem*," said a voice from under the table.

Bertram leaned over to check. There were four tiny people down there—tiny people with peaked hats that still wouldn't come up to his knees. He'd seen this race before, or at least statues of them.

"You're gnomes."

"Thanks for pointing that out. Did that half-horse giant say you were the best questor in here? We can't use you if you're getting too old for the job. We need the best."

"Big talk for walking lawn ornaments. What's the job?"

The little man jumped up on the seat opposite him, followed by the three others. "An evil wizard kidnapped our queen. We recently went to an oracle who said only the best questor in Sanctuary could help us rescue her."

"Is it dangerous?"

The little men looked at each other. "When we started, there were a dozen of us and we've already gone through two questors. You're our last hope. So, you the best or not?"

"I might not have made a good first impression," Bertram said. "I'm a powerful wizard and if I agree to your quest, I'll use all my power to complete it. I've never failed a client." He signaled to Chiron, who put four smaller cups on a tray and added a pitcher of beer to the order.

Bertram hunched over the table while the Gnomes told him their tale of woe. He'd worry about his skills as a lover later. Right now, he had better things to do.

It was time for another quest.

ABDUCTED
BY SHAWN COOK

David Ellis was positive he was in Hell. Perhaps during the drive into the mountains he'd suffered a heart-attack and careened headlong into a tree. Maybe, while he had been setting up his tent or preparing the campfire, an aneurism had struck with godlike speed and shut his brain off like a light switch. Maybe.

Maybe this was all real and he'd won the prize for being the unluckiest man in the world. Or, had he just been in the wrong place at the wrong time? It didn't matter to David at that exact moment. His eyes were fixed upon the whirring machine that nestled above his captive body; his eyes remained fixed upon the glistening blades and tubes that pumped bright green fluid.

His anxiousness was palpable and terrifying, as it hung ready to carve into his flesh and rend muscle from bone—all it needed was approval. The tension in the air was maddening and David's inert form shuddered involuntarily. A shadow passed the foot of his steel table. The shaking was worse, hysterical terror on a cellular level.

The alien creature stopped next to David's head and peered down with large black orbs. The slit of a mouth never twitched and the only form of expression came from body language—a quizzical cock of the head, a feather-light touch upon his brow. The sight of the thing—the Gray, David knew they were called Grays on Earth—unlocked the scream that had been hiding behind his teeth.

He screamed long and loud. Screamed until it hurt and black dots appeared in his vision. He tried to thrash his head and found that it was just as immobile as the rest of his body. The Gray placed a long skeletal hand upon David's chest, gave a slight squeeze of pressure. David whimpered at the feel of the alien skin; it felt like decaying orange peels left in the sun.

He began to beg and was not ashamed in doing so. When the Gray touched something just out of sight and the spider machine above began to decend, David began to gibber in almost absolute madness. Through the tears and horrified anticipation, he felt a soft touch across his brow.

A voice filtered into his mind.

Sleep, it said.

And all went black.

He dreamt.

David could smell the thick, humid scent of the trees that surrounded him and felt the rich loam cushion his footfalls across the forest floor. Ahead, something glowed in a brilliant white-blue that threw the forest into stark photo negativity.

The woods were quiet, completely silent as if nature herself held its breath. He pushed through the underbrush and thickets of trip-vines, the noise of his passing thunderous in his ears. He drew closer now. A faint, warm breeze wafted over his skin and gave a thrill of goosebumps. In the forest behind, somewhere among the green, lay his camp. A tent, sleeping bag, and dying campfire abandoned with ghost town precision.

He didn't remember leaving the warmth of his fire, had no recollection at all of getting dressed and working the contrary zipper that separated his abode from the outside. David had little recollection of anything until he drew closer to the light. His mind was hazy and his skin itched and burned from the haste with which he'd forced his way through the trees. He knew he'd been compelled to push through, press on as if summoned. The fear David felt was kept small and squirming at the back of his mind.

He crested a ridge and gazed in terrified wonder as the light pulsed in the valley below. A beam of solid light slammed into him, through him and transfixed him among the trees unable to move. Unable to flee as the shapes emerged from the foliage. Unable to scream as they grasped at him.

From somewhere far off he could hear someone else scream. It wavered from high and brittle to a throaty roar of agony and terror. It was enough to pull David back into the waking world.

Unfortunately for David, this was only the beginning...

* * *

He sat upright on the platform that served as his bed and gathered his thoughts as best he could; his mind was a whirling dervish of broken thoughts and vague memories. Outside of his small room he could hear the same frightful noises he'd heard almost everyday since his abduction. His fingers involuntarily played across the metal ring that lay across his Adam's apple, traced the odd metallic strap that held it in place as if searching for a flaw he could exploit in an attempt to gain his freedom. Nothing.

He barely registered the noise from outside his new home. He'd grown used to the roars and growls, the hisses and chittering that filled the air. Some he could recognize—a tiger from a cell farther down, for instance—while some punctured the air like nothing he'd ever heard this side of a nightmare. To David's ears they sounded as if they'd never set foot on planet Earth. He was sure this was the case. Another scream snapped David's mind into focus and he was shocked when he saw the figure in the cell directly across the hall.

Details emerged slow in the dim light, but the writhing creature appeared humanoid. No, it *was* human—if the form that lay under the sheer blue cover followed nature's earthly design. The thin material seemed to flow over her in a liquid way that clung to her curves but draped her body as if in a sheath of protective plastic. Tubes ran from her body to a whirring mass of machinery that hung suspended from the ceiling. A pink light pulsed in a slow strobe from the cell walls and she screamed louder with each wave.

David strained his eyes and paced his cell like a caged animal, trying to find a better vantage point. Around him the light faded in an approximation of dusk that mimicked the cycle of day and night.

He wanted to rush across the hall and into her cell, see and speak to another human being; even if only to comfort her. He resisted the urge. The front of his cell appeared wide open, with no door to hold him, but he knew from experience that breaking the threshold would garner him nothing but a painful shock and temporary paralysis.

He called to her, tried to reassure her that she was not alone among the monsters. As the cell around him grew to deep night, her screams turned to plaintive cries and weak moans. Eventually, she fell into a deep sleep, and as the night cycle deepened around him he listened to her ragged and labored breathing. His mind turned over and over, tried to fathom what kind of torture they were putting her through. He shuddered at the memories of his time in what he'd come to think of as *The Chamber*. Its chemical smells haunted him, and the gleaming blades...

He pushed those thoughts away. It had been quite a while since they'd taken him and he was thankful for that. Although, on occasion, he was subjected to a series of what he guessed were medical tests. Some were painful, while others were nothing more than annoyances.

He wanted to resist. He'd fight and claw and kill if given the chance, but the choker that pressed against his throat locked his muscles into place with snap of pain, denying him that option.

Through the long , empty artificial night David sat and watched the cell across the aisle. Aside from the occasional groan, the woman never stirred now. Above her, the machine hissed into the cool air. He spoke to her. In quiet tones he spoke words of encouragement that rang hollow to his own ears. He talked for hours, filled the empty space between them with whatever came to mind. The only reply came from the creatures farther down the aisle, the ones he couldn't—didn't want to—see. He eventually ran out of things to say and let the silence fill the air like a thunderclap. David's eyes grew gritty with fatigue and soon he was snoring softly upon the floor.

* * *

The sight that met him upon awaking was enough to strip any fatigue from his body. It stood above her, loomed in the faint light of the false morning like the specter of death. She lay motionless beneath the machine. The Gray placed a long-fingered hand upon her still form and pulled the sheet cover across her face.

The scream that tore from David's throat was one born of rage. The Gray recoiled in surprise, stepped away from the body, and gaped with a naked expression of fear towards David. That momentary slip of emotion from one of his tormentors was enough. He charged forward, heedless of the barrier, mindless of the collar he wore.

An intense wave of energy washed across his body and set every nerve alight. His fury and momentum pushed his rapidly numbing body forward. A brief sensation of freedom, a scorching flash from the ring at his throat, and then all went white.

The pain was immense. A bright, actinic flare scorched his retinas and the throbbing thrum of the field pulsed within his bones with violent intensity. From a thousand miles away he can feel his body push through the field before he was hurled back to land in a painful, tingling heap.

David twitched and convulsed, momentarily blind and dazed. His body felt as if thousands of electrified spiders danced through his veins and lit him up from the inside out. He sensed movement as the Gray entered the room and urged his unresponsive muscles to squirm away. The best David could manage was to flop around like a fish suffocating on shore.

He smelled the harsh odor of burnt circuitry and the skin around his neck felt burned where the collar sat. Above him, the Gray stood motionless and gazed down at him with blank and burning black eyes. The lipless mouth remained impassive as David rolled to his side and stared into that down-turned face, refusing to show fear.

Slowly, feeling began to filter back into his limbs.

The being backed away as David slowly gained his feet. He panted like a dog from the exertion, as adrenaline coursed through his body. He realized he'd never been this close to one before, not unrestrained, anyway.

David began to move forward, and the Gray waved its long fingers. David froze, every muscle clenched; he anticipated the paralyzing effect of the collar. It never came.

A vicious grin split David's face as he continued to step forward.

From his experience, David knew the Grays moved with a carefully measured grace, as if well aware of the fragility of those lithe and rail thin bodies. They moved gracefully but not quickly, and before it could turn to flee he's tackled and brought it to the floor. His hands wrapped around the pulsing neck and David had to exert all of his will to keep from recoiling in horror at how its skin felt. That image of rotting orange peels festering in the sun flashed across his mind again, and David clenched his teeth while bearing down.

Fighting back, the Gray's hands flailed but did no damage, and in an instant David felt something that wasn't quite bone snap in the creature's neck. It went limp beneath his straining form and David hurriedly clambered off the corpse.

He waited through several long and drawn out minutes, expecting alien reinforcements that never came. On shaky legs he stepped to the energy field. The choker no longer felt hot and he traced fingertips across the metal. What was once smooth and featureless was now pitted and warped in places.

He held his breath and stepped into and through the field without a tingle. He quickly scanned left and right and was shocked at how far down in both directions the hallway trailed. He could see no end in either direction. From his vantage point the walls stretched upward and out of sight. Every cell on the same floor as his was dark and empty, but every level that rose above him contained countless cells. Within each, movement of one form or another was visible. None appeared to be human; some were grotesque, while others were almost nonsensical.

Noise filled the air from a million throats. His level contained all manner of earthly animals, but no other human could be seen.

My God. He thought. *How long have they been doing this?*

He raced to the woman's cell and entered without problem. Slowly, he pulled the sheet from her face and reeled at the damage done. From a face horribly burnt stared one beautiful blue eye, its twin a milky white marble, shrunken and lifeless. Small patches of blonde hair poked from scar tissue and melted skin. David gagged, forced the bile back down and gently closed her remaining eye with a shaking hand.

A white hot rage he'd never felt before rumbled through his body and made every nerve come to life. He leaned heavily against the cool metal wall and slowly slid to the floor. Sobs wracked his body and warred with the anger that strummed through his soul. The rage won out. He stood, lay a hand upon the corpse, and bowed his head.

"I may never escape this hell, but by God I'll wreak enough havoc to atone for every second you suffered."

He stepped into the hallway, picked a direction, and began walking. He felt no fear; now that the collar was deactivated there was nothing to stop him. A thought flashed in his mind of ray guns and science-fiction technology, but he quickly squelched it. He'd exact his revenge or— *and*, he thought, most certainly *and*—die trying. He found that he was fine with that. Death was preferable to being a bug under glass or a zoo exhibit.

He walked until his legs began to tire. No opposition, no guards. Nothing. He was sure the smug bastards probably felt safe with their captives locked away to rot or be toyed with. David had passed a multitude of cells and each held an animal he recognized. Some were living, some were hooked to more murder-machines. More than a few were little more than carcasses. Almost all were injured in some way.

Between two cells sat an open mouthed tube that ran upwards into the dark. He stepped inside and his stomach dropped away as he felt his body being propelled upwards. Floors passed and David saw more of the prisoners that line the ship's cells. Some were little more than bands of flesh twisted in obscene shapes, a few were massive monsters full of tooth and plate. All those creatures observed him with eyes that burned with hatred and fear.

He reached the end of the line and stepped cautiously into an empty, well-lit hallway that extended outward from the tube in one direction. He traveled onwards past hydroponics labs, greenhouses, and what he could only guess to be a vast library. David could see books, tablets, cubes that shimmered in the air, and scrolls made from animal skins among other things. All in neat order and ready for study.

He slipped quietly inside and ghosted from aisle to aisle. Upon a low table sat a two foot long bone, covered with symbols that seemed to move when his eyes slipped across them. He lifted it from its resting place and tested its heft. It made a perfect bludgeon.

He wandered deeper among the shelves and tomes, his eyes scanning the aisles. Two rows over stood a Gray. Its back was turned and David could see one of those shimmering cubes floating before it, shapes playing across the surfaces like oil on water. He stepped close and swung the bone in a vicious arc. Thin skin split and black viscous blood sprayed into the air. The lithe alien form crumpled to the ground, its head a mangled mass of tissue. Deeper still into the library he went. He found and killed two more with the same efficiency and bloodlust.

He worked his way from room to room and slaughtered all he came across. They were perfect victims; slow, frail, and preoccupied. The trail of death was as subtle as a hammer blow, yet no alarm was raised. Aside from the thrumming of the ship, all was silent. The next room he entered was sealed with a thick metal door that lifted in absolute silence as he drew near. The inside was lit with a low light that brightened the farther in he went. It was huge, this room; immense and filled with an awful stench that assaulted his senses.

The shock at what lay before him was immense and sickening. It was a charnel scene of broken, bloodied bodies that lay in neat rows. The same black fluid that served as the Grays' lifeblood covered the floor, and David could see nothing but Gray corpses. He walked among row after row and found more than a few were badly burnt. Halfway across the room, he realized he didn't care. Not one iota. He quickly left the room and made his way forward, to the Bridge.

At least twenty Grays stood silently at control panels or at observation screens. None noticed David's presence as he entered. Every bulbous head and onyx eye remained fixed upon a large screen that covered the far wall. Upon the screen turned a glowing red world that swirled with firestorms and ash. David paid the screen no mind.

He stalked the first Gray, hefted the bone bludgeon, and set about the work of revenge and ruination. They never had a chance, nor did they fight back. Only when he began to wreck the computers did the surviving Grays move to restrain him.

He destroyed them, slaughtered them without a second thought, and moved about the wreckage of the room looking for survivors. He found one.

It lay in a bleeding heap beneath the remains of a control panel and David hauled the creature free. He dropped the gore covered bone and grasped the creature tight. Its head lolled to the side and he gave it a brutal backhand across that still and lipless mouth. Black eyes focused on his face. David leaned close and held its head in both of his hands, squeezing tight.

"Why?" He snarled.

It lifted a weak finger towards the viewscreen, where the wasteland turned below. David shook it like a dog shakes a rat until it sank once more to the floor. Above, an alarm started to wail. A faint vibration played through the floor and the surviving Gray shuddered.

From the bits of machine and body parts it pulled a small orb free and placed a finger upon a curved groove. From the center of the room a large holographic image of the Earth appeared, shrank as if a camera were being pulled away. More detail began to show as stars glowed in a dark tapestry. David watched the sun appear in the distance.

"Home." he said. "That's where I want to go."

One word appeared below the image.

DESTROYED.

"What?" He stammered. "What are you—"

A brilliant pulse erupted once, twice as the sun ejected a massive flare that arced across the vast distance of space to engulf his world. The leading edge was thin, and David watched as the ionosphere burned away in beautiful tracers of color. The main mass impacted shortly after and in seconds turned Earth into a flaming maelstrom. The wave of destruction continued onwards, growing upon the screen as it closed with the ship. The impact was devastating. More than half of the immense construct disappeared in seconds; the rest was set adrift into the airless void. His knees buckled and he had trouble finding enough air to breathe. The holographic display disappeared and was replaced by the image of the burned woman.

SURVIVOR.

Oh, God, he thought.

"What about me?" He asked faintly. "Was that torture?"

The Gray tilted its battered head; its breathing had become ragged.

MEDICAL ATTENTION.

"What?"

CANCER.

Oh. Oh, God. He remembered the blackish brown tissue that was pulled from his body by the machine as he lay upon the table. "It hurt so bad."

CANCER = TERMINAL.

ANESTHETIC = FATAL.

Realization hit home. They had paralyzed him but couldn't sedate him. The stress upon David's body would have killed him. They waited until the last minute and blanked his mind, erased his being with sleep to alleviate the agonizing memories. "The other creatures?"

SURVIVORS.

Another vibration ran through the floor, stronger than the last time, and lights began to flicker and die.

SHIP FAILING.

NO RESCUE COMING.

David started to shake. In his lust for revenge he had dealt the killing blow to an already damaged ship and slaughtered innocent scientists and medical staff. The air began to grow cold as more lights turned dark.

The image faded from the air as the last of the Gray's strength ebbed away. David's breath became visible as a plume of white vapor. He looked once more to the screen and said a silent goodbye to his planet and all he'd known and loved. Lights died faster, the hallway was almost pitch black and the Bridge was fading as well.

David Ellis, the only survivor of a dead planet, sat upon the floor and watched the burning Earth until the cold closed his eyes forever.

THE LONG VIEW
BY WILLIAM R.D. WOOD

"History waits for no man," said Terry.

"Except, perhaps, for us, yes?" said the Russian with a laugh.

Attaching the last few hardline connectors to the console was a clumsy affair using the bulky gloves of the suit. Still, he and Mikhail were far better equipped than their space-faring predecessors. Environmental suits had come a long way in the hundred years since Armstrong and Aldrin (and, in all fairness to Mikhail's homeland, Gagarin and Titov). Still, vacuum being vacuum, EVAs were always going to be awkward.

The multiwrench slipped from Terry's grasp in mid-turn and fell slowly to the ground. "Damn it." Gray dust plumed around the tool as it struck.

The Russian's hand clasped his shoulder as Terry stood from retrieving the wrench. "Patience, my friend. No rush is needed. Our families will sing our praises even if we—what is word—*dawdle,* yes?"

"I just want to get this done." The eighteen month buildup of the *Hemera* project was over. The whole mission would be over in hours now and they'd be on their way home. Two days later they'd be crawling out of the return module on the Kazakh steppe. And not long after, he'd be standing on the deck of his beach house at sunset, the chill winter wind in his hair, the salt on his lips.

The final connector slid into place as a vibration passed through the ground—just enough to stir the dust at their feet and set the cables to swaying. The tendency of the *Hemera* device to shake the ground a little and the civilian news media's unfailing feeding frenzy over such events had prompted the project directors to move the experiments somewhere more remote.

As the shaking subsided, the heads up display in Terry's helmet informed him all systems were online and the reactor was spinning up for test-level discharge.

The heads up display in Terry's helmet informed him all systems were nominal and the coils in the Ring were spinning up for transition-level discharge. "Finally."

"This is time travel, yes?" asked the Russian with a laugh. "What is hurry?"

The Russian was efficient and highly skilled, but the concept of urgency was alien to him. Here they were, on the surface of the Moon, unknown to all but a few scientists and bureaucrats on Earth, assembling a device that might or might not sling them across time, and the man's pulse was probably not a beat above baseline.

Terry wasn't quite so at ease. Buzzing around between the various inflatables in low Earth orbit, with an occasional jaunt to the higher platforms, was a thrill like no other. Still, those distances were measured in terms of altitude. One hundred kilometers. Two hundred. No one ever referred to the Moon as being at an *altitude* of four hundred thousand kilometers, though.

The full Earth hung almost four times the size of a similarly full Moon in the terrestrial sky. No, the *height* didn't bother him. It was the *remoteness*.

The main control console's monitor, a transparent plate of glass a meter wide and five centimeters thick, flickered, ripples like water expanding outward as it booted up. The illusion of a vertical pool of water against the stark lunar landscape was at once comical and disconcerting. And just plain wrong.

Terry ran down the checklists displayed on the console, cross-checking against his own lists in his heads up. Everything had gone perfectly and in the great tradition of space travel, it was time to start worrying. Another reason to get the tests done and get the hell off this chunk of regolith.

The image on the plate stabilized into three views of the Earth, each taken from the set of telescopes placed with the *Hemera* Ring. A close-up of the terrestrial horizon dominated half the display. Another showed a magnified dayside disc of the Earth and the last a series of computer-enhanced overlays of temperature, biomass distribution and industrialization. Status data scrolled along the edges of the display as a countdown in the corner signaled that optimum test conditions were minutes away.

"This is great day for Slavsky family, my friend."

The man was incapable of *not* mentioning his family every few minutes. The two weeks of their isolation together in transit and assembling the *Hemera* Ring had convinced Mikhail that the two of them were now brothers. *Brat'ya*. The Russian's incessant stories of *futbol* games and dirty diapers, though, had only convinced Terry the bachelor life was the only one for him.

A second vibration worked upward through his boots, twice the amplitude of the last.

"Geo-lock is good, yes?" In the lower corner of the largest display window, a tiny icon of the Earth with a padlock through it blinked.

"Two minutes."

The early models tested on Earth had flustered the project leaders. Despite unwavering certainty that the theory, calculations, and engineering challenges had been met, every practical test had ended with the mock-down Rings vanishing just as planned but not returning as *also* planned.

An undergrad had realized their mistake. Celestial movements as large as the Local Group had been accounted for, but not the latest models of the greater-verse that predicted movement through a series of hyperstrates. She'd received a personal letter of thanks from the President, simultaneously attaining a higher dimension of professional exile from those she was supposed to be learning *from*.

"Please to take picture for wife and kids."

Terry turned to see his partner a dozen meters away, arms raised in a triumphant Y, the smooth basin of Mare Vaporum stretching to the distant mountains behind him. Sunlight glinted gold from the cosmonaut's mirrored visor washing out his face, but, even in the bulky suit, something bold and perhaps a little brazen in the man's posture identified research-cosmonaut Mikhail Slavsky as surely as the Cyrillic letters printed on his chest.

Terry sighed loudly to ensure microphone pick-up. "Mikhail, they'll never see the picture."

"You are prude, friend Terry," scolded the Russian. "Must learn to live little, I think. *Hemera* will not *always* be classified. When project is public, children will see father as hero and you will wish I had taken picture of you too."

"Fine," said Terry selecting the camera option from the controls on his left sleeve. "Hold still and say—"

"*Cheese.*"

Hi-resolution stills of the Ring and various other components of *Hemera* displayed against the inner surface of Terry's visor, showing the images taken since their arrival. The camera blipped as dozens of shots of Mikhail streamed into the suit's memory. Standard departmental protocols called for all imagery from all devices to be simultaneously transmitted to all mission vehicles as well as Earth-side receivers, but *Hemera* was an exception. The only transmissions allowed were the line-of-sights between Mikhail and himself. Houston and Korolyov had decided to take no unnecessary chances with intercepted signals.

The secrecy was ultimately pointless and those in power knew that. Sooner or later an industrious Moon-gazer or automated telescope on Earth would spot the hundred meter Ring as well as the landing/living module. Even the assemblers they'd brought along were the size of small cars. Their little photo shoot would be nothing compared to the public's discovery of the three trillion spent on a project that might be nothing more than a new way to stir up dust on the ground.

"Satisfied?" asked Terry as he streamed the photos to the Russian.

"*Da*," said Mikhail lowering his arms. In several bounds, he skidded to a clumsy stop next to the nearest of the assemblers. "I find woman for you when we get home, friend Terry. Maybe my cousin Yuliya. She give you good children and she has the big—"

"I'll pass," said Terry. "Can't take a leak off the porch if there's a woman in the house."

"I think you miss point, my friend."

Terry had made the joke time and again that the only thing he feared more than disappearing like the previous devices was Mikhail's matchmaking skills.

A third tremor rumbled across the landing site.

"Sixty seconds."

"Holy hot damn, yes?" said the Russian bounding to his side and rubbing his gloved hands together. The numbers on the display counted down as sunlight played across the crystal blue waters of the Asiatic on the close up.

"We should say words," said Mikhail.

"Nonsense." Armstrong had flubbed his line and Terry didn't want to be remembered saying something that might not play as well in history. Of course, if things went badly, they would be gone and the few people in the know Earthside might get away without ever having to explain the new hundred-meter gouge in the lunar surface.

"Then I will," said the Russian, pausing until the various counters reached five seconds. "I am honored to be here at this time and all those to come."

Terry felt the vibration first through his boots, a second later through his hand on the console. Then the floodlights around the project site flared, throbbing in sync with his heads up display as the view washed out in a sea of milky white.

And, as though a celestial switch toggled back to home, the whiteness was gone and the ground was still once more. The heads up indicated all systems online and the viewing plate showed the same three views as before. Seconds passed before Terry realized he was staring into the sun which had changed position in the lunar sky.

"Better than Disney Island, yes?"

Terry gave the man a grin. Sliding his fingers across the monitor controls, he instructed the system to make comparisons between the readings a few seconds ago and the data coming in now. Icons blinked on and off as images flipped over one another. The main image of the Earth's horizon remained, but the view of the Earth's surface was now desert instead of the Adriatic Sea of moments ago. Terry felt his heart speed at the thought.

He'd not expected *Hemera* to *fail*. In fact, he'd *prayed* it would succeed and he was not a particularly religious man. Still, at some level, he'd just assumed the changes would not strike him as so dramatic.

One of the smaller monitor frames indicated star positions. Various vector-lines flashed between before and after sampling of key constellations. In the other frame, two columns of data shuffled, blinking as they aligned with their counterparts.

"Pollution index," said the Russian with a laugh. "Negligible!"

He slapped Terry on the back, prompting him to skip a step to control the momentum transfer.

"Habitation and development fractals—negative growth."

"I'll be damned," said Terry. *Hemera* was also displaying the postulated date. "July 20, 1869. Just as planned."

"*Now* you want to say words?" asked Mikhail.

The laugh that erupted from Terry's mouth startled him. He felt stunned, detached. Shaking his head sharply, he shook off the feeling before it could take hold. *Get thee behind me, hindbrain,* he thought, and that made him smile.

"Are you okay?"

"Yeah." Terry had to force the affirmation. "Just realizing what we did. Where we are—rather, *when* we are. No amount of training or psyche testing can prepare you for... this."

"*Da.*" Mikhail stepped to one side to look around the console at the disc of the Earth, steadying himself on a floodlight stand as a small after-tremor passed beneath their boots.

Terry took a deep cleansing breath. "I think I will make a go at the history books."

"By all means, my friend."

Terry keyed the voice recorder. "Like my comrade, research-cosmonaut Slavsky, I too am honored—humbled even—to be part of this momentous occasion. To everyone who helped bring us here and now—to everyone who has ever walked the shores of Earth or the shoals of the Moon—we stand on your shoulders today. My eternal thanks."

The Russian clasped him on the shoulder. "There is poet in my comrade, yes?"

"I guess." Still smiling, Terry called up the mission schedule, scrolling until he reached the list of temporal targets. "Next jump is 500 years."

"After we make calibration jump."

"Of course."

Terry swiped the controls for an immediate return to their present. The geo-lock showed green, as did the coils of the Ring. *Hemera* had performed perfectly. There would be time for in-depth exploration and observation later—probably by specialists and scientists yet to be selected—and Terry was fine with that. The ground shuddered beneath them, dust dancing in tiny static discharges at their feet. A flash of light and seconds later they were peering intently at the monitor, the sun no longer overhead.

"Star locations are off," said Mikhail, his voice uneasy. "Fractals at zero point one off target."

Terry linked into the console, comparing the star maps and the landforms manually. The main screen showed a sunset streaming through a brilliant cross-section of atmosphere. The colors through the airborne dust and clouds were amazing. Earth was a gem among the heavens no matter *when* you looked upon it. And the data discrepancies were nothing to be concerned about. "It's okay, buddy. We overshot a day or two is all."

The Russian nodded. "Houston must be shitting brick, yes?"

"No doubt." Terry scanned the emergency-only mission

frequencies. If anything went wrong, then future-Houston should know about it as part of *their* past. Sending a message back to them at this point in *Hemera* time was the plan should that happen. Since the frequencies were clear and no future versions of themselves had come bounding across Mare Vaporum to stop them, all was well. Terry made adjustments to *Hemera's* parameters. "A little tweaking is all she needed. Next stop, five hundred years."

"Very well." Mikhail took the controls in hand this time, confirming the computer's automated settings and engaging the program.

The floodlights surrounding the site quivered and brightened, sending eerie shadows dancing across the lunar landscape. Terry held onto the console with one hand and Mikhail's shoulder with the other. The tremors passed like a wave across the surface and, in a final flash from their displays, were still once more.

A bead of sweat rolled down his face and onto his lips. The taste of salt was strong in his tiny closed-loop environment. Someday someone would design a suit that could wipe your forehead or at least a helmet fan that could prevent perspiration.

Mikhail pointed at the screen. An ocean gleamed in the daylight, the sun now shining at their backs, illuminating Mare Vaporum as well. Icons flashed across the main viewer, motion tracking software identifying a pre-programmed *significant feature* and zooming in. Viewed from an oblique angle against a white-crested section of ocean, a wooden ship of brown and black plowed ahead, white sails billowing.

"Habitation fractals have almost vanished," said the Russian, looking from the viewer to a series of dynamic graphs. "Welcome to 1669—give or take year or three. Friend Terry, we should we make trek to Tranquility and leave note, yes? *Second place is bitch* or something like."

"You're a funny guy." These moments were the biggest in human history and the Russian was taking it all in stride. As tempting as it was to stay a while and turn the telescopes on other areas of the ancient Earth, they needed to move ahead. "Taking us back to the present."

The transition seemed worse to Terry, but only a little. Could be he was just more sensitive after the last one. He'd make a full write-up for the docs so the techies and theorists could make whatever refinements were needed. Time lag, they'd probably dub it. Hell, maybe they'd even name it after him.

While Mikhail busied himself with the mission checklist, Terry zoomed the main display onto a strip of coastline not unlike the one his own beach house sat on. Smoke billowed up in places. It had been a dry year and California was no slouch when it came to its reputation for seasonal brush fires.

"Temporal targeting still off," announced Mikhail. "Over a week this time."

"The techies are going to be busy when we get back."

"This is why *test* pilots test, yes?"

Terry laughed, the taste of bile rising in his throat for an instant. The schedule in his heads up blinked. "Next stop five thousand years."

"Forget that," said the Russian, shuffling toward the console, adjusting the controls. "We go for the grand prize, my friend."

Terry watched as the Russian scrolled down the list of target destinations in their linked systems. The bottom-most blinked once and dropped into the destination window. His hand hovered above the initiation icon on the main control console for only an instant. Terry thought the duration of a sixty million year jump ought to take longer than the two hundred or even the five hundred they'd already made, but just as mission scientists had predicted, the transition time was the same.

Seconds traded for centuries—now for thousands of millennia.

Staggering away from the console, Terry fought down a wave of nausea and dizziness, his gaze slowly rising to take in the darkened Earth hanging against a star-strewn blackness. Mare Vaporum was in darkness. Light from the floods crept out a few dozen meters beyond the Ring, but that was all.

Mikhail leaned on the control console, his breathing heavy on the radio connection. "Too hasty, I think." His voice was raspy as if his ever-present optimism might be at war with exhaustion.

Terry moved to his side and tapped the main display. All views of Earth were nighttime but as the telescopic enhancements overlaid the images one by one, all the theoretical details they'd both learned as children came to light. The continent of Africa was recognizable though more isolated. Asia, visible in the full-disc view, was missing the jutting triangle of India and the icy North American wastelands of their own time had formed a swath of land that swallowed all of Europe in a band of mountains and plains before fusing into Asia.

"Sixty million years," whispered Terry.

Their radio connection was nothing more than a whispery crackle and hum of white noise for a long time and, somehow, it made those moments more empty than any Terry had ever known.

"Terry, my friend?" Mikhail's look peaked in the wash of the floodlights. "I am ready to go home."

"Roger that."

Across such a large jump, Terry didn't attempt to compensate for the drift they'd experienced in the previous runs. They could fine tune with an additional jump or two once they got closer to their own time.

Right now, though, Terry just wanted to go home. He wanted to pack this site up, climb aboard the return module and get back to normal gravity. To a fresh breeze in his face that didn't come from a cabin fan. To the sounds of gulls and the smell and taste of the sea. To the sound of voices besides Mikhail's and his own.

Hell, when he got home, he might even let Mikhail hook him up. A smile tugged at the corner of his mouth as he touched the activation icon. Unlike their previous jumps, for several seconds nothing happened, as if the universe had lost track of them.

The ground shuddered and Terry watched a ripple from the perimeter of the Ring move inward as the floodlights flared and the white noise in his headset became deafening.

A blank white wall bloomed around him, snatching away every sensation and every thought. He woke as though from a drug-induced slumber. Dust coated half of his visor, sunlight refracting like tiny prisms.

With an effort, he pushed himself into a sitting position. "Mikhail?"

A groan crossed the connection. Terry shoved with his hands and knees to gain his feet, the first few steps clumsy as he made his way to his fallen friend and helped him up. A tremor, the worst they'd encountered since beginning their jaunts, knocked them both to their knees before they managed to stand side by side. Some of the floodlights had fallen, and super-cooled gases vented in the distance from a chiller near the Ring.

The Russian muttered something Terry could not understand, then, "What is happened?"

Rather than answer, Terry moved to the console. The main telescopes were still tracking and rebooting, having been thrown off target by the seismic component of the transition. The computer had already estimated their arrival point though, apparently using inputs from the return module's smaller scopes.

"Over shot by almost ten years," said Terry.

"Not bad," said the Russian, life ebbing back into his voice. "Should be easy—"

A flash of light filled the airless sky. In the distance, a plume of dust and rock erupted upward. Terry tracked a second streak of light and it impacted beyond the mountains, farther than the first. The impactors wouldn't leave large craters, but such events were so few and far between, the odds of them arriving during such an event were—well, astronomical. Maybe they were passing through a particularly dense field of cometary debris. They just needed to make a few calibration calculations and get out of there before any other surprises came their way.

"Friend Terry?"

Mikhail stood before the main console. Gouts of glowing red flashed and oozed on the display plate. Terry was reminded of both a magnified image of microbial life and an erupting volcano. The smaller inset image he couldn't make out.

"What are you zoomed on?"

The Russian pointed to the distant smear in the sky. "Not zoomed."

Where the Earth should have been was a shimmering mass, roughly spherical in the middle, and flaring out into a disc of molten red like the birth of a miniature solar system.

"No…"

Mikhail exploded into motion, hands flying across controls as the final telescopes came online, giving Terry a better view. "We must go back." The Russian twisted quake-loosened connectors back into place and Terry imagined he could hear them snapping home. A tremor passed under their feet as a smoldering shadow moved across the moonscape, blotting out the sun for an instant as it passed.

They were only ten years in their own future. Terry remembered the view of the clouds on their first return. On their second, the fires he'd assumed were the typical California scourge.

And now…

The icon of a tiny earth with a padlock through it blinked in the corner of the largest display window.

"We can't go, Mikhail."

The cosmonaut turned on him, brow knitted and fury in his eyes. "I will return to my family—you will help me." Blood ran from a contusion on the man's forehead where he had struck himself when he blacked out. The Russian grabbed Terry's working harness and lifted him. His fury had become madness.

"It was the geo-lock. We used the Earth of our time as our anchor." Their future Houston hadn't warned them because they couldn't.

The Russian blinked hard. Blood oozed down the inside of his faceplate. "And every time we use *Hemera*…it gets…worse."

Terry nodded. He'd seen pictures of his friend's family for months now, their smiling faces staring up from stills and video. The words were thick in his mouth. "They'll have more time if we just stay here."

Research-cosmonaut Mikhail Slavsky lowered his partner to the ground and dropped to his knees.

Terry sat down beside him in the lunar dust. The fiery reds of their broken world were not unlike a sunset.

The tiny fan in his helmet blew chill air across his face.

And his tears tasted of salt.

Into The Thick of It
by Martin T. Ingham

Ron and Joella were riding at a steady pace through the thinning pines. After a full day of riding, they were still in California, which amazed Ron, for he hadn't expected them to be this far from the arid Nevada town of Selwood, where he'd been abducted by this treacherous elf. Truly, she must have used some enchantment to transport them such a distance in a single day, or he'd been unconscious a lot longer than he'd suspected.

"Physical relocation is one of the few talents I have," Joella admitted when asked about the length of their journey, "but it's spotty. Some days, I can move a few miles with a thought, others I'm stuck on foot. Hauling you and these horses all the way over two hundred miles wiped me out. I doubt I'll regain enough mystic equilibrium to teleport anytime soon."

"So we're stuck doing things the natural way," Ron added.

"At least you've got a ride," Joella said, patting her brown steed. "Are you sure you want to go back to Selwood? From what you've told me, the sheriff was trying to keep you like Mactus wanted me."

"Not quite," Ron said, seeing some parallels, but far different motivations. "He gave me his word I could decline his offer after I thought about it. Well, I've thought about it, and I say no. Soon as I pick up my pistol that you left with that snotty elvish barkeep, I'll be heading someplace else."

"Any idea where?" Joella asked, right before a tree branch smacked her in the face. She wiped a hand over her eyes and spit out a few needles.

Ron laughed. "That'll teach you to get distracted."

"At least I'm tall enough to catch a branch," Joella quipped. "You'd have to run into a tree head-on before anything hit you."

"Yep, being small has its advantages," Ron said, turning her obvious insult around. He recognized her antagonism wasn't malicious, and let it roll off his back.

As the mid-morning sun crept upwards, the foliage began to thin, and the ground grew sandy. They were reaching the dividing point between forest and desert, Ron suspected. They couldn't be too far from Nevada now.

A few more hours of riding brought them to a grassy meadow surrounded by scrub brush. There, they stopped to give the horses a rest and refill their canteens from a trickling brook. Joella knew this trail well, and the desert was fast approaching. Soon, their trip would be determined by the handful of springs hidden amongst the barren hills and plains. Over a hundred miles of sparse vegetation and arid sand awaited them on the trip back to Selwood, assuming they could take a direct route, but under full sunlight they'd need to rest frequently. Without pushing the horses, their trip could take a few more days.

While he sat and nibbled on some hardtack, Ron spotted a glint of light in the distance. Atop one of the hills a few miles away, a spark of light caught his eye for a moment. Following that flash, he thought he saw a humanoid figure there, though the distance was too great for him to be certain. He kept his view on that general area as he ate, seeing if his eyes were playing tricks on him, but it soon became obvious he was right. Someone *was* there, and getting closer.

When Joella came back from a short visit to the bushes, Ron pointed out the approaching figure. Grabbing a pair of binoculars packed in her saddlebag, she took a closer look, and positively identified it as a pale man with black hair, dressed in brown leather attire with a star pinned to his vest.

The brief description told Ron all he needed to know.

Twenty minutes later, Sheriff Doliber came walking up to the watering hole, looking calm and relaxed, as always. He was lacking a hat, which was something unheard of for men on the frontier, though there were many things unusual about this law man.

"What brings you out all this way, Sheriff?" Ron asked with a mouthful of dried meat stuck in his cheek.

"I've spent the last three hours trying to find you," Doliber replied coldly. "I thought we agreed you'd stay in town for a while."

"I didn't exactly go of my own accord," Ron replied, standing up. His height reached the sheriff's chest, so he was still looking up at the man as their conversation continued.

"Yes, well, we can settle that later," Doliber said, reaching for a piece of paper in his pocket. "I've got a job for you."

"Not interested," Ron said instantly.

Doliber ignored his protest and continued. "It seems a pack of rustlers out of Arizona is riding our way. Marshal Kingsley is in pursuit, but he needs back-up, and I'm currently indisposed with another case. I figure this would be a good job for you to cut your teeth on."

"What did I just say?" Ron asked, tired of the sheriff's selective hearing.

"You said you weren't interested," Doliber replied with a hint of irritation, "which is fine. Jobs aren't always interesting, but we have to do them, nonetheless."

Ron sighed and walked over to his horse. He knew he couldn't get out of this, but had to try. "You're out of your jurisdiction, Sheriff," he mentioned. "It's not even Nevada, let alone Nye County."

"As a bonded deputy, you are under my jurisdiction, even when traveling abroad," Doliber stated.

"We fought a war over slavery," Ron growled. "Last I checked, it was abolished. I ain't bonded to nothing, and you can't force me to fight."

"Why are you being so obstinate?" Doliber asked.

"Why can't you just leave a man alone?"

"I can't afford to let you go," Doliber replied. "Not right now. Trust me when I say there are things happening which could have dire consequences for this great nation, and the entire world."

"And this relates to me how?"

"As a duly elected law enforcement officer, I must see to my duties of maintaining order and justice in this arid wilderness, but I can't do it all. Right now, I need you—yes, you specifically—to help me. I helped you not so long ago. Now, can I count on you to help me?"

Ron thought on it a moment, and considered what was being asked of him. Was it truly that outrageous? The sheriff was correct in his presumption of debt. Without Doliber's help, Ron would never have succeeded in bringing his brother's killer to justice. The present request was only fair turnaround.

"Okay, I'll do it," Ron said, "but after this one, we're even. If I don't want to carry on as your deputy, you'll let me go, agreed?"

"If I must," Doliber said, sounding less than enthused. "Now, I have a lock on the Marshal's general position, so I can send you to meet him immediately."

Doliber raised his hand in a preparation to cast the spell, but before he could, Ron halted him. "I don't even have my gun," the dwarf said.

"Oh, I took the liberty of retrieving it from Solen at the saloon," Doliber said, pulling the revolver and its ammunition belt out of his jacket pocket. The bulk of the object was far in excess of what you'd expect to fit inside that little slot, yet it had fit, and without even leaving a noticeable mark on the outside of the overcoat. Yet another one of the sheriff's mystic tricks, no doubt. "You really shouldn't leave something this important lying around."

"Yeah, thanks for the advice," Ron said, grabbing the trusty pistol and hooking the belt around his waist. It felt good to have his weapon of choice again, like being reunited with an old friend.

"Ready?" Doliber asked, eager to get him to Marshal Kingsley.

Ron put up his hand and turned toward his horse. Mounting the steed with an ungallant leap, he positioned himself for a ride. "Ready."

Doliber raised his hand again, prepared to activate his magic teleport.

"Wait," Joella interrupted sharply, causing Doliber to cringe. "That's my horse."

"Shoulda thought of that before you married me," Ron rebutted. He wasn't sure who was a preferable master, the sheriff or his new wife.

"Married?" Doliber said with clear amazement. "I'm sure that's one hell of a story, but it'll have to wait. You have some rustlers to apprehend." The warlock sheriff raised his hand for a third time to cast his spell.

"Stop!" Joella snapped. Walking up to the sheriff, she asked, "Say, Sheriff, how much does a deputy get paid in your county?"

"Depends on the workload," he replied. "But I can promise Ron will get ten dollars a head for the rustlers, dead or alive. Does that satisfy you, Missus Grimes?"

"Sure, if you give me a badge and the same rate," Joella replied.

Doliber looked at her as if she were joking. "Excuse me?"

"You want help. I'm volunteering. Deputize me."

"You're a lady," Doliber said incredulously. "You can't honestly think I'd send you up against armed men."

"It's either that, or you leave Ron Grimes here with me," Joella said, poking a finger in Doliber's chest most rudely. "And before you think about snatching him away against my consent, you should know we're bonded by a proximity tether. If we're separated by any significant distance, he'll be paralyzed."

Doliber wasn't pleased, and wondered if it was worth putting up a fight. Dispelling an elvish tether would be a tricky thing, and it would cause further delay. Every minute they waited, Marshal Kingsley was without backup, and that could prove deadly. This had to be resolved quickly, and there was only one obvious solution.

"Why are we even arguing this?" Ron asked. "Let's go!"

"Fine, I'll send the both of you," Doliber said, turning to Ron, "but it'll be on your head if anything happens to her." Raising his hand for the teleport, Doliber finally cast the spell, enveloping Ron, Joella, and both horses in a shimmering light that faded within seconds, sending them on their way.

* * *

The blinding light faded from Ron's eyes, and he became aware of his new surroundings. A rock outcropping was staring him right in the face, not ten inches from his horse's nose. Turning the steed around, he saw they were in a small canyon filled with rock and dusty soil. It could have been any number of places in southern Nevada, and the dwarf didn't know the region well enough to venture a guess.

Joella wasn't in plain sight, leaving Ron to wonder where she'd gone. She had to be nearby, for if she weren't that pesky tether of hers would be kicking in by now, leaving Ron as a limp sack of flesh. The teleport must have separated them somehow, but not by too much.

Directing the horse forward, Ron felt a lump in the seat of his pants. Reaching back, he pulled a folded hunk of paper out of his back pocket. Opening one of the many leafs, he could see it was a map. There were some pencil and pen marks over the lithograph, highlighting his position and nearby landmarks.

"Nice one, Sheriff," Ron mumbled as he refolded the map and tucked it away.

As Ron slid the paper into a front pocket on his vest, a gunshot spooked his horse. The steed lurched up and began to run, but Ron managed to stay seated, and fought against the charge. As another shot ricocheted on the cliff behind him, Ron managed to pull the horse to a stop and draw his pistol. Somebody was gunning for him, and he had to assume it was the rustlers he'd been sent to capture.

Hopping off the horse, Ron sidled up to the canyon wall, looking around. Those shots were likely coming from overhead, based on their trajectories. There were plenty of places up there for men to be perched, but none he could spot from his current vantage point. He had to move further into the open.

The horse helped to provide cover as Ron moved forward. The animal threatened to bolt with each gunshot, but his tight grip on the reins and reassuring whispers kept it from total panic. After a few steps forward, Ron grew convinced that the shots were not aimed at him, for his horse was too big a target to miss. That gave him some reassurance that he retained the element of surprise.

The canyon opened up as it curved, and Ron spotted two men hiding behind a sizeable boulder, being shot at from above. The shots were ricocheting against the stone walls, which explained the bullets that had made their way toward Ron.

One of the men behind the boulder stood up and fired a rifle, picking off one of the opposing men. A bearded man up on the canyon's edge keeled forward and dropped thirty feet onto a pile of rubble, twitching his last on the rock pile.

The man who'd stood up to take the shot received two bullets for his trouble. As the wounded man stumbled backwards and slid behind the boulder again, Ron spotted the silver shield pinned over his heart. That man had to be Marshal Kingsley.

Knowing whose side he was on, Ron took aim with his Remington and shot back at the men above the canyon. His aim was accurate, but the distance was far, and an uphill shot caused him to misjudge the target. His first bullet skirted the ground under the rifleman's feet, causing him to jump back out of sight.

The firing ceased for the moment, so Ron made a run for it, reaching the sheltering boulder without incident. There, he found a young man with a clean shave rushing to reload his nickel plated revolver, while the bearded Marshal bled silently.

Ron bent down to inspect the Marshal's wounds, and saw they were mortal. The man's breathing had already stopped.

Kneeling with his back to the wall, he heard a slight commotion from behind, and turned just as a pair of armed men came out of a cleft in the rock. By the time he turned around, it was too late, and they had him dead to rights. "Drop it," one of them said. He was a tall man with a brown mustache and a blued Colt in his smooth hand.

Ron set his revolver down slowly and gently, making sure not to make any sudden moves that might spook the gunman. Once he was unarmed, he raised his hands over his head and waited for his captor to make his next move.

"My name's Wyatt Earp. Who the hell are you?"

"I'm Boron Grimes, Deputy to Sheriff Doliber of Nye County," Ron replied.

"Last I checked, we were still in Clark County," Wyatt said, keeping his revolver pointed at the dwarf. "What are you doing down here?"

"Marshal Kingsley asked for help, so Doliber sent me."

"I believe him, Wyatt," the young man sitting behind the boulder said. "He took a shot at 'em, right after Kingsley was hit, helped scare 'em off."

Wyatt stood still for a moment, then raised his pistol. "Well, if Warren believes you, that's good enough for me. Nice to have you along, Deputy."

Ron reached out and shook Wyatt's hand, which felt smooth to the touch. The man hadn't seen much hard labor lately. "Pleasure to make your acquaintance. You ride with Marshal Kingsley long?"

"Not at all," Wyatt replied. "We just met up this morning. Turns out we were tailing the same pack of outlaws and ended up in the thick of it together." Pointing to the young man by the boulder, he said, "That's my little brother Warren over there."

Ron tipped his hat to the young man, and Warren did likewise.

"And this is Texas Jack Vermillion," Wyatt said, hooking a thumb over his shoulder.

Texas Jack was a slim man with bushy, black eyebrows and a bulbous nose. There was a perpetual scowl on his face, which may have been due to his current circumstances, though you never could tell. Many gunfighters out west were of the sour type, unwilling to lift their cheeks in the mildest levity.

As the men were getting comfortable with each other, a commotion arose from up the canyon, drawing everyone to the cover of the boulder. The sound of horses was quickly evident and they waited with pistols drawn, anticipating an approaching foe. Their guards diminished as the new arrivals came into sight.

Ron recognized the first rider immediately. It was Joella, looking a little shaken but none the worse for wear. Behind her, riding atop a grayish mare, was an emaciated man with reddened eyes and a shotgun aimed at her back. He smiled from behind an imperial beard and week-old stubble on his cheeks.

"Hey, Wyatt, look what I dug out of the rocks," the scrawny man shouted boisterously with a southern drawl.

"Damn it, Doc, shut up and get down," Wyatt growled back in a half-hushed tone.

"Aw, it's all clear now," Doc Holliday replied, bringing his horse to a stop beside the dead rustler. He glared down at the corpse on the rocks with his sinister eyes. "Who shot this one?" he asked.

"Kingsley did," Ron said, getting a dirty look from the emaciated man on horseback. Warren nodded confirmation which did nothing to relax Doc's expression.

Doc climbed down from the horse and tucking the shotgun under his left arm he drew his pistol with his right. With rapid ease, he fired the gun at the bloody body, adding an extra hole to its head.

"What did you do that for?" Joella asked.

"Never can be too sure," Doc replied, holstering his sidearm before going into a coughing fit. He clung to the reins of his horse for support until it passed.

"You don't sound so good," Joella mentioned.

Doc raised his shotgun again, and directed her to dismount. He moved both horses forward until they reached the men by the boulder. He jabbed Joella in the back with his shotgun and smiled at his friends.

"There's no need of that, Doc," Wyatt said sternly. "They're on our side."

"Like I said, you never can be too sure," Doc replied.

Joella walked over to Ron and wedged up against him in a reassuring manner. "Husband," she said so all of the strange men could hear. "Thank God you are all right."

"Well, ain't that peculiar," Texas Jack mentioned with a bitter connotation. "What's a deputy doin' bringin' his woman along on a ride?"

Doc Holliday cleared his throat and added, "Perhaps we could continue this conversation on the move, before those rustlers get too far ahead."

His friends agreed, and Ron posed no objection. The rustlers were on the run, and if they wanted to catch them they had to pursue. Sitting around in this canyon did no good, and only invited another ambush.

"Did you manage to find the other horses, Holliday?" Texas Jack asked.

"All but one of them," Doc replied as they started walking. "They're just up ahead. Figure Pete Spence must have gotten yours."

"Damn it, Doc," Wyatt interrupted.   "We're not tailing Pete Spence."

"Coulda fooled me," Doc replied, climbing onto his horse.   The walking was clearly too much for him.

"We all know Spence is hiding in one of Behan's cells right now," Wyatt reminded him.

"We'll see about that soon enough," Doc replied dubiously. Spotting the limp body by the boulder, he mentioned, "Well, Jack, I guess you'll have to use Kingsley's horse.   Doesn't appear he'll be needing it anymore."

The path out of the canyon was narrow and rough, and by the time they retrieved the horses in a side channel and reached open ground, there was no sign of their enemies.   The scraggly trees and the surrounding hills prevented a long view, though there were plenty of tracks. Half a dozen horses were on the move northwest, and that was their path to follow.

THE VENDETTA RIDE
BY MARTIN T. INGHAM

April nights were cold in Clark County, but the Earp party decided against a large fire. There was no telling how far they really were from their quarry, and smoke had the nasty habit of traveling on the breeze. They built their fire in a small depression nestled beside a steep hill, which provided the most cover they could find, and they kept it to a minimum, just enough to warm their beans.

The location was ideal, for there was also an active spring nearby. Water was life in the arid land, and without it a man and his horse weren't long for this world.

After building a fire and refilling canteens, the posse sat down for an evening's rest. The Earp party was growing acquainted with Deputy Grimes and his unlikely bride, and they all seemed to be getting on very well, with the exception of Doc Holliday, who refused to hang around and socialize. "Think I'd better tend the horses," he said, walking off and leaving his friends to babysit the new arrivals.

"What I wouldn't give for a good steak about now," Warren mentioned, rubbing his arms together.

"Here," Ron said, digging a hunk of jerky out of his saddle bags. He ripped off a fair-sized hunk and tossed it at the young man.

Grabbing the hunk of dried meat, Warren attacked it with savage fury, ripping and tearing with his teeth as if he hadn't eaten in days. Texas Jack leaned over and tried to snatch a piece, and nearly had his hand bitten in the process.

"Mind carving me off a hunk of that?" Jack asked after recoiling from the ravenous Warren.

Ron complied, and threw another piece of meat across the fire. Jack grabbed it and stuffed the whole thing in his mouth, munching with equal vigor as the young Earp.

Ron looked up and saw Wyatt standing over him, glaring with narrowed eyes. There was anger in him, though over what the dwarf couldn't fathom.

"Stay here," Wyatt told everyone, and then left the sheltered campsite. He headed around the side of the hill, keeping his eyes peeled for any figures lurking in the night. After getting a fair distance from camp, he saw a figure sitting beneath a dead tree. A brief coughing fit from the shaded individual positively identified him.

"How are you holding up, Doc?" Wyatt asked on approach.

"As fine as ever," Doc Holliday replied, breathing as deeply as possible, his chest wheezing. "Are you alone?"

"Near as I can tell," Wyatt replied, certain he had not been followed. "They're getting worse," he said, then related the last scene from camp.

"Can't let them have meat," Doc said, shoving a hand into his jacket to retrieve a flask. "It'll hasten the process."

"It was hard to avoid," Wyatt defended. "The dwarf gave it to them."

Doc Holliday made a disparaging sound and took a swig from his flask.

"We're going to have to tell them," Wyatt said calmly.

After taking a second nip from his flask, Doc asked, "Why should we do that?"

"Jack and Warren are getting worse every night, and we don't know how long it'll take us to catch these bastards. If we don't tell the dwarf and his elf what's going on, it could cause trouble."

"What makes you think they'll understand?"

"I see it two ways," Wyatt answered. "Either we can trust them and be honest, or we can put a bullet in Warren and Jack here and now, and I'll be damned if I'll do that."

Doc coughed a few times as he began his response. "I believe you're missing the third and easiest option here."

Wyatt waited patiently for him to provide it.

"We put a bullet in the dwarf and the elf, then continue on without worry."

"That's not an option," Wyatt said, spitting out the words with a violent growl. "After what scum like these rustlers have done to us, how can you even talk about killing an honest law man?"

"We do not know his character, so it's presumptuous of you to call him honest," Holliday said, tucking his flask away. "Now, if it were just a dwarf we were dealing with here, I would consider giving him the benefit of the doubt, but we all know how underhanded the elves can be."

Wyatt shook his head.

"We both know what low regard elves have for those in Warren and Jack's position. They would gladly see them dead, rather than cured."

"We don't know if Joella is of that persuasion. There are lots of different elves, with many different values. You're just bitter about Big Ears Kate leaving you."

"Do not bring that howah into this!" Holliday snapped, stomping his foot. "This has nothing to do with her. You know I'm right. We'd be better off without those two tagging along."

"Perhaps," Wyatt said, turning to head back to camp. "But would it be right?"

"You picked a fine time to find your conscience," Holliday replied.

"What about yours?" Wyatt asked as he walked away.

"I'm afraid I coughed mine out years ago," Holliday replied, moving to follow.

Wyatt had no trouble finding his way back to camp. The moon was more than half-full now, and there wasn't a cloud in sight. This crisp spring evening, he found his mind sliding back to a simpler time, to those same cool nights of his childhood in Iowa. Shaded by darkness, he could imagine these barren desert hills were those fallow fields waiting for the plow, and his brother Morgan was back in bed, waiting to help with the planting. So much he'd lost, all because of a vaunted sense of duty, coupled with monetary ambition.

He now wondered if it wouldn't have been better to stay a farmer, though it was too late for that. The die had been cast. He and his family would now have to accept the consequences of their actions.

When he returned to camp, Wyatt found Jack and Warren tucked in their bedrolls, sleeping off the savagery that he knew coursed through their veins. It was going to be another rough night for them, and it would keep getting rougher until they caught those responsible for their current condition.

The dwarf and his elvish bride were still sitting by the fire, talking quietly, though as soon as they spotted Wyatt they grew silent. He wondered what they'd been saying about him, and what secrets they could be hiding. They were certainly not the most ordinary pair. What kind of deputy brings his wife along on a ride, anyway? She had some cockamamie story about being deputized, too, but what sheriff would do that to any woman?

Yes, these two were strange. Perhaps that would help with the explanations.

"Dwarf, come with me," Wyatt said at the edge of the firelight.

"The name is Boron Grimes," the dwarf replied, standing up. "What's this all about?"

"We need to talk, alone," Wyatt replied, giving the elf a scrutinizing gaze. Holliday was right about the pointies, and he couldn't be sure how she'd react to the truth. It made more sense to take the dwarf aside first and gauge his reaction.

Wyatt turned to leave the camp, and Ron followed him into the darkness. As the men left the sight of the camp, they bumped into Doc Holliday, who decided to accompany them on their midnight stroll.

Once they were a sufficient distance from camp to avoid being overheard, Wyatt started the conversation. "What do you know about werewolves?" he asked, being direct.

"Just what I read in the newspapers," Ron replied. "Why?"

Doc Holliday growled at Wyatt, then threw up his arms in resignation, showing his disapproval of what was about to be revealed.

"These rustlers we're chasing," Wyatt started, "at least one of them is a werewolf. Maybe more than one."

It was a startling revelation, but Ron was careful to keep his cool. He was never one to show fear, even if the prospect of chasing contagious creatures of the night scared the hell out of him.

"Did Marshal Kingsley know?" Ron asked, putting on his bravest front in light of the new facts.

"No," Wyatt replied. "We only met him in the thick of it, and didn't have time to explain."

It made sense, and explained a few things, such as why Doc Holliday would shoot a dead man in the head, *just to make sure.* Werewolves weren't easily killed, and lead bullets would only give the illusion of death. There was only one thing that could put one down for good: silver.

The plague of lycanthropy wasn't a new thing, though it had been all but eradicated in Europe during medieval times. However, the disease lingered in the Americas, and many native tribes did not see it as a disease at all, but as a blessing. Of course, it didn't affect them as it did the Europeans. There was nothing more dangerous than an Indian werewolf, as they remained fully lucid and in control of their faculties, even as white men became unthinking animals in the same state.

It had only been recently that the disease of lycanthropy had become a problem in the west. Even among the Indians, it had been a rare gift, one they didn't want to share, until they realized the white man couldn't harness the power of the plague. Once that revelation became widespread across the frontier, they began using it as a weapon, inflicting settlers with seemingly superficial bites whenever the opportunity arose.

There was a growing problem with werewolves as a result, though it was still a rare affliction. Besides for special order military contracts, factory ammunition with silver bullets was virtually unheard of.

"They say Custer's face was eaten off at the Little Big Horn," Ron recalled, fighting to maintain his rugged façade.

"They were outnumbered and ill equipped to deal with their enemy," Wyatt said. "We're not so outnumbered, and we've made some effective ammunition. With any luck, we'll put these rustlers down for good, before they can poison anyone else."

"Got any silver .44 caliber balls?" Ron asked, tapping the revolver at his side.

"Have you got a mold?" Wyatt asked.

"Of course," Ron replied.

"Then we'll melt a few dollars and get you some balls."

"Don't suppose he's got his own change, do you?" Holliday asked. "Money doesn't grow on trees."

"You might ask Joella," Ron suggested. "I'm pretty tapped out."

Wyatt looked over at Holliday and both men exchanged questioning looks.

"I would not recommend that," Holliday said after an awkward silence.

"Why?" Ron asked, perplexed.

Holliday stepped up to Ron, so both men could see each other plainly in the faint moonlight. "How much do you really know about elves?"

It was a simple enough question, and Ron was prepared to give a quick retort about how much everyone knew in regard to the pointy-eared devils and their uncouth ways. Though, this wasn't a time for flippancy, nor for offhand boasts. This was serious, and giving the question serious thought, Ron realized he didn't know all that much about elves. They were an ancient and mysterious culture who largely kept to themselves, and few outsiders bothered to learn their ways.

For a moment, Ron felt ashamed of his ignorance in the matter, though he soon dismissed it as an unavoidable result of his upbringing.

"A lot of elves do not look kindly on lycanthropes," Doc Holliday explained. "Their old world superstitions paint werewolves as the leper, incurable and damned by God. They do not accept the fact that it is a disease; rather, they paint it as a sign of divine punishment. They'll kill anyone who is infected, without a second thought."

"So?" Ron asked, seeing no problem with eradicating criminal rustlers for the greater good. It wasn't like they were innocent women and children minding their own business. These were diseased vermin who needed to be put down.

Wyatt gave Holliday another look, and after a coughing fit the sick doctor just shrugged.

"There's one other thing you should know," Wyatt said, sounding reluctant. "Today wasn't the first time we tackled with these rustlers. Truth is, they first hit us down in New Mexico, which is why we're here now."

"I figured there was some reason you'd come all this way. What'd they do, kill some of your posse?"

"Not exactly," Wyatt continued. "We were at the train station in Albuquerque, on our way to Colorado, when these bastards ambushed us. One of them bit Warren and Jack, almost took a bite out of me before we chased them off. We pursued them clear across Arizona afterwards, and here we are, still at it."

The picture was getting painfully clear for Ron as he pieced the facts together. A single bite from a werewolf was all it took to infect someone, and then you were cursed for life. To become a slave of that mystic plague was a fate no honorable man could wish on his worst enemy.

"You understand why we can't have your wife killing every lycanthropic victim," Wyatt concluded.

"But what other option is there?" Ron asked. "If I had a choice between being a werewolf and being dead, I'd take a bullet any day."

"There is an alternative," Holliday interjected. "I believe there is a cure for lycanthropy. It has not been widely pursued by modern scientists or mystics because the plague was nearly extinguished centuries ago. Though, as you know, modern times are seeing a resurgence of it. Therefore, the old treatments are being revisited by some healers outside of the mainstream, you understand."

Hearing him speak of a cure, Ron wondered if Sheriff Doliber wouldn't be of help. The sheriff was a journeyman warlock of impressive skill, with connections to an esteemed guild of sophisticated wizards. If there were a cure, he'd probably know it, or know where to find it. "If you're looking for a cure, I may know someone who can lead you to it." Ron said.

Doc Holliday grunted. "I've already got the cure. I merely need the source of the infection before I can concoct an antidote."

"You?" Ron asked. Based on the man's gruff demeanor, he'd assumed the title "Doc" to be purely ceremonial.

"I was a learned man before the curse of tuberculosis deterred me from my chosen profession of dentistry. During my illness, I've sought out treatment with little success, but the journey has taught me a thing or two about other ailments and their cures. Unlike my own affliction, lycanthropy is treatable, but I must find the man who infected Warren and Jack to do so."

"Then we'll find him," Ron said, feeling bold. He was starting to get a taste for helping people, and the thought of ending the scourge of lycanthropy was appealing. There was a purpose to this pursuit, more than simply policing men. It was no longer a matter of justice, but of saving lives and bettering society as a whole. *That* he could understand, and appreciate.

"But, like I said," Doc added, "elves do not believe in curing lycanthropy. That's why we can't tell your wife about this."

Ron could see his point, but wondered if it were valid. Joella wasn't your typical elf, and though Ron didn't know her all that well, he had the feeling she'd be more open to possibilities. He'd lived this long by relying on his gut, though his instincts also told him not to argue with these men.

"What should we tell her?" Ron asked. "We can't leave her completely in the dark."

"We'll tell her what she needs to know," Wyatt interjected before Holliday could reply. "We'll tell her these bandits we're chasing are infected, and we've got to stop them before they hurt anyone else."

"Agreed," Ron said, feeling it would suffice. So long as she knew what they were up against, she'd be all right. They could worry about the rest of it later.

"Now that we've cleared the air, I think it's about time we got back to camp," Wyatt said. "We've got a long day ahead of us tomorrow."

* * *

They were on the trail before dawn, saddling up as the faint glimmer on the horizon vanquished the twinkling stars. They'd have to be swift if they wished to catch the pack of rustlers and find the werewolf among them.

The trail was easy to follow, almost as if their quarry wanted to be chased. Though, it was more likely a sign of desperation. These rustlers knew they were being tailed, and after weeks of hard riding they'd failed to shake their pursuers. By now, it was obvious their hunters would not stop until they were caught, and if they were caught, they'd be dead soon thereafter. Yesterday's shootout had proven that.

Wyatt looked over at the dwarf riding beside him, and wondered how the little man would feel if he knew the full story behind this ride. He hoped not to find out.

The cool of the night quickly vanished with the rising sun, which caused them to slow their pace and give their horses rest. It wasn't convenient, but it was necessary in the heat.

The rolling hills soon flattened out, giving them a good view of the terrain up ahead. There were still dips and canyons that could conceal the rustlers, though there was only so long they could hide. The Earp party was determined to catch up, and nothing could deter them.

At mid-morning they slowed down as the trail got vague. Several different riders had come through these parts recently, so they had to do some figuring, and pick a set of tracks to follow. Jack was a decent guide, and Joella offered to accompany him as he rode ahead to assess the situation. They were half a mile across a rocky plain before any word was spoken.

"There," Jack said, pointing to a few deep hoof prints dug into hard clay. "See them markings? Unshod ponies. Most likely Indian tracks, not our guys."

"The other set was heading north," Joella mentioned.

"Yep," Jack replied, "so unless we're way off, that's them."

The two rode back at a steady pace, trying to keep their horses fresh for the next leg of the chase. As they neared their companions, Joella had the urge to satisfy a point of curiosity. "So, where are you from in Texas, Jack?" she asked, seeking to open up a polite dialog.

"I'm from Virginia," Jack replied, keeping his eyes on his friends up ahead.

"Oh," Joella said, feeling the brush-off, but unwilling to accept it. "Then why do they call you *Texas*?"

"It's a long story," Jack said. "Let's just say that some Yankees don't know the difference between one southern accent and another."

The last hundred yards of their ride was done in silence. Wyatt rode up to meet them as they returned, and Jack explained what he'd deduced.

"They must be headed for Vegas, hoping to bed down for the night," Joella remarked after Jack's explanation. "It's the only settlement within range, and Army presence is sporadic. I'm not sure who's stationed there at the moment."

"You seem to know a lot about these parts," Wyatt replied, rubbing dust out of his mustache.

"I've been all over this part of the country," Joella said, leaving out the reason for her past travels. Her late husband, Vincent Lafayette, had been an unscrupulous character, one who'd dragged her along on his early travels.

Joella cherished that first year of their marriage, for she'd actually felt wanted. Their relationship had seemed right then, even when she was sleeping on the ground or hanging back while Vincent rode off on some criminal venture. Theirs had been a real partnership for a time, though the honeymoon period hadn't lasted.

After a year of riding together, Vincent had had his fill of marital bliss, and he subsequently dumped his wife off at home, preferring to share a prostitute's bed when coming in off the trail. Joella had seen him less and less, and grew to hate the drunken scoundrel. By the time of his death, she'd been glad to see him go.

The marriage had made her strong in many ways, and the early traveling had given her a working knowledge of southern Nevada. That information was proving to be invaluable.

The pursuit continued across the land of dusty soil and sparse weeds. After a few miles, the tracks disappeared onto a well-ridden trail, which continued in a northerly direction, but Joella advised a detour. Having ridden this route before, she knew the main trail wasn't the shortest route to Vegas. It curved toward the west over a span of ten miles, adding significant distance. If they skipped the path and made a direct bee-line for Vegas, they could cut several of those miles off the journey and possibly catch up to the rustlers.

The ride was rough over rocky hills, but the horses handled it well. Within two hours, they were back on the road, and within sight of the Vegas outpost. They were at least a mile off, but so was the group of six men they spotted coming up the road behind them.

"Ready for it, boys?" Wyatt asked as he drew the revolver from his belt.

"As ever," Doc replied, taking a quick nip from his flask before drawing his own pistol.

The others followed suit, arming themselves for the coming confrontation. Ron and Joella stood ready, though their effective ammunition was in short supply. Six silver balls were all that Ron had been able to make from the spare change in Joella's pocket. Fortunately, Joella's revolver took the same .45 Schofield cartridges that Jack's current revolver used, so he'd been willing to share a few rounds, but only a few. There would be no reloading for them, so they'd have to make each shot count.

The rustlers abruptly stopped about a hundred yards away. Spotting the Earp party which stood in their way, the men quickly dismounted, clearly done with running. They set their horses in front of them, building a defensive wall of equine flesh.

"Good, we can finally get this over with," Jack said, clicking his revolver's cylinder to check that he was fully loaded.

"They have nowhere to run," Joella mentioned, suspecting these rustlers knew as little about this area as Wyatt's men did. Unless you knew where to look, it was hard to find water in the arid lands, and Vegas Springs was the only mapped source within short riding distance. Death by gunfire could be preferable to lethal dehydration.

Everyone on both sides held their fire, waiting for the other side to shoot first. Rifles and pistols glistened in the sunlight, cocked and at the ready. The range was far, but each man knew the art of killing well.

"What are they waiting for?" Warren asked, as he trained his rifle on one of their horses.

Seeking to end the stalemate, Wyatt shouted to the rustlers. "We're after Pete Spence," he said, giving Doc a dubious look. "Send him out, and you can ride on."

"Pete's not here," a deep voice replied.

Wyatt turned back to Doc. "I told you, Spence is locked up in Tombstone."

"No!" Doc growled. Standing up and raising his pistol, he shouted, "I'll prove he's here!"

Doc's first shot skirted the ground directly in front of the line of horses. The rustlers replied with a volley of bullets, most of which went astray, but a few sank into Joella's horse. The wounded animal lurched to the side as it tried to run away, but fell in the attempt. Joella was almost caught under its heavy mass, but managed to dart out of the way.

The Earp party responded in kind, sending bullets at the wall of horses. Two of the animals dropped quickly, but four more continued to provide cover for the rustlers. Warren got a clear shot with his rifle, and picked off one man's head as it poked up for a look, but the others were too shielded.

"We need to get closer," Jack shouted as ricocheting bullets kicked dirt onto his feet.

"Good luck with that," Doc said, firing again. His latest shot managed to hit one of the fallen horses, doing little good.

As the volleys of gunfire continued, Joella noticed Ron standing behind his horse, watching the exchange. "Why aren't you firing?" she asked as she took aim.

Ron didn't reply, but continued his quiet observance. He had yet to fire for very good reason; he was waiting for a clear shot. As the bullets burned through the air around him, he stared at the rustlers, saw their cover diminish as horse after horse collapsed. It wouldn't be long before he had his chance to end the conflict. Patience was the key. He was going to save his bullets for when they'd really count.

The rustlers weren't terribly accurate, but one finally had a lucky shot. Warren screamed in agony as a bullet sank into his shoulder, forcing him drop his rifle. Nobody had time to check on him, not in the thick of it.

The final of the rustlers' horses whinnied in protest after being hit, leaving the five standing men relatively exposed. That was what Ron had been waiting for, and he stepped forward to take aim with his Remington. He shot round after round, taking careful aim at his opponents. Wyatt joined him, while everyone else reloaded. One by one, the silver bullets found their targets, and when both men had emptied their cylinders, silence finally prevailed. The gunfight was over.

As the dust settled, Joella tended to Warren's wound while the other men marched forward to inspect the dead and dying rustlers.

They came upon the band of rustlers and studied their faces, looking for someone familiar. Doc rolled a man over with the toe of his boot, hoping to see Pete Spence, only to be disappointed. The man was unfamiliar, a total stranger.

"Damn it, Spence has to be here," Doc said after seeing the last of the rustlers.

A peculiar chuckle came from one of the wounded men who still clung on to life. Everyone turned to see the source of the laughter, an Indian leaning against his dead horse.

"Indian Charlie," Wyatt said, pointing his gun at the wounded man who continued to laugh, even though it clearly pained him.

"I told you, Pete's not here," Charlie said with amusement. The bullets in his chest would soon silence him, but he didn't seem to care.

"You look pretty happy for a dead man," Wyatt challenged, cocking his pistol. "I already killed you once. This time, I've got the right bullets to make it permanent."

"You murdered my friends, hunted us like dogs," Charlie said, growing bitter in his tone. "What sort of law is that?"

"You bastards killed my brother Morgan, and tried to kill me! Now you have the nerve to lecture about the law?"

Charlie paused a moment, and then replied. "I shall have my revenge. Your friends will never be free of the wolf-spirit. Death will be their only recourse."

"Not if I have anything to say about it," Doc said, digging around in his vest pocket. He removed a piece of linen and unfurled it, revealing a tiny sprig of wolfsbane. He waved it in front of Indian Charlie, and the wounded man cringed.

"Yep, as I thought," Doc said, waving the dried plant in front of Charlie again, just to watch him squirm. "Assuming you're the source, it should be easy to formulate an antidote for Warren and Jack."

Even the presence of the wolfsbane couldn't stop Charlie from laughing at Doc's assertion. Wyatt kicked the chuckling Indian and demanded an explanation.

"I am not the one who bit your friends," Charlie said. He coughed up a bit of blood and struggled to stay conscious.

"Who did?" Wyatt asked.

Charlie looked up and smiled, leaving the question unanswered.

"It was Pete Spence, wasn't it?" Doc said, stuffing the wolfsbane back in his pocket. "I knew I saw him in Albuquerque."

Charlie stopped smiling, clearly discontented at Doc's deduction.

"I don't get it," Jack interrupted, pausing from his looting of the bodies to join the conversation. "I thought Spence was in protective custody. What was he doing in New Mexico?"

"He came for revenge," Charlie answered, "to assure you would pay for your crimes. As Pete was the one to bite your friends, only his blood can serve your needs for a cure, and only until the next full moon completes their transformation."

"You son of a bitch," Wyatt said. Full of rage and adrenaline, he pulled the trigger at point-blank range, putting a silver bullet into Charlie's forehead. The Indian slumped down as the final breath passed his lips.

With the last of the rustlers dead, Wyatt put his gun away.

The answer was becoming clear, though nobody said it. This entire run had been a diversion, a way for Pete Spence and Indian Charlie to assure they'd get their revenge. All this time, Wyatt's party had been chasing the wrong men, taking them further and further away from the one man who held the key to a cure. It would take them days to get back to Tombstone, assuming that's where Pete Spence was hiding, and by then the moon would be in decline. It would be too late for Warren and Jack.

Doc grabbed a handkerchief out of his pocket and began sopping at the bloody wounds on Charlie's body. "I'll see what I can do," he said. "Maybe we'll get lucky."

* * *

The Earp party rode into Vegas Springs an hour after their bloody gunfight. As they approached, a dozen soldiers rode out to greet them. The authorities were ready for battle, understandably so, though Wyatt flashed his badge and gave them a brief explanation which allayed their concerns. Most of what he said was true, though he left out the personal motivations behind his actions. The commanding colonel let them proceed into town, though assigned two of his men to keep an eye on them.

Ron had a funny feeling about these alleged law men, as more of the truth sank in. None of this seemed terribly lawful, their pursuit of the rustlers or the execution of Indian Charlie. It was clear that Wyatt had sought vengeance, rather than justice. Ron could relate, having dispatched his brother's killer not so long ago, but that didn't mean he could trust any of his new acquaintances.

There wasn't much to Vegas; a dozen houses and the army barracks near the life-giving springs; little more than a way-station, and a depository of goods for a handful of ranchers in the surrounding area. It was hard to believe there was much farming going on in this part of the country, but Joella said the land was suitable for subsistence living in certain places. It was also plausible that amateur magicians made a living augmenting the poor soil and assuring adequate moisture for the crops. With the blessings of magic, any land could be inhabited.

It was mid-afternoon by the time they got settled at the local flop house. The place was drafty, but the beds were clean. Ron felt it was as good a time as any for a nap, so he left the others to their business and caught up on the sleep he'd lost over the past few nights.

The room wasn't much more than a hole in the wall. The bed took up most of the space, and it was hardly large enough for a full-grown man. Fortunately, Ron was smaller than your average lodger, so it suited him just fine. He shut the door and flopped down on the lumpy mattress, feeling ready to doze off in spite of the full daylight shining in through a small window. He'd learned to rest at odd hours over the years.

As Ron felt the curtains of slumber tugging at his consciousness, a hollow voice echoed around him. "Deputy Grimes, status report!"

It took him a minute to realize it was Sheriff Doliber's voice interrupting his rest.

"I was about to get some sleep. How's that for status?" Ron replied impertinently.

"I know," Doliber replied. "I've been watching you remotely for the last hour."

"Just an hour? I thought you'd be spying more often," Ron said, suspecting this outing to be a well-monitored test.

"I've been busy," Doliber's voice answered. "That's why I sent you in the first place, so I could attend to other matters. Now, what happened?"

Ron rolled over onto his side and felt a lump of cotton digging into his shoulder. "Can't this wait? I'd like to get some shut-eye."

The sheriff's voice disappeared, and Ron started to drift off to sleep. Before he could, the voice returned.

"I see," Doliber mentioned.

"See what?" Ron asked.

"Why you were reluctant to explain the situation," Doliber said with crystal clarity. His voice had suddenly lost its echo, and sounded much closer, unlike the remote tone it had been.

Ron opened his eyes and saw Doliber standing beside his bed, looking very imposing with his tanned leather outfit and exposed gun-belt. The startled dwarf rushed to attention, sitting up on the edge of the mattress.

"Oh, don't get up on my account," Doliber replied, turning to look out the tiny window at the foot of the bed. "By all means, get some sleep."

Ron grumbled to himself and stood up. The opportunity for rest had passed, as the sheriff's disturbance had snapped him awake. There was no way he'd be able to fall asleep now, not in broad daylight and a jolt of adrenaline coursing through his veins.

"So, what do you want to know?" Ron asked, wondering how much Doliber had deduced.

"Oh, I have what I need," Doliber replied, tapping his temple with two fingers. "I scanned your mind."

Ron frowned and stood up. "Ain't nothing off-limits to you magic meddlers?"

"I needed information, and you weren't being forthcoming." Doliber saw Ron shooting daggers with his eyes. "Don't worry, it was only a passive reading. Your deep, dark secrets are safe, other than those you did over the last day or so."

"I do a lot of thinking," Ron said, wondering how many questionable concepts flowed through him on a regular basis. He was a man, after all. So was Doliber, but that didn't mean he had the right to pry on another man's daydreams. Ron had no idea how much the sheriff had seen of his involuntary imaginings, but to think he'd seen any of them was unpleasant.

"Yes, I realize that," Doliber answered, looking thoughtful. "But a passive scan only reveals sensory memories, what you saw and heard... maybe a touch of emotion comes through. Now, can we get down to business?"

"What would that be?" Ron asked, being purposely obtuse.

"We have a pair of potential werewolves downstairs," Doliber reminded. "That could be a problem."

"Can't you take care of it? Spin a little magic remedy for what ails them?"

"I'm afraid not," Doliber replied. "There are a lot of diseases that magic has yet to cure; lycanthropy and consumption are among them."

"My Uncle Brizban was shot three times at Gettysburg, and the Medlocks patched him right up, even healed a shattered leg. How is it you can't conjure up a cure for these folks?"

"Knitting tissue and bone is a lot different than curing plague. There are still a lot of things we don't know about the human body, and I'm not a warlock of medicine at any rate. So, that leaves us with one option."

"And what's that?" Ron asked.

"We wait to see if Doc Holliday's miracle cure really works," Doliber replied.

* * *

Joella was alone in Miller's Restaurant, the downstairs portion of the boarding house. A dozen tables were crammed together into a cramped eating area, and a counter sat opposite the door. The small establishment doubled as a saloon, with a rack of whiskey bottles set against the back wall. There weren't any drovers or cowboys in town at the moment, so the place wasn't seeing much business.

The peace and quiet was nice after a day of hard riding and getting shot at. She'd just spent the past hour cleaning everyone's guns, which entailed pouring scalding water down the bores and pulling oiled patches through to remove black powder residue. If left uncleaned, the filth would corrode the metal.

A bell rattled as the door opened, and Wyatt came inside. Joella didn't pay him much attention as he sat down beside her, and simply nursed the glass of water she had in front of her.

The proprietor of the establishment, Erwin Miller, Jr., came slouching into the room after hearing the bell. The middle-aged man with prematurely-white hair didn't look terribly enthusiastic as he came over to see what his newest customer wanted.

"Coffee, black," Wyatt requested, slapping a nickel down on the counter.

"Big spender," Erwin mentioned with disdain, grabbing the five-cent piece and eyeing it suspiciously. A large 5 sat surrounded by thirteen stars on one side, and a striped shield occupied the other. He shook his head slightly and slid the coin into his pants pocket before leaving to fill the order.

"Where are your friends?" Joella asked.

"Doc's taking care of them," Wyatt replied. "I hope you don't think we're ungrateful for your help, but as soon as Warren's patched up, we'll be leaving on our own."

"Oh?" Joella asked politely.

"We were headed to Colorado before these rustlers got in our way. My brother James went ahead of us to secure accommodations, so we've got some time to make up."

"What's in Colorado?" Joella asked, getting nosy.

"Nothing in particular," Wyatt said, avoiding an explanation.

"Hoping to get some peace and quiet for a change?"

"Something like that," Wyatt said as Erwin returned with his coffee. He waited until the surly barkeeper was back in the kitchen before adding, "I reckon I've seen enough bloodshed for a while."

They sat and sipped their drinks for a minute, until Doc Holliday came bursting through the doors. The withered man collapsed on the floor, gasping for breath with congested lungs. Wyatt helped him up off the floor and set him in one of the nearby chairs.

"It was the wrong blood," Doc uttered between gasps and coughs.

"What's happened?" Wyatt asked, gripping Doc's shoulders to keep him from falling over.

After the coughing fit subsided, Doc answered.   "They've succumbed to the infection."

Wyatt stepped back and brushed a hand over his hair in a shaky manner.

Joella downed the last of her water and joined the conversation. "What is he talking about?"

"I am so sorry, Wyatt. I never thought the wrong blood would have that effect," Doc said, starting to tear up.

Wyatt said nothing, but reached for his revolver. Joella thought he was going to pull it on Doc for a minute, but as the weapon was drawn, the law man turned for the door. Time became palatable as Joella watched him clomp to the exit and push his way outside. She had to see what was happening, and know what Wyatt would do next, so she pursued, leaving Doc Holliday alone to nip at his flask.

A woman's scream greeted Joella as she ventured out into the sunlight. She turned her head to see a pair of ladies racing along the side of the road, holding up their cumbersome dresses as a large silver-gray wolf sprinted after them. The beast had blood dripping from its teeth, revealing it had already tasted prey.

As the women ran by, Wyatt took aim and shot at the wolf. The bullet skimmed the top of the beast's shoulders, but that didn't slow it. The wolf zipped past, getting dangerously close to the women it pursued. In moments, a wicked curse would be spread to the women, assuming they survived the mauling.

Wyatt stiffened his stance and took careful aim, holding the revolver with both hands. Squeezing the trigger, his shot proved more accurate, sinking a bullet behind the werewolf's skull. The savage beast collapsed in mid-stride, as did one of the women who caught a piece of ricochet in her calf.

The werewolf twitched in the throws of death, and as the life faded from the creature, a metamorphosis occurred. In a matter of seconds, the hairy exterior and dog-like features vanished, replaced with the naked body of Texas Jack Vermillion.

Joella walked over to look upon the dead man, remembering him just an hour ago, and suddenly realizing the truth these men had been hiding from her. The true purpose of their mission was not one of justice or revenge. Dread filled her as it all sank in. "How could you keep this from me?" she shouted.

"We didn't know how you'd react," Wyatt explained as he came over. The gun was still in his hand. "Elves are known to kill werewolves on sight."

Joella turned around and tensed her arm, feeling the urge to punch someone. "Bigoted rumors spread by petty men!" she cursed. "I could have saved him!"

"You what?" Wyatt asked, maintaining a cold front.

"My clan has used magic and alchemy to exorcise lycanthropes for decades. If you'd told me the truth..." She trailed off, shaking her head in dismay.

"I can't believe that," Wyatt said. "I've known plenty of elves, and I've never heard of any cure!"

"You obviously knew the wrong elves. If you'd known anyone from Clan Talus..." Joella stopped as her eyes spotted a hairy figure slinking in the distance. She pointed over Wyatt's shoulder, and he turned to see what she'd spotted, a wounded werewolf staggering on three legs. It had to be Warren. The bullet hole through his shoulder had not healed with his lycanthropic transformation. As such, he was sluggish and disabled, a much easier target.

Wyatt raised his revolver, ready to fire.

"It's not too late. I can still save him!" Joella shouted.

Without a word, Wyatt pulled the trigger.

Joella closed her eyes as the shot went off, unwilling to see this law man kill his own brother. The very human scream that followed prompted her to open them again, and she saw a uniformed Army corporal staggering to the ground, dropped by Wyatt's bullet. A second round was fired from Wyatt's gun, and this time a young private screamed and gripped his shoulder, dropping his rifle on the boardwalk across from the boarding house.

With the soldiers out of the picture, Wyatt looked over his shoulder at Joella. "You'd better be telling the truth."

Joella nodded her response, and they both ran over to Warren the werewolf, who growled and snapped at them when they came near. His mind was totally suppressed, and every shred of humanity was gone. All that existed at that moment was this transformed animal which instinctually sought to spread its disease.

"All right, Mrs. Grimes, time to weave that elvish magic of yours," Wyatt said, keeping his revolver aimed at the wolf.

"That's Grimes-Talus," Joella corrected as she put out her opened hand. "Give me some silver. A coin, a bullet, anything!"

Wyatt reached his free hand down to his gun belt and pulled a cartridge out of a loop. He handed it to Joella without taking his eyes off the wolf that continued to growl and glare back at him.

Gripping the cartridge in her hand, Joella closed her eyes and began to hum. The calm and steady meditation allowed her to focus her limited mystic abilities, which she channeled into the silver bullet. A pale blue glow emanated from her hand, and she opened her eyes wide. The light burst from her hand and followed her gaze, striking the werewolf directly on the snout. In response, the beast leapt up on its hind legs and stared up at the sky, howling at the midday sun. The metamorphosis that followed occurred much like it had for Jack, quickly and completely, only this time it wasn't caused by death.

When it was all over, Warren stood there, stark naked, dazed and confused in the middle of the street. Glancing around, he spotted his brother right in front of him and asked, "Did it work?"

"What do you remember?" Wyatt asked, directing his brother to head for the boarding house.

Warren lowered his head, trying to think. "Last thing I recall, I was swallowing this dirty concoction Doc had mixed up. It burned my throat pretty bad. I must have blacked out after that."

A shot was fired, and a bullet sailed past Wyatt's field of vision, missing his nose by mere inches. He looked up and down the street, and spotted one of the soldiers he'd wounded crouched against a porch post, struggling to aim his pistol.

"We've got to get off the street," Joella said.

"We've got to get out of town," Wyatt replied, "before the colonel comes back and has us all hanged."

"Somebody mind explaining to me what's going on?" Warren asked, flinching as another bullet zinged by his head.

"Doc botched the cure," Wyatt said, as they reached the boarding house door. "I had to shoot Jack, and would've shot you if not for Joella here."

"I managed to arrest the symptoms," Joella explained as they walked into Miller's dining room. "For a lasting cure, we'll need to see the medic in Ravenna-West."

Doc Holliday was standing beside the door when they entered, and kept an eye on the street from his vantage point. "So, we've declared war on the Army now?" he asked condescendingly.

"It was that or let them kill my brother," Wyatt said. "It was self defense."

"I doubt they'll see it that way," Doc replied, watching the wounded private collapse half a block away. As the wounded soldier hit the ground, a shimmer of light surrounded him, and in seconds he was gone, spirited away in a flash of magic.

Doc cursed after seeing the display, fearing the worst. "Damn Army's got a 'lock in the ranks." He stuck his head out far enough to see where the corporal had fallen, but saw only an empty patch of street. Both men were gone!

Wyatt could tell his run was nearing an end. For all they had done—the miles they had ridden and the men they had killed—it was about to result in a prison cell, the last place a former law man wanted to be. It was a dreaded defeat, but there was one positive result from it all.

Gripping Warren's arm, Wyatt said, "There's no need for you to stick around. Go with the elf and that dwarf of hers. Get out of Vegas, and keep riding until you're where you need to be for the full cure."

"The hell with that, Wyatt, I wanna fight!" Warren protested.

Wyatt shook his head. "We spent all this time hunting those rustlers down so you could live. I'm not going to have all our efforts wasted."

"Nor am I," Doliber's commanding voice said, snapping everyone to attention.

Sheriff Doliber came down the sturdy flight of stairs that led up to the bedrooms. Accompanying him were Deputy Grimes and the two soldiers Wyatt had shot. The enlisted men weren't injured in the least, though they didn't look very happy as they took a position in front of the bar.

Wyatt sized up the situation, and came to a likely conclusion. "So, you're going to bring me in, Sheriff?" he asked, spotting the star pinned to Doliber's chest. "It's okay; I'll go quietly, just leave my brother out of it."

"No," Doliber said.

"But Warren's got nothing to do with this. He didn't shoot those soldiers, I did."

"That's not what I mean," Doliber continued. "I understand what you were trying to do. Corporal Baines here was about to shoot your brother, so you did the only thing you could to stop him. If I'd been in your position, I might have done the same."

"So now what, the Army gets to hang me, instead?"

"You're free to go," Doliber said.

"But I shot those men," Wyatt said, seeming interested in condemning himself. The guilt of his vendetta ride was influencing his judgment, even if he didn't realize it.

"You may have shot at them, but I made sure the bullets didn't cause any real damage. Oh, I provided the illusion of injury, so I could gauge your true reaction, but I'm satisfied with the way you conducted yourself."

"That's it?" Wyatt asked, wary of Doliber's motivations. "What about them?"

"I've talked it over with the boys here," he said, hooking a thumb at the soldiers. "They'll cover for you, and so will I under one condition. Leave Nevada, and never come back."

"You don't even have to ask," Wyatt said, finally willing to accept the acquittal.

Their run was at an end, and Wyatt saw no reason to press his luck by sticking around a minute longer. With Doc Holliday and Warren in tow, he headed for the door, eager to kick up some dust and ride for the State line.

"Head for California," Joella advised as the men stepped outside. "When you reach Mono Lake, ask for directions to Talus County. You'll find what Warren needs there."

"Much obliged, ma'am," Wyatt said, tipping his hat in farewell.

As the Earp posse headed for the stables, the two soldiers stepped outside to watch them go. It was their assignment to keep track of the men while they were in town, and that's what they continued to do. Doliber and Ron went out to see to it that was all the soldiers did, and watched as Wyatt, Warren, and Doc trotted out of town.

"You're really gonna let 'em ride out?" Ron asked.

"Of course," Doliber replied. "This county's not my jurisdiction, and even if it were, I wouldn't feel inclined to arrest a man for defending his family."

"Even if that entails shooting soldiers and protecting a werewolf?"

"Obviously," Doliber said. "But I saved the soldiers, so no harm done."

"You're a good man, Sheriff. Maybe I'll stay on as a deputy for a while, after all," Ron said, finding the allure of the job outweighing his past reservations. He could make a real difference in this wild country, and get paid for it. The time had come for Ron to accept his fate.

"I'm glad you're finally coming around," Doliber said, looking down at the short man. There was satisfaction painted all over his face, which covered up the worry that lurked beneath the surface. The answers he'd been seeking in the stagecoach robbery were finally unraveling to his mind's eye, and that spelled trouble.

DOING TIME
BY BARBARA AUSTIN

The guard handcuffed me and chained my ankles. Then he led me from my cell on death row down a putty-colored hall to the visitor's room.

A woman in her mid-twenties was sitting in one of the two chairs welded to a metal table. The clock on the wall had a white face and black hands that pointed to bars instead of numbers. The thin red second hand jerked along its relentless path. Time had begun to fascinate me. I heard clocks ticking throughout the prison, twenty-four hours a day. It's not many men who know in advance the precise time and manner of their death.

She rose and held out her hand, from habit I suppose. She was nearly six feet and built solid. Her light-weight wool suit was designed for air-conditioned offices. In here, the AC labored to keep the temperature below eight-five. She was pretty with silky brown hair and greenish eyes, but the last thing on my mind was hitting on her.

She lowered her hand. "My name is Paulina Gibson."

I didn't need to tell her mine.

The guard said, "I'll be right outside the door."

We sat down.

Paulina laid her mobile phone on the table.

"We don't have much time," she said in a voice that was too small for her.

"I've got exactly eleven days if the governor doesn't commute my sentence."

She arched an eyebrow. "I meant we have a lot to arrange and only thirty minutes in which to do it."

"Don didn't give me any details. Just said he had one more rabbit in the hat. You don't look like a bunny," I quipped, followed by a grin.

Paulina frowned.

"Sorry," I said.

"Don told me you're guilty. But he doesn't want to see a client fry. It's bad for business."

"I wouldn't want that on my conscience." My conscience was overloaded already. I could hardly sleep or eat or breathe. I deserved to die, but, damn it, I didn't want to.

She hunched forward. "We're going to establish an alibi."

"How?"

"I'm going to send you back in time."

"You're kidding."

Her eyes locked with mine. Close-up, hers were a murky yellowish-green, like a pond full of granddaddy catfish and water moccasins.

"Can you follow instructions?" she asked.

I wondered if she was a lunatic, but Don had sent her.

"Do you want to live or not?"

She looked so serious, I started to believe her. Hell, I wanted to believe her. "What do I have to do?"

She crossed her arms. "The price of my services is one million dollars."

I laughed, the only real laugh I'd enjoyed in months. I'd liquidated my assets and paid every penny to Don for defending me.

She threw me a no-nonsense look. "Once you're acquitted, the insurance company will pay out the policy you took on Travis McWilliams' life."

What did I have to lose? "It's a deal. Do you have a paper for me to sign?"

"The guard wouldn't let me bring in a pen. But don't think you can double cross me. If you don't pay up, you're a dead man."

What else was new?

She took a notebook out of her bag and flipped it open. Her lips moved as she read the page to herself. She raised her eyes.

"Listen carefully. You're going back to the night of October 25th, two years ago. You'll arrive at the Longhorn Tavern at 10:00 pm. Sit at the bar and talk to the bartender so he'll remember you. Don't go anywhere. Stay put until 11:00 pm. Then you'll be zapped back to the present."

"If I'm at the tavern, I can't kill Travis. I won't need an alibi, because he won't be dead. I can't be in two places at once."

She smiled impatiently. "Think of it like an anomaly in the space-time continuum. For a brief period there will be *three* of you. You can't undo the murder. Don't try or you'll screw up everything. Trust me, certain acts are too heinous to change. But the testimony of the bartender at the Longhorn Tavern will plant reasonable doubt in the jury's mind. You'll be acquitted."

I glanced at the clock.

"How can I be gone an hour when we have only seventeen minutes left?"

"You'll be gone from the present for only four minutes. The *third you* will be sitting here across from me until you return."

I wasn't a sci-fi buff. My literary tastes ran more toward mystery— at least, until I had become the villain in my own true crime story. But I'd seen enough Star Trek episodes when I was a kid to believe that what she said was possible.

"Are there any side effects?"

"Time travel activates cellular activity at the molecular level. One of the side effects is partial memory loss."

I wouldn't mind losing some memories. "Any others?"

"Time travel causes a reversal in the aging process. The effect varies depending on the individual. I would estimate you'll come back ten years younger. You would be surprised to know how old I am."

If she was on the level, I would be twenty-five again. Young enough to start over

She picked up what I had mistakenly thought was a mobile phone. "Press your right thumb on the screen."

The movement was awkward with handcuffs.

She referred again to the notebook. "I'm typing in the temporal and physical coordinates of your destination. What's your social security number?"

* * *

I was standing in front of the Longhorn Tavern on a chilly, damp night in Austin. A pickup swerved close to the curb and splashed my trousers from the knees down. I laughed. It was good to be free again. To feel the rain. No handcuffs, no leg irons. I leapt into the air like a puppy.

Bars and pool halls stretched out in both directions. This was Sixth Street. I was miles from the gated community of Rob Roy, where I had killed Travis. All I had to do was have some drinks and make sure the bartender remembered me. I felt around in my trousers pocket and found a wallet. I pressed a wad of green bills to my nose and sniffed. The dirty, wonderful, scent of money. With drinking money in hand, I ambled through the old-fashioned swinging doors of the Longhorn

Tavern.

The tavern resembled a long, narrow pine box that had been stained dark by cigarette smoke. The bar ran the length of the long side. The place smelled faintly of beer and puke. A few rickety-looking tables were scattered around in the shadowy interior

I hoisted my ass onto a bar stool.

"A Bud, please."

The bartender pushed a frosty mug of golden beer towards me. It tasted like nectar from heaven.

The loud, vintage soul music hurt my ears. I had become accustomed to silence on death row. The only sounds I had heard for the past six months had been the clanging of the metal doors, the shuffle of feet in leg irons, and the occasional sob from another poor bastard in the middle of the night.

There was a gold watch on my wrist. I'd been back for ten minutes. All I had to do was stay glued to the bar stool, keep my nose out of trouble, and in fifty minutes I would have an alibi. My attorney would be able to establish reasonable doubt. I would be a free man.

I ordered another beer.

The saloon doors swung open and a girl walked in. She wore a short suede jacket, a pair of low-hung jeans clinging to slim hips, and cowboy boots with high heels.

She tottered to the bar and hopped onto a stool further down, leaving one empty stool between us. Up close, I saw she was older than my first impression. There were fine lines at the corner of her eyes, and her neck had lost the tautness of youth. But she was gorgeous. Long hair so blonde it was almost silver. Blue eyes like the sky I could glimpse through the bars on the high window at the back of my cell. She caught me looking at her and smiled, putting dimples in her fair cheeks. A woman like that could almost make me forget about money. A woman like that would take a lot of money to maintain.

"Can I buy you a drink?" I asked.

"Sure. White wine." She flashed an even bigger smile.

I moved over one stool. Her complexion was like white marble, as if she'd never been exposed to the Texas sun.

"Are you alone?" I asked.

She laughed. "If you mean am I here with a man, I am not."

I wanted to know what a woman like her was doing at the Longhorn Tavern alone on a Saturday night, but the question would have sounded like something from an old movie script.

"My name is Jimmy."

"Iris," she said.

We clinked glasses. After exchanging some one-liners, we moved over to a table in the back so we could talk without the bartender hanging over us. An after-game crowd surged into the bar about the same time. They were already drunk and noisy. They kept the bartender hopping. But I didn't worry about depending on him for an alibi, because now I had Iris.

I looked at my gold watch. It was 10:20. At this moment, my original self, the one that belonged to the past, was arguing with Travis at his spread in Rob Roy. We had been watching football on his wide-screen television and drinking beer for hours. Travis was my business partner and my best friend since our freshman year at college. He'd inherited money, and because of that he was stingy about the small things: light bulbs and splitting the bar tab, but he'd surprised me on my birthday with plane tickets to Aruba. He could afford to be idealistic, too; something he'd caught in college, like a chronic disease. His idealism was a sore point between us. I wanted our company, TLC Software, to be run like a business, with budgets and regular financial statements. But Travis was a salesman, and he held the purse strings.

We were drunk and the argument got out of hand. He slapped my face and I saw red. I knocked him out with one punch, then dragged him out to the pool and threw him in. I honestly don't know if I wanted to drown him or wake him up.

The murder would happen in twenty-five minutes. It wasn't premeditated but the jury thought differently because of the million dollar life insurance policy I'd taken out on Travis the month before. He had taken one out on me, too, but only at my insistence. That was the reason I got condemned to die instead of a life sentence. I regretted leaving Travis to drown. Of all my friends who didn't visit me in prison, I missed Travis the most. Paulina Gibson had told me to let things be. That the murder could not be undone. I wondered what terrible thing would happen if I stopped myself from killing Travis.

"What are you thinking about?" Iris asked.

I shrugged.

She gave me a look full of empathy, a look I could fall in love with.

It occurred to me if I didn't kill Travis tonight I wouldn't get a life insurance payout. I wouldn't be able to pay Paulina Gibson her fee of one million dollars. That was what she wanted to prevent.

Iris bombarded me with questions, which I duly answered. I was born in Mineral Wells, got a degree in computer science at UT, and was the brains behind TLC Software. Travis was (or had been) the image man, the one with the charisma, the one who brought in investors and new business. Uninteresting small talk, but she hung on every word I said. I was flattered though confused. I was only average looking. My jokes were usually met with nonplussed stares. I wasn't rich. I couldn't understand what she saw in me.

"What time is it?" she asked, when I stopped talking to take a breath.

"10:30."

"Are you sure?"

"I'm sure," I said, as sure as I could be considering I'd zapped in from the future.

"I've got to go," she said, jumping up with such force I half expected her to leave a boot under the table.

"Where are you going?" I asked.

She smiled a little anxiously. "My taxi is outside. Can I give you a lift somewhere?"

I scanned the crowded bar. I couldn't see the bartender over the wide shoulders, crew-cuts, and cowboy hats. This was my chance to set things right.

I rattled off the address in Rob Roy.

The taxi headed towards Town Lake, rode up the ramp onto Mopac for a short piece, and turned north on 360. Iris and I sat on opposite sides of the back seat. She stared out the window and fingered the fake leather seat cover. We had run out of small talk and didn't know each other well enough to go deeper.

Ten minutes later the taxi dropped me off at the entrance of the gated community.

Then she said something strange. "You won't forget me, will you?"

"Never," I smiled.

The taxi flipped a U and sped away.

Luckily, the guard station was deserted. I was about to scale the wall when a car driving at a high speed without lights barreled towards the gate from inside Rob Roy. The electronically controlled gate swung open just in time to let the car plunge through. I jumped out of the way before my other self could run me down, and I slipped through the gate as it slammed shut. My heart was thudding in my throat. I sprinted along the dark street. On the right were houses set back behind circular drives. Curtains were pulled tightly shut. The hill on the left side of the road was too steep to build houses on, but it was the home of deer, armadillos, and coyotes. Animal eyes followed my progress down the street. The sweet fragrance of wet cedar filled the air.

None of the yards were fenced, which made it easy for me to go around the back of Travis' house to the solarium that housed the pool. The thick warm air stank of chlorine. He was floating face down, arms spread. It was 10:48. He hadn't been in the water for more than three minutes. Without stopping to remove the gold watch, I dove into the water and nudged him to the edge. It took a good thirty seconds to get him onto the deck. I started mouth to mouth.

He sputtered and coughed.

"Hey what are you doing?" he gurgled. "Get off me."

He sat up, rubbing his chin.

"Sorry I hit you," I said.

He looked mad as hell for a moment, then sighed.

"I deserved it. Let's go in the house. I'll lend you some dry clothes."

My watch had stopped, but it must have been close to 11:00.

"I don't want to drip on the floor. I'll wait here."

"Okay, I'll be back in a minute." I watched as Travis walked towards the house, his shoes squishing. I wondered if I would still be there when he came back.

* * *

I was lying on a king-size bed. A ceiling fan buzzed lazily overhead. On my right were three big windows with wooden shutters. Golden sunlight shifted through the slats. A door to my left was ajar. Turquoise tiles on the floor, white tiles on the wall, and a Jacuzzi. Twenty feet from the end of the bed was a door with a shiny gold handle. Next to it stood a curved black console table. I didn't know where I was, but I for sure wasn't on death row.

Light footsteps sounded outside the door.

Iris entered with a tray. Her silver-blonde hair was cut short. There was color in her cheeks that reminded me of strawberries. Her eyes were the same incredible blue as her nightgown. Pregnancy agreed with her. She was eight or nine months along judging by the size of her belly. She set the tray on the table, brought me a cappuccino and the newspaper and snuggled next to me.

She placed my hand on her belly. I could feel the baby kicking.

I felt awkward, as though I had no right touching her. She was practically a stranger. I politely withdrew my hand, noticed the wedding band on my finger, and opened the *Austin American Statesman*. I didn't dare look at Iris, but I sensed her eyes observing me.

The date on the newspaper was the day Paulina Gibson had visited me on death row. My brain began to process the data. I had prevented the murder and altered the course of events. Iris and I had married. If I could afford Iris, this bedroom, the Jacuzzi, and the house that must go with it, TLC Software had grown more successful than I could ever have dreamed.

The two years I'd spent in prison began to fade from my memory, but there were no memories to replace them. Two years of my life had slipped into a void.

Iris moved closer and stroked my thigh.

I rolled away and got out of bed.

"What's the matter, Jimmy?"

"I've got to go out"

"For a run?"

"Yeah, a run." Where were my jogging shoes? I went into the bathroom and opened a door to a walk-in closet bigger than most bedrooms. My nose crinkled at the smell of dry-cleaning fluid and perfume. In the men's corner, I found a faded t-shirt, a comfortable-looking pair of training pants, and running shoes. The outfit fit perfectly.

"Take your keys in case I'm in the shower when you get back." Iris handed me a key ring with what looked like house keys or office keys and a key bearing the BMW logo.

As far as I knew, I hadn't jogged in two years, but my condition was excellent. We lived in a new development further west than Rob Roy, I judged. The lots and the houses were even bigger. Though the hills were steep, I ran up them effortlessly. The air was fresh but prickly. By nine it would be at least eighty degrees and climbing. I could already hear the zoom of traffic in the distance.

I was curious how Travis and TLC were doing. After my run, I would shower and go to work.

* * *

TLC Software had moved. A CPA occupied the two-room office suite we had leased on Spicewood Springs Road. I went in anyway and asked the girl behind the desk if she could look up an address. In a few minutes I was on my way to the new location, a ten-story building with the TLC logo on top.

The executive offices were on the top floor according to the building directory. I stepped into a private elevator that whooshed me straight to the penthouse. Reception was covered with a pristine white carpet, so clean I wondered if I should take off my shoes. The sleek furniture looked like black glass. Travis was chatting with the receptionist who wore a white dress and black pendant earrings that matched her desk.

Travis blinked his eyes. "Did you go to the spa or something? You look--rejuvenated."

"I slept like a log last night." I couldn't say the same for Travis. He looked like he hadn't slept in years.

"Ready for the big meeting?" he asked, looking me up and down.

"You bet," I mumbled and darted to the door with my name on it: James Harwood. I closed the door, leaned against it, my heart pounding. What big meeting, I wondered?

I turned on my laptop. It wanted a password. I pushed the chair out of the way and crawled under the desk. A list of passwords was written in pencil on the underside of the drawer. All were neatly crossed out except for the last one. It was reassuring to know my working habits hadn't changed.

I consulted my Outlook calendar. No appointments until 3:00 when there was a meeting with Angel Software. Angel was the biggest software development company in the world. They were interested in buying our new personal health software app. Not because it was better than theirs, but to protect their market share. Ours was just as good and half the price. But TLC could make more money selling the app to Angel (who would quietly bury it) than marketing it at bottom prices ourselves.

How did I know this? The only explanation was that my revised past life and my future were starting to merge. I spent the next couple of hours getting acquainted with the contents of my hard drive; my appointments over the last two years, the date of Iris' birthday, the projects I'd been involved in. I was curious about the sales figures for TLC, but there were no financial statements on my hard drive, which didn't surprise me because I had always left money matters to Travis. Except for the time I'd talked him into buying the key employee life insurance policies.

Just before lunch, Travis phoned. "We have to talk. If you have lunch plans, break them."

I acquiesced, then hastily checked Outlook. No lunch plans to break. He drove me to a Mexican restaurant about a half mile from the office.

We were seated at a booth in the back.

I ordered the works—tamales, chili con queso, beef enchiladas topped with sour cream, Spanish rice, and fried beans. No more bland prison food. I hoped Travis wasn't going to spoil my meal. We munched on corn chips and hot sauce while we waited for the margaritas.

As soon as the drinks had been served, Travis took a couple of long chugs, set down his empty glass, and picked up mine. A drinking problem would explain the charcoal bricks under his eyes, the loose jawline, and the red blotches on his cheeks. He wore a wedding ring that was too tight for his pudgy finger, and I wondered if he'd finally married Jen. She had been devastated at the murder trial.

"What did you want to talk about?" I asked.

"I want to make sure you're ready for the meeting with Angel. I don't have to tell you what's at stake."

I must have looked puzzled, because he sighed deeply. I'd never seen anyone guzzle rock salt and crushed ice before.

"You really are a geek, aren't you? Don't you know what's going on?"

"Tell me," I said cautiously.

"The financial viability of TLC hangs on the deal with Angel."

"We're broke?"

"A cash flow problem."

I was incredulous. But on reflection, I could guess where the cash had flowed to: the penthouse office suite in the prestigious building, my BMW, his Cadillac. My multi-million house in the hills overlooking Austin. I wondered if Travis still owned the mansion in Rob Roy or if he'd traded up.

Travis ranted, "The real estate market has collapsed. Our building is more than half empty. We can't afford the interest on the bank loan. Software sales are a fraction of what they were. If we don't get cash fast, salaries won't be paid next month, which means all the employees will quit."

"Is TLC incorporated?"

Travis gave me a withering look. "Jesus, what's gotten into you! No, we're not incorporated, and don't say you told me so."

If we'd been incorporated, the bank wouldn't be able to seize our personal assets. Now we stood to lose our homes, too. Travis had sworn he would never become a part of an anonymous corporation. He didn't want to hide behind limited liability. I wondered if he still had the sign on his desk that said "The buck stops here."

I was mad enough to kill him.

"I hope your memory improves by three o'clock," Travis sneered. Guacamole dip coated his front teeth. "As good as I am, I can't make the sale without your support on the technical specs."

I bristled at his threatening tone. It wasn't my fault I could remember nothing about the personal health app. If only the meeting was scheduled for tomorrow. Maybe by then I would be fully integrated into my old self.

* * *

But the Angel team had flown to Austin the night before. Their IT director, procurement manager, and attorney arrived promptly at three, and the grilling began. Their expressions morphed from friendly to courteous to puzzled. Travis couldn't see through the technical smoke I was blowing, but he knew what "no deal" meant.

Our disgusted guests left in a taxi for the airport.

Travis and I were alone in the boardroom, which was equipped with a TelePresence conferencing system, a remote control that operated the lights and the temperature, and a well-stocked bar.

You could have heard a software app drop. I nervously admired the view of north Austin from ten floors up.

Finally, Travis said, "What the hell is wrong with you?"

"I'm a little off today."

"A little off!" he thundered, his eyes as hard as marbles. "We're finished. The bank will take everything that's left, and it won't be enough to pay our debts."

"I'm sorry, Travis."

He stood up abruptly. His hands smoothed the creases in his jacket, trying to recapture some of his dignity. He walked over to the bar and tossed a shot of Wild Turkey down his throat. "My inheritance is gone.

All I have left is Jen." There were tears in his eyes.

"I have Iris."

Travis looked at me with pity. "Iris isn't the kind of girl to stick around. As soon as she finds another rich sucker, she'll be gone. Mark my words." He didn't say it in a mean way, which made me think it might be true.

I felt like shit. Had I saved his life only to ruin it?

When I got home, a sports car was parked on the circular drive directly before the front door. Its roof was so low I couldn't imagine an adult could sit upright inside it.

I went into the house. No sign of my wife or her visitor. "Iris?"

She peeked out of the study, slipped out, and softly shut the door behind her. She reminded me of a deer venturing into a clearing during hunting season.

"What are you doing home?" Her voice trembled.

"Who's in the study?"

"Let me explain first." She looked so guilty I expected the worst.

I brushed Iris aside, rushed towards the study, and flung open the door.

Iris' visitor was Paulina Gibson.

Her mouth curled into an unfriendly smile. "You've moved up in the world since we last met. Only this morning, by the way. The house is a vast improvement over death row. You were naughty, but I won't punish you as long as you pay me what you owe. I was just discussing the situation with Iris."

"Leave my wife out of it."

Paulina chuckled. "She's part of it."

Puzzled, I glanced at Iris. She didn't look a day over twenty. I had noticed her youthful appearance this morning, but I had heard that pregnant women glowed. The truth was I had been too preoccupied today to give Iris much thought. When I'd met her at the Longhorn Tavern, even in the shadowy bar, she'd looked closer to forty than twenty.

"Darling," Iris said, "let me refresh your memory. Two years ago, you murdered Travis, and I murdered my husband. Don Newsom defended us both, and we both got convicted. You were sentenced to death. I got life in prison. Paulina's time machine was our only hope of getting our convictions reversed on appeal. The bartender was supposed to be our alibi, but you left the Longhorn Tavern early and prevented the murder of Travis."

"And you?"

Her eyes darted away. "I followed Paulina's instructions. I was afraid of what might happen if I stopped myself from shooting my husband. You testified at my trial that we were together until 10:45. You were my alibi."

My head swung around to Paulina. "You sent two murderers back in time to the same bar on the same night! Wouldn't that have looked suspicious if we had both needed the bartender as an alibi?"

Paulina alighted on the edge of my big cherry wood desk. My eyes ran down her long legs to her purple pumps with narrow ankle straps.

"I admit it wasn't ideal, but the license for my time machine was about to expire and I needed money fast to renew it. If I don't renew before midnight tonight, I'll have to pay a huge setup fee for next year. The economy's in a recession. Demand for time travel has dried up." She pulled a gun out of her handbag and calmly pointed it at Iris.

I still had to come to grips with the fact that Iris was a murderess.

Iris must have seen the anguish on my face because she began to sniffle. Or maybe she was plain scared.

"How much do we owe?" I asked.

"A million dollars each."

"Iris, do we have two million?" I thought I already knew the answer.

"We invested the money from my husband's life insurance policy in TLC. Your salary comes in, and it goes out."

Obviously, I hadn't received a payout from Travis' policy. And TLC was bust.

"No worries," I lied. Maybe I could buy some time. "Paulina, if you'll give me your bank account number, I'll have the money transferred from the TLC account this afternoon. All I have to do is make the phone call."

"That's more like it," Paulina said, letting down her guard just a bit, but it was enough. I walked slowly towards the desk, and as I reached for the phone, I suddenly changed direction, lunged, and grabbed at the gun. It flew out of her hand and skidded across the wooden floor.

Iris got to it first. She scooped it up, and in one fluid movement, without a moment's hesitation, took aim and fired. Paulina appeared to be dead when she struck the floor.

"Why did you do that?" I cried. My heart pounded. Visions of prison bars flashed through my head.

"I know the TLC bank account is in the red. There was no other way. We would have been watching our backs for the rest of our lives, which would undoubtedly have been short. I had to think of our baby." Her eyes were pleading.

From where I stood, she had reacted instinctively without thinking of the baby or anything else. Goosebumps erupted on my arms. She was still clenching the gun. I wrapped my hand around the barrel, pointing it away from me. Her fingers loosened, and she let me take it.

A pool of blood was expanding next to the body and with it a nauseating coppery smell.

"We'll have to dump the body," I said. Travis' family owned a ranch near Dripping Springs—a perfect impromptu burial site. "I'll get a blanket to wrap the body in. You get a mop and a bucket of soapy water."

Iris told me where to find the blankets, and we hurried out of the study heading in opposite directions.

I got back first

I couldn't believe my eyes. The patch of floor that had hosted the pool of blood was dry and untainted. The body had vanished. All that remained of Paulina was the skirt, jacket, panty hose, underwear, and purple pumps that she had been wearing, heaped on the floor in the approximate position they would be if her body was still wearing them. The ankle straps were still fastened. Her handbag lay on the desk where she'd left it when she pulled out the gun.

Iris entered the study, bent over to one side by the weight of the bucket full of steaming water. In the other hand she held the mop. She stared.

I felt faint.

Iris set down the bucket and sank onto a chair.

Then a crazy idea struck me.

I trotted over to the desk and rummaged in Paulina's handbag. How could she have found anything? No time to waste. I shook out the contents: a bunch of keys, bulging billfold, hairbrush full of brown hair, sunglasses, frayed tissues, and, underneath, the time travel device.

I perused the user-friendly menu. The software version was dated twenty-seven years in the future. On the back of the device was the familiar logo of Angel IT.

I slipped it into my pocket and headed towards the door.

"Where are you going?" Iris asked, tears sliding down her cheeks

"To the office. If I can duplicate the time travel software, TLC's cash flow problems will be history. With my programming skills and Travis' marketing talent, we'll be back on top."

"What about us?"

We needed time to get to know each other. Maybe she'd had good reason to shoot her first husband.

I blew Iris a kiss.

LIFE OR DEATH
BY STACEY JAINE MCINTOSH

Briseis ran blind. The stars overhead looked like tiny crystalline orbs in the night sky. The moon was void, making it harder to see what was ahead of her, and many times she tripped and almost fell. The third time she did fall, but she didn't hit the ground.

Strong and muscular hands gripped her shoulders, as dark, probing eyes bore into hers. Briseis felt as if he could see into her very soul, had she possessed one. Leaning in, he tucked a loose strand of her hair behind her ear, his fingers lingering on the pointed tips.

Briseis shivered under his touch, and felt the presence of something cold clamp around her slender wrists. It radiated a heat that wasn't all that unpleasant, until it began to burn. Her skin hissed as the metal touched it. *Iron?* Surely, the humans hadn't evolved enough that they knew the fey's biggest weakness? She only knew of one other creature, besides herself, that could pass as human, and that was a werewolf. But, as she had been told many times over, they were the enemy.

She sank to her knees in agony, as the world slipped away from her and tumbled into darkness. The stars overhead were snuffed out, as if they had been no more than meager beeswax candles than crystalline orbs.

"Well, well. What do we have here?" He touched her again, rousing her from her stupor. His index finger traced the line of her jaw, from her eye to her chin, and tipped it up so she was forced to look at him. If she hadn't been bound at the wrists and rendered almost too weak to move, she would have slapped him. Instead, she settled for second best and spat; the spittle landed just above his nose before it zigzagged along the contours of his face, to his stubbled chin.

"Rather feisty for a faerie aren't you?" He wiped his face with the sleeve of his jacket while Briseis remained silent.

Her hands jerked, the cuffs biting into her wrists as she tried, and failed, to reach the contours of her ears. "Stupid glamour," she muttered. It was a tricky magic to master, and not all fey, managed to grasp its complexities, despite their preternaturally long lifespans.

He pulled on the cuffs, nearly dislocating her shoulder in the process, and all but dragged her over to the edge of a makeshift camp, not too far from where a fire was burning. She could smell the damp earth and dead leaves, as well as the wood as it burned to ash.

"Sit." He commanded before disappearing into the darkness and returning with a length of chain in one hand. "You didn't run, maybe there's hope for you yet, little faerie," he said, as he worked to attach the iron chain to her cuffs and slammed a metal spike into the ground with the heel of his boot.

He sat down next to her, but not too close. Despite the darkness and distance, Briseis was able to study him in detail. Given her keen eyesight, she noted from the color of his eyes and the shape of his face that he wasn't a full blooded werewolf. So, what was he doing here amongst them?

"Let her go, Zack," a stranger walked up to the two of them and stood opposite Briseis. This one was definitely a werewolf, she thought. All the indicators, including those that were missing in the half cast, were present in this new specimen.

"No way, Fenris! I *found* her and I get to *keep* her. She's mine to do with as I please, so keep your dirty paws to yourself."

"I don't think so. She's not some bone that you can toy with she's a—"

"Faerie?" Zack asked. "And we're wolves which makes her *prey*."

"You, a wolf?" Fenris scoffed. "You're no better than the human your half breed mother mated with."

Briseis didn't even whimper and the two men stared at her in surprise.

"I won't be a part of this, Zack. If Markus finds out that you brought one of *them* here, he'll skin you alive and sell your pelt to the highest bidder. Is that what you want?"

"Of course not, but Markus isn't here and won't be back for three days. I reckon we could have some fun between now and then."

"Because a dead faerie is so much better than a live one," Fenris scoffed. "Really, Zack, you can be so stupid sometimes, you know that? *Let her go!*"

The last three words were no more than an unintelligent growl but his stance said it all. It was menacing, primal, but more importantly it said *obey*.

"No!" Zack replied, baring his teeth.

She didn't struggle; instead, Briseis sat perfectly still, watching as the two wolves fought over her. She only screamed at the very moment they phased from human to wolf, from shock more than anything. She'd never seen a werewolf up close before.

"Then, as the pack's Beta, I give you no choice. Let her go. That's an order!" Fenris said after he phased back into his human form.

Zack whined; even in the dim light Briseis could see him lower his head and expose his throat, in what she assumed was a submissive gesture. When he strode over to her and unlocked the cuffs at her wrists, she simply sat there, stunned. Since when had the wolves allowed fey to get up and walk away? All the tales she'd grown up on had said they were the enemy, and yet here she was, free again, when she hadn't counted on that at all.

"You're not leaving?" Fenris' voice rose an octave as he continued to stare at her. "Why aren't you leaving?"

"I came here to die," Briseis answered.

"You came here and deliberately put yourself in the path of a pack of wolves, just so you could die? Are you insane?" Fenris asked.

It was obvious to Briseis, in that moment, that Fenris wouldn't be easy to convince. Killing her was against his better judgement, which was funny because they were supposed to be enemies. It was kill or be killed. Guess the rules had changed.

"That's irrelevant," Briseis snapped. "I came here to die. So, you can either help me, or not."

"Faeries don't die, it's a well-known fact. You outlive everybody, except the parasites."

"Why should we help you to *kill* yourself?"

Why? Why not? Last she'd checked, werewolves despised the fey. Killing them came naturally. Or, at least, it was supposed to. Briseis huffed, blowing stray strands of hair out of her eyes. As she struggled to find the right words, her mother's own came bubbling up from within. *Life is a continuous cycle. There is no beginning, nor end. Death is merely a doorway...*

The words faded away. She needed to die if she had any hope, at all, in gaining her soul. Of course, admitting that she wanted a soul in the first place seemed somewhat trivial. There was no way Fenris or Zack would understand her desire to become more like them—more human.

"It's just something I have to do," she said, with a small shrug of her shoulders. "Think of it like a rite of passage."

"You have to die?" Zack asked, again. Minutes ago, he'd all but talked freely about taking his pleasure in killing her for the fun of it, but now he was questioning *her* motives. Gods, he had some nerve.

Briseis only nodded.

"I won't help you." Fenris replied, while one look at Zack told her that he was clearly still processing everything she had just said, so Briseis waited.

Finally, Zack responded with a quick shake of his head. "It seemed more fun when I thought you were scared." His voice shook, alerting her to the fact that Zack was scared. What on earth did he have to be afraid of? She was the one who was going to die. Perhaps that was what Fenris meant when he had chosen to mock Zack about his status as a wolf.

"Then I'll do it myself," Briseis said, knowing full well she sounded more confident than she felt. Death, when you lived as long as the fey, suddenly felt rather perplexing and alien to her.

Without a word she stood up and walked calmly from the fire and back into the dark night. Turning her back on the woods, she hit the hard bitumen street. It was slightly better lit than it had been in the werewolf camp near the woods, but for Briseis to be taken by surprise, given her keen eyesight, came as a complete shock even to her.

The human stood under the eaves of the corner building, cocked her head to one side, and smiled, reminding Briseis of one of her own, while instincts told her that this *thing* couldn't have been *one of her own*. Fey, no matter how diluted their blood was, possessed a little extra charm, and this girl's natural ability fell ever so slightly short.

"Underestimating me was your first and last mistake, darling," the girl said. "Not running was your second."

Briseis shrugged. "So, kill me already. I'm not scared. In fact, I want to die."

The girl took one step forward, the light of the streetlamp cascading over her, which allowed Briseis to see her clearly. She was blonde, had green eyes, and freckles ran across the bridge of her nose. Pretty, in an all-too-wholesome way, really. Of course looks could be deceiving.

"Tell me, why does such a young thing like you want to die? Your life—such as it is—is only just beginning."

"Oh, it's just something I've always wanted to try, is all." Briseis' tone was laced with sarcasm.

"Well, beggars can't be choosers," the blonde girl said as she flashed Briseis a fantastic smile, exposing razor sharp teeth.

In that single moment, panic shot through Briseis' entire body, rendering her both mute and paralyzed at the same time. She wanted to scream, but when she did no sound came out. This girl was definitely not human; in fact, she was nothing like any of the creatures Briseis had heard of or seen in her entire life.

"Go ahead and run, I won't stop you. In fact, it will make this *situation* all the more exciting."

So Briseis ran—again—only this time she was thankful that she was running on flat ground. It afforded her only a small advantage, and just like last time she stumbled and fell, landing herself in a man's strong arms again.

Zack? What was he doing here? Not that she wasn't glad that he was, but wasn't his place with a pack, not roaming the streets of some nondescript country town alone?

"Looks like you could do with my help in staying alive after all."

"I'm doing just fine on my own, *thank you*."

"Sure as hell doesn't look like it," he said as he released her. "You're running, as in *away* and I'm telling you now, you don't want to die by that *thing's* hand. Trust me, there are nicer ways to off yourself than to be bitten by one of those."

"Shouldn't you be with your pack or something?" Briseis asked, answering his question with a question of her own.

"If you could call that menagerie a pack, but help me understand something, because I just *don't* follow your reasoning at all. Why do you want to die so badly?" Zack paused, looking at her with fervent scrutiny. "Believe me when I say you don't want that girl to get her hands on you. A vampire's bite is one of the most excruciatingly painful ways to die. I've witnessed a few members of the pack die that way. It's almost like you're burning from the inside out."

"What's your point?" Briseis had her hands on her hips

Zack reached out for her wrists, taking both of them in one of his own large hands. "The cuffs... they didn't *hurt* you?"

The iron had hurt, hurt more than any other pain she had experienced before in her entire life, but she wasn't going to admit it aloud. She frowned and pulled her hands out of his. "Go away, Zack!"

"Aww, I'm hurt," he mocked, as she turned away from him. "No... hang on a second, we're not finished. I just saved your arse, missy, yet again, and this time from someone far meaner than me. Show me a little gratitude, at least."

"Briseis. My name is Briseis," she said, turning around to face him. "And, for what it's worth, you didn't save me, Zack. You just kept the lure of death at bay for a little longer."

"Briseis," he repeated, trying to wrap his tongue around it. "I'll help you die *if...*"

Briseis squealed in delight. "You'll help me, like, really help me?"

"You haven't heard my condition yet. I said if. I'd help you *if.*"

Briseis nodded eagerly. "Okay, so what's your condition?"

"Tell me why you want to die."

Briseis sighed. "We have to experience death so we can receive our soul. We're not born with one, you see, and not every fey wants to possess one. It's because we don't have a soul that we are set apart from the mundane."

"So, it's some sort of soul quest?"

"Yes," Briseis paused, she wasn't going to sugar coat it. "So now that you know, will you help me?"

"You're not giving me a choice, are you?"

"No. Either you kill me or I let the vampire do it," Briseis said, watching as Zack's mouth turned down in a frown. It was either him or the vampire. Was it really that hard? Briseis thought it an easy choice, given what he'd told her and how painful a vampire's bite could be. Did he really want to put her through that?

"Fine," Zack said at long last. "But hold still, this may hurt a little."

Briseis exhaled, having been unaware that she'd been holding her breath until the idea of pain registered, and right there and then she wanted to leave death and dying to the mundane folk. Fey had no business messing with a cycle they clearly didn't understand.

"Briseis?" Zack asked, looking more closely at her. "You still with me?"

She nodded once but said nothing, as her thoughts whizzed a mile a minute through her head. It occurred to her then that she hadn't even asked how he was planning to kill her. She should have asked. A normal person would have asked. *But you're not normal, Briseis, you're fey,* she chided herself. And fey were higher up on the hierarchy compared to that of werewolves, supposedly, remembering her lessons; Fey, werewolves, and humans. Although, she supposed it now went something like fey, werewolves, vampires, and humans. Perhaps she ought to have already known how Zack planned to kill her.

She closed her eyes, and concentrated on her breathing, in a miserable attempt to quell her overactive mind, along with the latent fear that had practically come out of nowhere.

"On three. One... two... thr—" Her eyes flew open as Zack plunged the knife into her chest.

So, that's how...

She slumped to the ground in the same instance that the world around her went black.

* * *

Light returned.

As Briseis came to, blinking slowly, Zack simply stared at her, with a mixture of what looked like shock and awe. Standing up, she brushed gravel from the back of her skirt and finally without so much as a second thought, pulled the knife awkwardly out of her own chest and let it fall, with a clatter, to the bituminised road. There was a slight hiss as her heated skin met with the coolness of the outside air.

"So that was, um, weird," Zack offered, breaking the uneasy silence.

Briseis held her injured hand with the other; she'd have to bypass the lake on the way back home. It was weird, she agreed silently, but also kind of freeing. "It was good of you to help."

"Better me than some nasty vampire," Zack agreed. "So, I guess you go back home and collect your soul now, huh? Finish the quest and all that?"

"Something like that," she said over her shoulder, walking away from him for the second time in one night. Without meaning to, she found herself wondering if their paths would cross for a third time, or ever again. She shouldn't have. After all, fey and werewolves were true enemies.

Even if Zack no longer wanted to kill her, even after he'd done what she'd asked, she couldn't be sure if he was acting of his own accord, or on the directive of Fenris, the pack's second-in-command and acting Alpha. It didn't mean that he'd completely gotten the blood lust out of his system. Werewolves were built to kill, whereas fey weren't. A werewolf killed more for the fun of it, which is why they had made a sport out of killing fey in the first place.

Of course, payback was always a fun pastime.

No, she thought, shaking her head. Going back to the werewolf encampment now would be nothing short of suicide.

* * *

The Hedge was a trifle harder to navigate than Briseis had anticipated. Having bypassed the Lake, she'd been able to cool her injured hand and think with a clearer head. But still the rumours that circulated around Faerie about Arawn were infamous. He was a no nonsense sort, capable of giving you your heart's desire in one moment, while ripping it right out of your chest in another.

That was just his style, and she hoped that when it came to the matter of her soul that he would be easier to deal with. A small part of her found it very unlikely, but it couldn't hurt to dream.

"And what do I owe the pleasure of a summer fey's company? I thought your sort were above the need of my services."

"I believe you'll find that talk to be nothing more than misguided rumors," Briseis said boldly, staring into Arawn's dark eyes. Two giant white hounds sat by his feet, tongues lolling from their mouths. They looked friendly but, Faerie dogs could turn vicious in a matter of seconds.

"Misguided rumors," Arawn laced his fingers together and rested his chin on his hands, as if to consider the words he'd spoken. "And what is it you want most in the world?"

"My soul."

"Your soul? My, my, such a hefty thing to ask for one so young. You'll do just as well—better, in fact—without it. Do you have a reason for wanting to possess a soul?"

Arawn was staring at her, his head cocked to one side, making Briseis uncomfortable and more than a little frightened.

Solitary fey are almost always benevolent. But Briseis wasn't convinced. The two hounds, despite their placid demeanour, looked ready to gobble her up where she stood. "I did not think that I required a reason."

"Did not think you required one? How unfortunate that I can't gift you something as precious as a soul without some sort of payment. I suppose I could feed you to my hounds, wait and see if you get spat back out and survive the ordeal." Arawn looked down at the two white hounds and scratched both behind the ears, one after the other.

"I've already died once today, I have no desire for a repeat performance," she said. "I doubt very much I'd survive death the second time around."

"A wise decision, I'd wager, but that still leaves you one gift short."

"M-my wings," Briseis said. "You can have my wings. Will that be a sufficient gift?"

"The wings of a summer fey? Not my first choice. I have little use for such things, but given how it's such a personal gift, I dare say I'll accept."

"Does that mean I get my soul now?"

"Patience, my dear, patience," Arawn said looking past her to the two barely there wings that rested flat against her back. "Besides you owe me a gift."

"So, take it already and give me my soul!"

"Ah, uh," Arawn waggled his pointer finger at her disapprovingly. "What did I say about Patience? Ordinarily, I admire a girl who knows what she wants. But rudeness is not a trait I tolerate well, if at all. You'll bite your tongue as long as you remain in my company, or you can turn around and march yourself back to whatever hollow you crawled out of."

"I—" Briseis closed her mouth. Thinking that it would be more prudent not to talk back to the only fey she knew, rumoured or otherwise, that was capable of giving her a soul.

"Much better," Arawn sidestepped Briseis and began circling around her slowly, his thumb and forefinger stroking his chin slowly. "Now, I've never actually extracted the wings from something that still has a beating heart, so this might hurt. Scream, if you have to, it makes no difference to me."

Briseis sucked in a nervous breath. The air around her grew warmer, while behind her Arawn pulled at the gossamer like threads of glamour that bound her wings to her. Once completed, she'd be wingless, but at least she'd have a soul.

The heat surrounding her quickly turned to a blazing inferno, and despite her best efforts not to, Briseis screamed. A slash of red flashed before her closed eyelids and she felt herself slip, but the world stayed. Although not in focus, it didn't go black, and she was forced to endure the blinding pain and the uncomfortable sensation of her wings being pulled from her. She wondered now if this price was worth the pain, all for want of a soul, something she could have done without.

"It is done," Arawn said, breaking the otherwise eerie silence, while Briseis panted, a cold sweat having broken out across her brow.

"D-does t-that mean I h-have my s-soul?"

"Not quite."

"What do you mean *not quite*?"

"I take souls *away*, my dear; I am not in the habit of bestowing them, at least not to just anybody. You cannot merely gift someone with a soul. It's a lot more complex than that."

"If you can't give me my soul then I'd like my wings returned."

"I'm not in the habit of returning gifts that have already been given. You paid the price..."

"And exactly what is it that I get for the price I paid?"

"The reassuring knowledge that you are still the same soulless creature you were before you came," Arawn stated matter of factly. "Without wings, of course."

"You... you *tricked* me!" Briseis fumed.

"Yes, it appears I did do that, didn't I? If it's a soul you're after, might I suggest trying the art of meditation? It seems to work remarkably well for the *humans*."

Briseis crossed her arms over her chest and huffed. She knew the solitary fey were often difficult, but Arawn took things to the extremes.

"Enjoy your walk, and do try not to get lost in the Hedge on the way out, won't you?"

Rolling her eyes, Briseis turned and walked away from Arawn. It wasn't going to be easy explaining why she'd lost her wings, especially when she had nothing physical to show for it. Her wings had been what had separated her from the humans, and now... well, she might as well have been one of them.

* * *

"So, was your little trip into the mundane successful?" Artemas asked. His sarcasm wasn't lost on Briseis, who stood in the middle of the clearing that was to the south of her home.

"Are you asking me if I failed, brother?" she asked. "Because I did not."

"Not at all. I was merely asking after your well-being, little sister. You died. Regardless of how you look at it, it's got to take some time to get your head around that."

"I'm fine, really. No nasty lingering after effects whatsoever."

"Are you sure about that?" Artemas' eyebrows shot up in surprise, as his lips turned up in what she knew was a smile.

"Yes!" Briseis huffed. Damn Arawn for taking her wings. If her brother had noticed, it wouldn't take long before everybody around her knew as well.

As with all elder siblings, Artemas was fond of overstepping his role as *big brother*. Sometimes, Briseis thought that she might one day suffocate from the overabundance of brotherly affection. "Now, go away, I'm supposed to have complete silence if this next phase is to work."

"I never did understand the concept of meditation," Artemas said as he stepped back.

"Which is why, dear brother, you've yet to attain your soul."

"A soul makes you weak."

"Spoken like a true fey who has yet to possess one," Briseis taunted.

Artemas huffed. Crossing his arms over his broad chest, he looked down at his sister, who sat crossed legged on the grass before him. His long, blonde hair was fanning out on either side of him. "You'll be singing the praises of werewolves next."

So what if I do? Briseis wanted to tell Artemas to stop being so silly, that werewolves and fey would never be friends, but something gnawed at her, telling her otherwise. Yet, she couldn't figure out what.

"That doesn't look very much like meditation to me," Artemas said, invading her all too deep thoughts. She looked up, wrinkling her brow. "Your mind's too active."

"I told you not to bother me."

"You were already bothered before I'd even left. Some small gem of a thought won't stop nagging at you," he said expectedly. "Will it?"

"Oh, go away, you soulless cretin!"

Artemas smirked. "Soulless cretin? Is that the best you can do?" He chuckled. "At least I'm not off running with wolves."

If her brother's aim had been to dig the knife in and then twist it, then he'd succeeded. Pushing her emotions further down, she squared her shoulders and tried her best to make her next words as flat and emotionless as possible. "I'm gaining my soul, not a pet."

The less Artemas knew of her changing attitude towards werewolves the better; it wasn't as if he'd understand. Artemas was too set in his ways to easily commit to change—of any kind.

"You do remember what happened at the last fox hunt, don't you?"

Briseis shivered at the memory, as images of Lacey's shredded body flashed before her eyes. The story went that several fey had gone into business supplying unsuspecting human girls for the wolves to chase. By the end, there had barely been anything left of her body to burn.

It was hard to think of Fenris and Zack as no more than the bloodthirsty animals they were, but she had to accept that, because the next time she died she wouldn't be coming back.

"Eventually even the nicest of wolves will turn on you Bri. Remember that."

Her brother's parting words were enough that they got under her skin, and soon she was pacing the length of the clearing. Pushing all thoughts of Lacey aside, she was determined to get back into meditating on her soul.

Closing her eyes, she focused on the rhythm of her breathing, with her mind newly empty, it was easy to see what didn't belong, and all too soon there was a figure walking towards her.

It was an effort to open her eyes, but when at last she did, the figure was still there, still advancing. And when *he* was close enough, she found herself staring into the piercing gaze of Fenris' golden eyes.

"What am I doing here?" Fenris asked

"I—" the last thing she'd been doing was meditating over her soul, not thinking of Fenris, or Zack. It didn't make sense that he was here. "I don't know. What do you remember?"

"Everything. You leaving. Wanting to ring Zack's bloody neck for being so stupid," he said, running his hands through his unruly, dark hair. "I even remember walking through the woods, but not how I got to be standing before you."

"You won't remember having been here once you leave, either," Briseis mumbled. It was the way of her world. So why were the two colliding now? "I think we should—"

Artemas' voice exclaimed, "Briseis, what in the name of—"

"I didn't bring him here, Art, I swear! I was sitting here, minding my own business, focused on meditating when suddenly he's walking towards me, like for real."

"Perhaps the wolf has got something to do with her soul," Briseis turned in the direction of her father's voice.

Briseis turned and saw her parents approaching, their still-youthful faces staring at her with concern.

"Don't be absurd Cass!" her mother said. "That's the most ridiculous thing I've ever heard."

"It's not that far-fetched," her father defended.

"You're talking about my daughter's soul being mixed up with a living, breathing *werewolf*! I think that's about as far-fetched as things get."

"Living?" Briseis asked as Fenris swallowed, practically gasping for air. His skin looked almost as pale as hers was naturally.

"The souls of most fey who attain one usually receive them from the likes of deceased animals. Given your soul's receptacle is still living, it makes things more complicated."

"I won't kill him," she said, her eyes darting from Fenris to those of her parents.

"You won't... are you insane?" Artemas roared. "They kill our kind for fun, or at least they used to. He could still turn on you."

"He won't."

"You don't know that."

"Yes, I do. Besides, it's my soul. Living or dead, I'm pretty sure the decision is up to me, and me alone," Briseis said.

"Fine," Artemas grumbled. "But try and remember that that thing has your soul. Treat it like a pet and nothing more."

Briseis would have laughed at what her brother was insinuating, had Fenris not chosen that moment to speak aloud. "You don't really keep werewolves as pets, do you?"

Briseis shrugged apologetically. "Some fey do. Much in the same way Zack tried to keep me."

Fenris swallowed. "I think if it's at all possible, I'd like to leave now."

"I'm coming with you," Briseis said, watching as Fenris' mouth opened but no words came out. His eyes roamed to the space behind her. The space where her wings should have been but weren't.

"I guess without your wings you'll fit right in, but I wouldn't go announcing that you're a wingless fey to anyone in the pack. Best to let them think you're a half-breed like Zack than admit to being fey."

"It's almost like being branded 'wolf-runner.'"

Fenris snorted. "Wolf-runner?"

"My brother's idea of an insult. I called him a soulless cretin and he retaliated by saying that at least he wasn't off running with a pack of wolves," Briseis shrugged. "Around here, something like that has a tendency to stick."

"It's not so bad, really. I kind of like it."

"You..." but her voice got stuck in her throat. Clearing it, she said, "You're a means to my soul, Fenris, nothing more."

"Oh, believe me, if I was looking for a mate—which I'm not—you'd be the last girl on my list."

"That's, uh, good to know," Briseis said, while mentally shaking her head. She hoped Fenris wasn't always so blunt. "We'll get out through here."

Ahead of them were rows and rows of trees.

"How?" Fenris asked. "You can't even see past the trees, they're so thick."

"Watch," Briseis said, and Fenris did. Ever so slowly, the trees bowed down at right angles making room for the two of them to step across, and leave Faerie behind for good.

CURSE OF THE BOTTLE
BY NYE JOELL HARDY

There are many things you should never say to someone you love because you can't ever really take words back—and I had said most of them to my ex-girlfriend, Mica. That was why I was trudging through Central Park that day, going to meet her at our old favorite deli, so I could pick up the key to my apartment.

It was over. I was sick to my stomach over it. My head knew I might enjoy life in the future, but my heart was offended by that kind of optimism. Yeah, she'd been a bitch sometimes. Yeah, she couldn't ever make up her mind over anything, from how many creams in her coffee to whom to vote for president. Yeah, she'd stepped out on me at least once—well, all the time, really—but I couldn't help feeling I'd made a terrible mistake by kicking her out.

It was in that self-pitying frame of mind that I was going down a grassy slope and something hooked my foot. I didn't just trip on it, I did one of those flailing movie "Wa-a-AA-AHHs" before I crashed face first in wet grass, followed by my own backpack smacking my head. It didn't do very much damage to my dignity because I pretty much didn't have any left, so I just looked back at what had caused my downfall. I saw the long neck of a green bottle—maybe a wine bottle— jutting above the lawn like an evil little periscope. Testing the ankle that had taken the hit, I stood up.

Some damn kids had probably buried it in the dirt. I had a grass skid mark straight down the middle of my favorite t-shirt. I could also feel a bruise puffing around my ankle. Sighing, I figured I'd better pull the hazard-to-all-ankles-everywhere out and throw it away before it up and killed someone else less lucky than myself.

Walking up to it, I saw there was a wax-sealed cork on it, and working it out of the soft dirt, I saw it was really a small jug, not a bottle. Despite being sealed, there was no liquid in it... but maybe some dead leaves... no, a wobbling stick... an insect? No, a... I brushed off the dirt and peered in close, closer, closer...

A pair of pale eyes met mine.

"What the—" Insert the swear word of your choice here, because I honestly don't remember what I said. I couldn't make myself think or move. I just held the jug in front of my nose and stared at him.

He was a tiny little living man, long dark hair, long dark beard, and not a stitch of clothes on him. Nothing; not even sneakers. Naked as the sun is bright, he leaned forward, his palms against the concave glass, nodding and smiling at me. It was a long, long time before I could manage anything other than staring.

"You're a pixie?" I asked. "A fairy?" I wondered if he really had green skin, or if that was just the color of the bottle, but it seemed rude to ask.

"A genie," I distinctly heard him say.

His accent hinted of many languages. *Old* languages. He grinned happily at me. I blinked, mostly because my eyeballs were getting dry from staring.

"The three wishes kind of genie?" I asked.

"No, not that kind."

"Oh. Are you the James-is-now-having-a-psychotic-break kind of genie?"

The genie shook his head, which could be taken as a "yes," if this were in fact a psychotic break. Great. Here I was, standing in the middle of Central Park, holding a bottle up to my nose, talking to it. I glanced around.

Yep. People were watching me.

In a really weird sort of slow-motion panic, I tucked the jug into my backpack and jogged the rest of the way to the deli.

* * *

Mica came walking up as I turned the corner. All over again, my heart shriveled up and rotted like a monster in an old stop-action horror movie. I loved the way she walked—I love the way all women walk—but her pace, the sway of her hips, her shapely torso swathed in cable knit because she was always cold; they were the backbeat of romance for me. It hurt in so many ways, I felt like I was drowning. A thousand words jammed in my throat like the musty bricks of the Berlin Wall.

"Here's your key," she held up a small manila envelope. She could see my feelings were running too high. "Everything okay, James?"

Well, my world was over, and I was carrying a hallucination in my backpack... or I had just acquired a naked genie my ex-girlfriend would probably screw in a heartbeat if she had half a chance.

"It can't get any worse," I said.

She dropped the key into my waiting hand. "It wasn't my fault." She stared at me for a moment, and turned around. Then she was walking away, filling and breaking my heart at the same time.

I groaned and closed my eyes.

"Hey," said someone faintly, from inside my backpack.

Fine, I thought to myself. *I'll talk to the genie. It's better than being the lead character in a bad love song.*

I took the genie back to my apartment, my lousy small New York apartment which had seemed bohemian and cool with Mica there—two people in love, squished together in love—but now it was just a stunted caricature of an actual home. I put the jug in the sink and began to wet-sponge the dirt off it. The genie looked up at me, expectant. The nudity was getting to me, though.

"Can you put some clothes on?"

He nodded, and suddenly was wearing a tie-dye shirt, cut-off jeans, and flip-flops. A tiny beanbag appeared behind him, and he flopped back into it, and crossed his legs. I toweled off the glass and carried him back to my lovese... uh, sofa, and put him on the shelf next to the TV so we could both sit to talk.

"So you're not the three wishes kind of genie?" I asked.

He shook his head.

"Because I could really use three wishes right now. I've known two of them since I've been a kid, and I have a third one I just found out about that I need really, really badly."

"Sorry," he said.

"So, what can you do?"

He gave me a hopeful look. "If you let me out of this bottle, I will give you... three *curses*."

I think my shocked expression said what I thought about that.

"Yeah," he added. "I know. It's a hard sell."

"Okay. Right. Can't I just let you out and not take anything in return?"

He shook his head. "Against the rules, I fear."

"What rules?"

"The curse that put me in this bottle."

"Someone put you in there? When?"

"Oh," he thought about it. "Fifteen hundred years ago, give or take a fourscore."

"Ah, uh... what did you do?"

"Unfortunately, I made the error of cheating on my wife..."

Suddenly, I realized that Mica had left nail clippers, her crazy eye-scalding magenta nail polish, and a bottle of perfume—the perfume I'd given her for Christmas, in fact—on the shelf. There it was, right behind the genie's jug.

"Has anyone cheated on you?" the genie asked. "Because one of your wishes could be to put them in this bottle once you let me out."

"Yes... No! No, no. I don't want to do that. Really, I don't want to curse anyone."

"Are you sure? It could just be a small curse. Like leprosy."

"God, no!"

"Or psoriasis. I am given to understand that's not nearly as bad."

"I..." I shook my head. The genie steepled his fingers contemplatively at me, so I added, "I... I really need to think about it. I've never thought about being able to curse people before. I don't think it's something one should do lightly." Against my will, the song Genie in a Bottle went through my head. I wondered then: Why couldn't I get the Barbara Eden kind of genie who wants nothing but my happiness? Why did I have to get the hippie, curse-y kind of genie?

"I'm going to have to sleep on it." *Because I think I hit my head too hard on the grass, and I am really hoping the swelling and you will be gone when I wake up in the morning.*

"Okay, man. I understand. But, could you leave the TV on for me?" he asked. "I get bored."

"Um, sure. What do you want to watch?"

"Law & Order is fine, any of them. Or HGTV."

* * *

In the morning, I'd made a point of seeming too busy to talk to the genie, although I acquiesced a little—after telling him to put some damn clothes back on—by changing the TV to "Judge Judy" just before I left for work. He'd looked pretty bummed.

Now, sitting at my computer—does it not seem that, regardless of your education, desires, or skills, you will in fact be spending most of your days stabbing your fingers at a keyboard and staring at a coldly glowing screen waiting for something to happen?—I started looking for some way out of my predicament.

A curse, according to Wikipedia, was "any expressed wish that some form of adversity or misfortune will befall or attach to some other entity—one or more persons, a place, or an object." Also, it could "refer to a wish that harm or hurt will be inflicted by any supernatural powers, such as a spell, a prayer, an imprecation, an execration, magic, witchcraft, God, a natural force, or a spirit."

That didn't really help me. Was there anyone I wanted "adversity" or "misfortune" to befall, even just a little bit? I'd thought of old school bullies, insensitive relatives, domineering bosses, a couple of girlfriends (yeah, Mica too), and even a dog that had bitten me when I was a kid.

Heck. The dog was probably dead by now. They don't live that long. And cursing a place or an object just seemed to have too many possible unforeseen ramifications. It wouldn't be responsible, I worried. Life always seemed to mete out its own brand of justice: did it really need me doing it, too?

"James." It was Manny in the next cubicle over. "You okay? You look like shit. Girl troubles got you down?"

I half-nodded.

"Anything I can do?"

"Man, what would you do if you could place three curses on anybody?"

Manny snorted. "That's an odd question. But three Kardashians immediately come to mind."

"No, seriously," I said. "Who would you curse?"

"Why in the hell is this a serious question? You're not planning to do something to Mica, are you?"

I shrugged. "I have a genie in a bottle back at my apartment. If I let him out of the bottle, he'll give me three curses."

"You can't just leave him in the bottle?" That was the cool thing about Manny. He would roll with anything.

"It seems kind of cruel to just leave him in there."

"Okay. Well, pedophiles and murderers and drug kingpins come to mind. But wouldn't it just be easier if he gave you three wishes instead?"

"You're telling me," I said.

"Yeah," Manny said. "But come to think of it, in all those old stories getting your wishes didn't make your life any better: it just made you realize you couldn't wish yourself out of your own life."

That started me thinking on what curses would make out of my life if I did them on someone else. It also made me wonder why, in fifteen hundred years or so, *no one else* had let that genie out of his bottle? I was so fretted up by lunch time, I needed to take the rest of the day off. When I started on my way home, I knew that, unless I was gunning for a full-blown ulcer in two days, I had to do something about that stupid genie.

* * *

I'd been so eager to get out of the apartment earlier, I'd forgotten my keys. I was about to go dredge up the apartment manager, when I remember Mica's key. I'd put it in my backpack, like I do most everything—well, except my own keys, this time. I found the little manila envelope she'd given me the day before. With a shake, the key dropped into my palm.

Looking at it, I knew it was the wrong one. Too small, too old, not enough teeth.

She gave me the wrong key. I turned again to go find the manager when a horrible thought came to me. I stopped. I tried my own doorknob. It was the most sickening sensation to feel it turn and click open.

Mica had been there, all right. From the doorway, I saw my dresser drawers spilled open, and she'd also taken a whole bunch of books—not necessarily hers, either. She'd found her nail clippers and her nail polish, but she'd left the perfume I'd given her.

Oh, and the genie and the long-necked jug were gone.

The thoughts that followed were not especially cogent: *That bitch, that bitch, that thieving bitch, bitch, God I can't believe she did this, now she knows about the genie, did she ever love me or was I just a stupid schmuck, she took the genie, I wonder what else she took, the genie, the genie, GOD, she'll probably let him out and sleep with him just to get back at me, I'm sure he was naked again, that asshole, damn it, well, now at least I don't have to worry about having to think up three curses...*

At that, my brain locked up dead solid like a seized engine, and what the "Engine Trouble" light stated very calmly in glowing red letters was: *No, you idiot. Now you have to worry about what kind of curse she's going to place on YOU.*

Uh…

I could become a human Voodoo doll any minute now.

I dared not call her—things always went sideways fast over the phone when we were upset—so I decided to take the bus over to her sister's house, where Mica had told me she would be staying. It was possible she would not be there, but what choice did I have? It could already be too late, but I had to find her.

Standing at the bus stop four blocks from my apartment, my skin was crawling like a force field waiting for the first torpedo to hit. Every sound made me jump. As the bus pulled up my hands were shaking so much I dropped my change twice.

Maybe she gave me a horrible degenerative disease. That's why I'm shaking. I hiccupped at that, which immediately felt like a heart attack. The little old ladies on the bus were gripping their canes tightly, waiting to do battle, staring at me.

My curse is I am going to be beaten to death by little old ladies with their canes because they think I'm deranged?

Oh, wait. I am deranged.

Embarrassed, I went to the back of the bus, hugged my backpack, and tightly closed my eyes. I was still trembling. *Die like a man. Die like a man. Die like a man,* I kept thinking to myself. I wasn't quite sure what that all entailed, but I was pretty sure it did not involve screaming and crying like a six year old beauty queen who'd lost to the fat kid—because that's what I really, really felt like doing.

Every time the bus jerked to a stop, I felt some organ jerk loose in my body, but I was strangely alive when we finally arrived in Mica's sister's neighborhood. Getting off the bus, I tripped and nearly busted my knee on the pavement. Death, I realized, might not be the only curse on Mica's mind.

There were no end to the sorrows that Mica could visit upon me, and for the first time, I wondered if I shouldn't have been a little nicer about throwing her out of the apartment. I mean, she'd been a harpy and a slut, but I could have taken the high road. Then, maybe…

I saw her sister's row house, and went up the stairs. Before I knocked on the door, I peeked in the window.

Through the lace curtain, I saw Mica, sitting cross-legged on the couch, the long-necked green jug in her lap, a fraught expression on her face. I couldn't see the genie from there, but I did see the waxed cork was still in place.

Oh, thank God. I thought. *Thank God she's completely incapable of making a decision.*

I knocked on the door in what I hoped sounded like a civil manner, and waited patiently. There was no answer—of course, she knew it had to be me. "Mica?" I called in the gentlest loud voice I could muster.

"Mica, honey. I'm not mad. I understand you're upset. I just want to talk."

I heard nothing. A little alarmed, I peeked through the window again. She was frantically trying to peel back the wax around the cork.

Panicking, I looked around and saw a pot of geraniums near the handrail, snatched it up, and hurled it at the window. Before my brain even caught up with what I was doing, I was pushing my way through splintered wood, long shards of glass, and lace. I staggered toward her, yelling, "That doesn't belong to you!"

Stunned, Mica had cringed back, hugging the bottle against her breasts. I could see the genie, surprised at my arrival. He was wearing a tux and his long black beard had turned into a trimmed goatee. Yeah, he knew how to work the ladies.

"Give it back to me!" I yelled again. I froze then, seeing how frightened she was. Her eyes were gigantic, tearful, and furious as well.

"You're a psycho!" she screeched. "I'm going to call the police!"

At that, the genie tried to intercede. "It's okay, really. I'm fine. Mica has HBO!"

"Please, for God's sakes, Mica," I said. "He's really dangerous. Don't let him out."

"Jeez, James." How many times had I heard that? "He's been in this bottle for an eternity. It's not right to leave him in there."

"Okay, okay." I tried to kick lace curtain off my leg, and failed. "Mica, let me take him. I'll put him back where I found him..."

"Back in Central Park? What if a gang member or someone awful finds him?"

"No one else has thought it would be a good idea to let him out, either—" I saw the retort she was preparing. "But, hey, what... what if I gave him to someone who would know how to work safely with him? Like a church, or something?"

"I beg of you! No!" the genie cried out, tragically. "Why do you think I've been in this bottle so long? I've been locked up in cathedral catacombs for centuries! They'll never let me out!"

Diamond tears started to roll down her cheeks as Mica began ripping at the old wax with her lurid magenta fingernails. "I'll think of something," she muttered.

Every muscle fiber in me wanted to lunge at her and wrest the jug from her, but it was so wrong to physically attack her. My still flip-flopping broken heart wouldn't hear of such travesty. Besides, I might break the bottle and free the genie by accident.

I watched the last curl of wax fall away.

"Please don't curse me!" I cried out.

Mica stopped. Her hands dropped. Still tearful, she looked at me, and in an odd way, the deep sadness that overcame her also seemed to relax her a little. "I would never put a curse on you, James."

I just looked at her, not sure why I was chagrined, feeling helpless.

Her voice was at its most tender. "Why would I curse you? You're the most..."

My heart was beating so loud I was sure she could hear it.

"...the most..."

I felt dizzy.

"...the most cursed person I know," she finished.

At that point, I had really been expecting a declaration of undying love and the begging of my forgiveness. I stared at her, not just a little disappointed, but pretty damn raw, in fact.

"No one is more miserable than you are, James," she continued. "You are not exactly the-glass-is-half-full kind of person, if you know what I mean. Nothing makes you happy, and you imagine all sorts of crap when there isn't anything readily available. Nothing ever goes your way, and you don't ever figure out that it's you making sure that's the case. I don't need to curse you. You're already cursed."

We were both silent.

All I could think was: *She's right. She's right.*

I thought of all the accusations I'd ever made at her. In the beginning, they'd been without any evidence. It was only later when...

I felt tears in my own eyes. I looked up at the ceiling, so Mica wouldn't see me about to cry.

"If it helps, I know some great curses," the genie said.

"Give him to me, Mica," I said, still staring at the ceiling. "I don't want some unforeseen consequences hurting you by unleashing any curses. These things can go really badly if you don't word them very carefully; think them all the way through, I think. I'll figure out something safe to do with him. I promise."

Finally, I was able to look at her again.

As usual, she was unable to make up her mind. She looked down at the genie, who met her gaze with an ingratiating leer. I had always hated the way she looked at other men.

"Please, Mica."

Silently, she held the bottle out to me. "Here. And you're paying for that window, right? If you don't, Annie will hunt you down and gut you like a salmon."

Before she changed her mind, I scooped the green glass up into my arms. "Call the repair guy. You know my credit card number," I said. "I know I told you I changed the numbers, but I didn't."

I disentangled myself from the curtain and left through the front door. The genie was silent, anxious about his fate. Glumly, I walked back down to the bus stop, sat down on the bench, and put the jug beside me. I looked around. The neighborhood was very quiet, no one was on the street. Distant traffic was the only noise. I sighed.

"You better keep your clothes on," I told him.

I pulled out the cork. It came out slick—my arm flung wide and I almost threw the cork into the street—no difficulty at all, a low-rent version of Excalibur's sword, with me as the foretold (and cursed) wannabe-hipster Arthur.

And there he was. The genie, standing right before me. I had thought he would be much taller. But he was very short, very wispy, pale as a vampire, large eyes fairy green, mercifully still wearing his impressive black tuxedo. And he was as surprised as I was. For the first time in fifteen centuries, give or take, he was experiencing the air, the sun, the ground, the entire world. He must have felt a newborn colt shivering at the new planet he'd arrived on.

Softly he said, "Give me your curses."

"Okay. I'm putting all three of them on myself." I took a deep breath. "Number one. I want a 1963 cherry red split-back window Stringray Corvette in mint condition."

Long black hair flickered by a breeze, the genie stared at me.

"Number two. I want a legitimate winning lottery ticket for at least twenty million dollars. And number three, I want to live the rest of my life with my true love."

He looked at me sadly. "Those sound like those three wishes you wanted, not the three curses I needed."

"You heard what the lady said. I'm a loser. I turn everything into a curse. So I might as well start with what I want, since it's going to end up being a curse, anyway." I told him.

The bright green eyes dimmed a little and he looked away. I thought he might be afraid of returning to his jug. "She did say that." He fell quiet.

"What happens, now?"

"I don't know. I've never gotten to this stage before." Worriedly, he shoved his hands in his pockets. Then, he pulled his hands out again like he'd made a terrible mistake. "Hey. These must be for you."

He showed me some silver keys on a white rabbit's foot keychain. I accepted them, as surprised as he was. We both looked around. There it was in its glistening cherry red glory, a vintage Corvette Stingray, split window included, parked directly across the street from us. Great rims, too.

He took the other hand out of the other pocket. "And this."

I read the slip of paper he handed me. It was a New York State lottery ticket with the next day's date on it. We goggled at each other, both feeling an amazing giddiness. I realized that we had not heard anything from the third "curse." I looked down the street.

The street remained empty and quiet. No one came out of Annie's house. It should have been upsetting, I suppose, but instead I felt a weird wash of relief.

"I guess you're getting a new girlfriend," the genie said. He hugged himself, hands on his elbows. It was a little boy's gesture that made me smile. He added, "Come to think of it, *I* want a new girlfriend. And a hun-burger... because I'm really, really hungry."

"You mean a hamburger?"

"That's not what Attila called them," he remarked with a smile.

"Okay, come on. I'll take you." I jiggled the car keys at him. "I've got wheels."

I'LL COME BACK FOR YOU
BY A.C. HALL

It happened in a swift series of violent moments. The door being kicked in, the heavily armored men rushing inside, the screams of the young couple who lived in the house, the brief struggle as they fought back, the way they were pinned down and bound, the dragging out to the waiting vehicle. A minute before, they had been curled up on the couch, in the midst of a movie and a quiet evening at home together. Now they were prisoners, their deaths not far off if all of the rumors were to be believed.

"Why is this happening? Why us?" Beverly cried.

"Just stay calm, we'll find a way out of this," Harold told her.

They had been blindfolded and she couldn't see his face, but it was all too clear from his tone that he didn't believe his own words.

"Both of you shut up," a gruff voice barked.

The increase in abductions by this group was covered daily by the news, but like most people Beverly and Harold never thought it would happen to them. No one knew for sure who they were or why the government hadn't stepped in to stop them. It was the perfect atmosphere for rumors to grow and that's precisely what they did. In just a few short years the group's reputation had grown to mythical levels. Some of the most popular beliefs were that they were a government sanctioned group that abducted and experimented on whoever they wanted. Others reported that they brainwashed those they took. The only known fact was that anyone who had been taken by them had never been seen or heard from again.

The vehicle made three more stops and each time more people were abducted and shoved into the back. One woman couldn't stop crying. A heavily armored man stalked towards her, stepping on the prisoners without a care. The woman's cries stopped and she gasped for air. The sound of her being choked to death went on for minutes longer than Beverly thought was possible. Finally, mercifully, the woman fell silent. Her lifeless body was flung on top of the rest of them. Beverly scurried out from under it. Tears began flowing from her eyes but she forced herself to stay silent.

Harold held her tight. From time to time he'd whisper reassurances to her, trying to keep her spirits up. Beverly used to think that any situation would be okay as long as she was in it with Harold, and it was true that having him with her now helped greatly, but she struggled to believe escape or survival were possible.

He tightened his grip on her. Harold had always been able to read her moods, they had felt connected the first night they met, and he sensed her despair.

"Do you want me to try to break us out of here?" he whispered.

Beverly was surprised he had waited so long to ask, but was glad he hadn't acted on the thought without verbalizing it. As much as she liked the idea of escape, everything was in the favor of their captors right now.

"Let's wait," she whispered back. "Maybe we'll see an opening when we get to wherever they're taking us."

It was impossible to know how much time passed as they were taken to their destination. Beverly fought against dark scenarios in her mind, trying everything she could to keep a small ray of hope alive within herself. At last, what must've been hours later, the vehicle stopped and they were pulled out. The air smelled different here and there was a low roar. They were near the ocean.

A tear escaped from Beverly's eye as she realized this. Harold had proposed to her on the beach. They were planning to get married in the same spot.

"Move," a man said as he pushed her.

She stumbled forward, arms out in front of her. Panic was setting in now that Harold wasn't holding onto her.

"Harold?" she asked quietly.

"I'm here, right behind you."

"No talking!" someone shouted.

Her foot caught on something and she fell. Rough hands gripped her and yanked her up. They were herded into a building of some sort and then gathered together. Harold found her quickly and again pressed himself against her.

"It's going to be okay, I'm here," he said.

She fought against her doubts and struggled to buy into his reassurances. Before she could respond, jets of water slammed into them. All of the prisoners huddled together as they were hosed down, the water battering them. Finally, it stopped, and they were led from the room. Their soaked clothing hung on them, immediately chilling them as the temperature in the drafty building steadily plunged.

The sound of metal gates opening and closing could be heard. Beverly was shoved forward and she fell onto a hard stone floor. Someone crouched on top of her and removed the bindings on her hands. Another crash of closing metal rang out. Then the sounds started moving further away.

"Beverly?"

"I'm here, Harold," she said.

She heard him crawling, then felt his hands on her face. He lifted her blindfold. Her vision was blurry and it took a few moments for her eyes to focus. Harold offered her a weak smile and she appreciated the effort. With their hands free they embraced fully now, then separated to take in their surroundings. They were in a prison cell. The walls were made of solid concrete but there was a barred window on each of them. Beverly moved to the window on the back wall and looked out.

"The ocean," she said. She took a deep breath, trying to get a lungful of the refreshing breeze. Harold approached and studied the bars.

"Those are pretty far apart," he said as he stuck his arm between two of them.

"We're on a cliffside and it's hundreds of feet down to the water. Even if we could get out we'd probably fall into the rocks and die," Beverly said with a frown.

Harold had his whole arm out now and was wiggling, seeing if he could get his shoulder through.

"Maybe we could clear the rocks and land in the water. At least we'd have a chance," he said.

Beverly was about to argue with him, to try and talk some sense into him, when they heard a loud voice. It was coming from one of the nearby cells. They went to the side window and peered into the next cell. Three young men were there, and all of them were gathered at their own window, watching something unfold in the next cell down.

"What's going on in there?" Harold asked.

One of the men turned towards him and answered. "Men in protective clothing are doing something to the prisoners. They're filming it."

"What do you mean doing something?" Beverly asked. "What does that mean?"

"Nothing yet, just poking and prodding and— "

"Something's happening!" one of the other young men said.

The man who had been talking to Beverly and Harold returned his attention to the window. A moment later a wet explosion could be heard. The three young men leapt back in unison and screamed out. One of them fell to the floor while another ran in circles yelling. "GOD IN HEAVEN!" he repeated.

"What is it?" Beverly yelled, trying to get one of them to snap out of it long enough to tell her. "What did they do to the prisoners?"

None of the men answered and Beverly's hard fought control over her panic started to slip away. Her heart was pounding and black scenarios assaulted her mind. Harold could sense her distress and put his hand on her shoulder.

"Try to stay calm. We just need to..."

A loud metal scraping sound cut him off as the door to the neighboring cell opened. Harold and Beverly watched as the three young men scurried to the back of their cell.

"No!" one of them screamed.

Four men entered. Three of them wore black containment suits that covered their whole bodies. A fourth man, wearing armor and strapped with weaponry, stood guard at the door.

"Stay away from us!" one of the young men yelled.

The three men in the containment suits steadily came closer. One of them held a small camera and filmed, while the other two had strange objects in their hands. A blue liquid shot out from one of the objects and covered the young men.

"AHHHHH!" one of them screamed.

Seconds later the three of them exploded. Blood and gore decorated the walls and the ceiling. Piles of entrails and nastiness were all that remained of the three young men. A stomach turning odor washed over them, almost causing Beverly to puke. It smelled like a mixture of sewage, burnt rubber, and dish soap.

"We have to get out of here!" Harold yelled.

Beverly was frozen, her knuckles white as she gripped the window bars and stared at the horrifying mess in the next cell over. Harold tore her away and lightly slapped her, trying to snap her out of it.

"We have to get through the bars!" he yelled.

She watched as he moved to the back window and again stuck his arm out of it. He grunted and wriggled, and a moment later his shoulder popped through as well. He was having trouble fitting his head and sweat ran down his face as he struggled to get it through the bars. The sound of a key being inserted into their cell door spurred Beverly into action. Her heart was threatening to leap from her chest and she rushed towards the back window.

"What can I do?" she asked frantically.

"Push!"

She placed both hands on his head and pushed as hard as she could. The loud scraping of their cell door being opened gave her new strength and she shoved with all that she had. Harold's head popped through the bars and he nearly lost his grip on the outside of the window and fell to the ocean far below. He pulled his leg through and was then fully clinging to the outside of the cliffside prison.

"Now you," Harold said. "Stick your arm out first."

Beverly could hear the men coming up behind her and she knew. A tear rolled down her cheek and she shook her head. "It's too late," she said.

"No!" Harold shouted. "Just stick your arm through and I'll pull you out."

Over her shoulder he saw the three men rushing forward. His eyes went wide with panic as he realized Beverly was right, that she wasn't going to make it.

"I love you, Harold," Beverly said quickly.

"No, no, no, don't you say that!" he yelled. "Don't give up!"

Beverly turned and rushed the three men, trying to block them from the window.

"Jump, Harold!" she shouted.

He reached in through the bars, trying to grab hold of her, but she was too far away. He tried to squeeze his shoulder back through, to get back in, but it was impossible to do from the outside. Beverly fought and clawed at the men as they tried to get to the window. Her eyes met Harold's and she gave him the briefest of smiles.

"Jump," she said calmly.

Tears poured down Harold's face. "I'll come back for you, do you hear me?" he said.

"We both know I'll be dead," Beverly said. "Just go and live your life."

"I'll find a way to save you!" Harold raged. "I will come back for you!"

The men knocked Beverly to the ground and moved towards the window.

"I swear it, Beverly. I'll come back for you!"

"Jump!" she screamed.

Just as their hands reached for him Harold jerked backwards. He fell towards the ocean far below and they watched until he disappeared from view. The three of them huddled together and spoke in hushed tones. Beverly laid her head against the cold floor and sobbed. Part of her was relieved that he had escaped but now she felt completely and totally alone.

She closed her eyes and resigned herself to her fate. She pictured Harold living out the rest of his life, happy and healthy. She watched in her mind as he grew older, found another person to fall in love with, had a family. Beverly smiled, ready now to die.

A strange buzzing sound caused her to open her eyes. The armored man guarding the door was convulsing, as a blue laser beam bored into his head. A moment later he dropped to the ground, giving her a clear view of the perfect circular wound that went all the way through his head. An odd figure cloaked in a prismatic robe stepped into the doorway holding what looked like a small pistol. Trying to focus on the clothing hurt her head, as it shimmered brightly.

The three men in containment suits turned to face this mystery person. The robed figure raised the laser pistol and fired three times in quick succession, burning a hole through each of the men's heads. They fell to the ground, dead.

Beverly looked up at this unknown rescuer, trying to see the face below the heavy hood of the prismatic cloak. The figure reached up and pushed the hood away.

"Harold?"

She could hardly believe her eyes. It was him but in a way it wasn't. Gone was his smooth, twenty nine year old flawless skin. This man's face had wrinkles, weathering, and a nasty jagged scar down one cheek.

"You're as beautiful as I remember," Harold said with a smile.

Beverly slowly stood up, never taking her eyes off of him. She stared at him hard and it was like staring into the future.

Tentatively, she reached her hand out and touched the side of his face. "Is that you, Harold?"

He brought his hand up and touched the back of hers. As soon as she felt his touch, Beverly knew. Somehow, someway, this was her Harold.

"It's me," he said, tears forming in his eyes. "It's me."

"But… how?"

Loud footfalls rang out in the hall and Harold pushed Beverly into the corner of the cell.

"No time to explain. I only have a small amount of time here and I used most of it getting to your cell."

He pressed her into the corner and stood in front of her, facing the door. Two armored men rushed into the cell but Harold dropped them quickly with his laser pistol.

"Put your arms around me and hold on as tight as you possibly can," Harold said.

A million questions rushed through Beverly's mind but she did as he said.

"No matter what happens, don't let go," he said.

"Okay."

She wrapped her arms around him and held as tightly as she could. Her face was pushed into his back but she heard him fire and kill three more guards. Then there was a blinding white flash, and the world around her was gone in an instant. She closed her eyes as tightly as she could, but the light found its way inside. Beverly wanted to scream. It felt like her brain was being cooked inside her skull, but no sound came when she opened her mouth. Just as the pain became unbearable, the light faded and she fell into a state of deep and profound unconsciousness.

* * *

Beverly opened her eyes slowly but was met with nothing but darkness. She moved her fingers, struggling to get them to obey. Her whole body was stiff and as she tried to sit up she felt as if she was emerging from a coma. Her thoughts moved sluggishly in her brain and, as she got shakily to her feet, she groped into the darkness.

"Hello?"

The only answer was her voice bouncing back to her in what sounded like a very small room. Flashes of where she had been, the cliffside prison, and what had been about to happen, came back to her. Beverly panicked and moved forward as quickly as she dared in the dark. She found the wall and slid down it, feeling all over for a window or a door. Her hands found a door knob and she yanked it open.

The hallway was barely lit and she rushed down it, looking for any signs of an exit. Just as she neared an intersection she heard voices. Beverly skidded to a stop, then took off in the opposite direction. Visions of heavily armored men and men in head to toe black containment suits haunted her memory and she ran from them. Her bare feet slapped against the concrete floor as she continued her flight.

Several random turns later, she spotted an exit. Beverly pushed herself harder, disregarding any thoughts other than the ones that urged her to escape. She slammed through the door, and immediately her eyes were assaulted by an unfamiliar site and her lungs assaulted with a foul, sulfuric air. The door swung shut behind her, and she covered her mouth as she looked around at her once familiar hometown.

Immediately recognizable was Mount Gregory, the small mountain that the town was built around. But the cityscape she had grown up in, the place she and Harold had called home, was barely recognizable. Many of the larger buildings were partially destroyed, some were in flames. She turned in a slow circle, realizing that she was at the location where the mall should be. Instead, it looked like some sort of a military installation.

The earth beneath her feet shook and Beverly held out her arms, startled by the minor quake. It passed quickly, leaving her gazing up into the orange, dirty sky, wondering what was wrong with her town.

What had started as a minor burning in her lungs slowly grew to be a horrible pain and Beverly covered her mouth with her hand. It grew worse with every breath and despite her great desire for escape she moved back to the door she had come from and pulled on it. It was locked.

Each breath was harder to take than the one before and her lungs screamed out at her for more oxygen. A thin blackness played at the edges of her vision, then grew larger, threatening to overtake her. Beverly fell to her knees and clutched her throat.

"Beverly!"

She barely heard the voice, but she felt the strong hands pulling a mask over her head. Soon she could breathe again and slowly the burning in her chest subsided. She allowed herself to be helped up and then turned to look into the face of her savior.

"Harold," was all she could say.

It came back to her now like remembering a dream—the prison, his pledge to come back for her, and then his almost immediate return in older form. She looked upon him, at the aging on his face, the scar on his cheek. This was the same Harold who had rescued her from the prison.

"It's not safe outside today," Harold said, placing a reassuring hand on her back. "Let's get you back in the complex."

Gunfire rang out in the distance, towards what appeared to be the front gate. Harold frowned. "Get inside now," he said sternly.

Beverly did as he said. A young woman wearing combat fatigues opened the door as they approached. She clutched a machine gun in her hands and had a laser pistol hanging from her belt.

"Thank you, Amelia," Harold said as they passed her.

"Of course, Commander."

Beverly raised her eyebrows. She looked over at Harold questioningly, but he looked away. He led them down several corridors and then into a large, well furnished room. He pulled off his mask and she followed suit. Her eyes never left him as he moved to a safe in the wall and opened it. He removed a pitcher of water and poured two glasses, then offered one of them to Beverly.

"How old are you?" she asked.

Harold looked at her strangely for a moment, then forced a smile onto his face. "That's your first question?"

Beverly's cheeks flashed red and she took a long drink of her water to cover her embarrassment.

"Easy," Harold said, "we don't have much water left."

She stopped drinking and nodded.

"Please, sit down," he said.

Beverly sat on the edge of the couch and continued to stare at the man that she loved. He sat in a chair across from her, studying her face. Finally, he leaned back and took a deep breath.

"I'm fifty."

She tried to process this information. They were both twenty-nine years old, their birthdays were six months apart.

"But you're Harold," she said. "You're my Harold."

He smiled and nodded. "I'm your Harold."

"The prison, it was…"

"Twenty-one years ago," he interrupted. "The worst day of my life."

Beverly's mind was overloaded as she tried to piece together what was happening, what had happened.

"I watched you fall," she said. "They rushed the window and you let go. But then, just moments later, you were back and... older, and you saved me. It wasn't twenty-one years ago, it just happened."

She wasn't sure why but tears had started filling up her eyes. Harold frowned as he watched her.

"For you, it just happened. But for me it has been twenty-one years since the prison. Twenty-one long years."

An unexplained anger was growing inside of Beverly. "But I was just there!" she yelled. "And so were you!"

Harold nodded. "This me was just there, that's true. Twenty-nine year old me was splashing down in the ocean at the time," he said.

Beverly stood up, on the precipice of a mental breakdown. "How is that possible?"

He got to his feet and took her hands in his. Part of her felt strange being this close to him, but another part felt comforted.

"I said I'd come back for you, remember?"

Deep down she knew what he was saying, that what he was implying had happened, but she couldn't allow herself to believe it.

"I've spent the last twenty-one years developing..."

"Don't say it," Beverly pleaded.

"... time travel."

She pulled her hands from his and backed away. She shook her head as tears began falling from her eyes.

"The men that took us that day, they were more powerful than you can imagine," Harold said, pleading for her to understand. "But I organized a resistance and we fought back against them. We purged them from the face of the planet. And all the while I kept the most brilliant scientists and physicists working on time travel, so I could come back for you and save you from your horrible fate in that prison."

Beverly kept backing away until she was up against the wall. "This can't be happening," she cried. "It can't be real."

Harold slowly walked towards her, his arms outstretched.

"I know it's not ideal, Beverly, and I know I'm not the same as I was back then. I'm fifty and you're not even thirty, I know it's weird, but I swear to you I tried to get back to you faster," he said. "But those bastards, they were imbedded in every level of our society. It's a miracle we were able to beat them at all. They slowed my research, but I never gave up hope. No matter what the obstacles, I never let anyone stop my development of the technology that could send me back to save you."

He extended his hand, hoping that she would take it.

"Excuse me, Commander," a sharp voice said from across the room. "I'm sorry to interrupt, but an attack on the complex is imminent. Your presence is needed in the command center."

Harold sighed, then nodded. He let his hand fall back to his side. "I'll be right there."

"I thought you said they were beaten, the ones who took us that day," Beverly said.

"They are; there are none of them left. This is... someone else."

She could sense the tension in his answer but didn't call attention to it.

"I have to go deal with this," Harold said. "Please, just stay here and try to calm down. I'm sorry this is so strange for you. I promise I'll answer any more questions you have when I get back."

Beverly nodded and watched as he strode from the room. She was glad to be alone and returned to the couch. She closed her eyes and attempted to make sense of everything that she had just learned. Despite her best efforts not to, she felt herself falling asleep.

* * *

Beverly's eyes shot open and she sat up quickly. She had no idea how long she had been asleep on the couch. Looking around, she saw that the room was still empty. She got to her feet and went to the door. The hallway was empty as well, and she moved down it slowly, totally unsure of where she was going or what was even housed within this complex.

At the intersection at the far end of the hall she saw a line of soldiers sprint past, weapons at the ready. The sound of explosions and gunfire outside were faintly audible through the thick walls.

She was just about ready to accept that she was lost when she heard Harold's voice.

"You're out of your mind!" he screamed.

Beverly came around the corner and saw the large command center. There were computer stations set up all over and in the middle stood Harold. He was addressing a dark-haired young man on a video screen.

"Out of my mind?" the man laughed. "That's a hell of a thing for you to say to me."

Originally planning on going inside, Beverly stayed just outside of the room, fearful of the scene currently playing out. Something about the way Harold was standing made him seem frightening to her.

"Do your people even know what you've done to this planet?" the dark-haired man asked menacingly. "Do they know that you're the one responsible for the quick death of the Earth?   Or are they so brainwashed that they believe only what you tell them?"

"Most of my people have been with me since the revolution!" Harold shouted. "They and countless like them fought and bled and died by my side, so we could rid our world of the tyrants that had silently taken it over! You're free today because of what I did, you ungrateful little bastard!"

The man on the screen laughed bitterly. "Ever the conquering hero, huh, Harold?"

Harold stalked closer to the monitors and pointed a threatening finger at the screen. "Wipe that smirk off your face," he commanded. "I freed this planet, and ever since I've had to deal with uprising after uprising. Well, I crushed those who came before you and I'll crush you as well. I'll paint the countryside with your blood!" Harold looked like a mad god as he sneered at the screen.

"I've never disputed that you saved us all, but that doesn't excuse what you've done to this world since then," the young man said. "Your secret project has killed the planet from the inside out, all so you could reconnect with the love of your life."

The young man paused and leaned closer to the screen, his face growing even larger. "But I must say, she's quite beautiful."

Beverly froze as she realized the man could see her. Harold spun around and his eyes went wide as he saw her standing there. The crazed look on his face slowly faded away.

"My men will lay waste to your complex and everyone inside," the man on the screen said. "If you come out and give yourself up, I will spare your people."

Harold didn't even hear what his opponent was saying. The crushed look on Beverly's face hit him like a bullet to the chest. He stepped towards her but she took a step away. He opened his mouth to speak but she cut him off.

"You caused everything I saw outside?" Beverly asked.

"There may be ways to heal it," Harold said. "I've got people working on it around the clock, but this little pissant and his revolutionary army have been hounding me for years. It makes it hard to sustain research."

"What did you do, Harold? Why would you cause such destruction?"

"I did what I had to do! Whatever was necessary!" he shouted, causing her to jump. "The only power source on the planet strong enough to supply the needed energy for time travel was the planet itself."

He realized he was yelling and paused to calm himself.

"We've tapped into the Earth's core, but it wasn't supposed to cause so much damage. We're not sure why it happened."

Beverly shook her head and took another step away. "You doomed the entire planet, all because of me?"

"I swore to you that I would come back."

"At the cost of damning the entire human race?" Beverly shouted.

"I couldn't just leave you there to die!"

He rushed towards her, but she turned and ran.

"Please, just hear me out!" Harold said as he chased her down the hallway.

Beverly ran blind, taking every turn she came to as Harold continued to chase after her. Before long, the hallways began sloping downwards, taking them into the bowels of the complex. Above, it had been more of a military installation, but down here were laboratories and huge banks of computers. And then she saw it. A giant room, and in the center a machine that could be only one thing. She adjusted her course and ran for it, knowing that the love of her life had left her with no other choice. Harold saw what she was doing and ran faster.

"No, Beverly!"

She sprinted through the door, then turned and slammed every button on the control panel. The heavy metal door slid shut just as Harold reached it. Beverly studied the control panel, piecing together how to lock the door. She manipulated the buttons that were by a picture of a lock and listened as the door sealed shut. There was a small window in the middle of the door and Harold's face appeared there.

"Don't do it, Beverly. You don't know what power you're messing with."

She turned away from him and approached the machine. It was a circular apparatus, and tens of thousands of wires fed into it from the ceiling. A large control panel stood in front of it, and she began looking it over, trying to decipher how it worked.

"You can't just go back in time. There are consequences you can't even imagine," Harold yelled through the door.

"I won't stay in this future that you've ruined because of me!"

"This can be our world, our time to be together," Harold pleaded. "Come out and work with me. Let's undo the damage together."

She punched buttons, familiarizing herself with the map layouts and the time gauge. The machine was still set to the same time and space coordinates Harold had used when he'd gone back to rescue her in the prison.

"What do you think you can accomplish here, Beverly?"

"I'm going to go back, and I'm going to convince you not to come back for me."

He slammed his fist into the door. "Don't you understand what that will do? It'll change this timeline, it will erase it. Once your time in the past runs out, you'll have no future to return to."

Beverly paused as she let his words sink in.

"Even I don't know what that means," Harold said, desperately hoping he was getting through to her.

She returned her attention to the control panel and pushed a few final buttons. Flashing red lights and an alarm sounded out in the chamber.

"No! Beverly don't do this! I waited so long to see you again!" Harold screamed.

Beverly saw one of the prismatic cloaks that Harold had been wearing when he'd time traveled, and she quickly put it on. She had no idea if it was essential to the time travel process or not, but decided not to chance it. She stepped onto the platform and then looked out at Harold. He was raging against the door, smashing it again and again with his fist, but when their eyes met he stopped.

They stayed that way for a long moment until finally he spoke.

"I promised I'd come back," he said. "No matter what I had to do, no matter the terrible price I had to pay, I did it for you." Tears streamed down his face and he pressed his palm against the window. "I did it because I love you."

"I know you do," she replied. "I never doubted that for a second."

And with a blinding white flash, she was gone.

* * *

Harold twisted as he fell towards the rocky shore. As he got closer he could see the jagged rocks pointing up at him, waiting to greet him.

He tried to contort his body, anything to angle away from them. He was almost upon them now, and he grunted as he arched his spine in a desperate final attempt to alter his trajectory.

He slammed into the water and rocketed downwards. Even though he'd managed to narrowly avoid the rocks, the water wasn't very deep, and he crashed into the ocean floor like a missile.

All of the precious air escaped from his lungs, and his vision went blurry from the impact. Everything hurt, but he knew if he didn't swim up to the surface soon he would die. The light in his eyes began to fade and he started to thrash wildly. Every movement triggered a thunderstorm of pain, and he was unsure if he was going to make it to the surface before his breath gave out.

Harold felt hands gripping him, tugging him upwards. He thought of the men in black containment suits, but even if he'd wanted to fight against whoever was holding him, he couldn't. His back was in agony, and he found he could barely move his arms or legs.

The mysterious person pulled him above water, and Harold gasped in lungfuls of air. He was dragged onto the shore, and as his wits finally started to return he craned his neck to look up at the person who had pulled him from the water.

"You're an angel," Harold said, smiling as he took the sight of his beloved Beverly in. She was cloaked in shimmering sunlight, but under the bright hood he could see her face. He tried to sit up so he could see her better, but pain shot from his back down into his legs.

"Sit still, Harold. Just sit and listen."

He shook his head. "We have to get out of here. I have to get you out of here."

Beverly adjusted the prismatic cloak and knelt beside him. She put her hands on his shoulders to calm him. She knew she should hurry, that there was no time to waste, but she couldn't stop herself from taking a moment to soak in the sight of him. This was *her* Harold, the way she remembered him, the way he was supposed to be.

"You need to listen to me very carefully, because I don't have a lot of time and this is going to be hard to understand," Beverly said.

She swallowed hard, suddenly overcome by the enormity of what she needed to do. With no idea of how much time she had left before she returned to the future, or if there even was a future for her to return to, she jumped right into it.

"I need to tell you about the future."

THERE'S AN APP FOR THAT
BY CHRIS ALLINOTTE

Ricky tightened the topmost nut one last quarter turn. If the time machine wasn't perfect *now*, it never would be. The machine had started to rattle when he flipped the switch to power it up a few minutes ago. With this final adjustment, he was ready... almost.

While the physics and quantum mechanics of bending space-time to his will were undoubtedly the trickiest part of the problem, they at least had been *finite;* there had been a definite end to the process, and it had come when he'd sent his hamster, Nico, forward in time by five minutes. He'd adjusted the containment beam and lased the time marker strapped to his pet for precisely thirty seconds while the computer did its calculations. On precisely the thirty-first second, a beam of green light shot out from the apparatus in the middle of the room and bathed Nico in crackling energy. With the smallest of squeaks, Nico had vanished. Five minutes later, he reappeared. His fur had been standing on end, and he became manic for awhile, darting from his exercise wheel to his water bottle three times in quick succession, but otherwise, he seemed unharmed. That had been two weeks ago—before he'd gotten himself tangled up in a logistical mess.

Ricky had wanted to continue the success of Nico's temporal voyage with his own time jump. It was reckless, but after five years of work, and no apparent ill effects to Nico, he was tired of waiting. *Now we'll get to see if this thing is worth the years I put into it.* First, he'd removed the quarter-sized sensor from Nico's belly, receiving a nip on his finger in the process. Rodents were so *touchy.* Next, he fastened the sensor to his own chest and was about to engage the beam when he had his first doubt. It wasn't about the trip itself. That much he'd settled. For years he'd been obsessed with Woodstock. His uncle Charlie had stoked this passion with years of tales that had only gotten more detailed, and much dirtier, as Ricky had grown.

"Sure kid," his uncle had growled, "We were all there for peace. Down with Nukes, the whole thing. But don't let *anyone* tell you it wasn't about getting laid too. Smokin' grass and getting some trim. *That* was Woodstock." Ricky had been enthralled. He'd read everything he could get his hands on about the festival, talked to as many people as he could that had been there, watched the movie—he was ready.

His finger was on the button when he suddenly had the thought that would ruin his day.

It was a simple thought: *I can't go dressed like this.*

That, however, led him down a winding road of problems that he had to think about before he could even attempt to go back to 1969. Not only would he have to make sure he was dressed appropriately, he had to make sure that wherever he appeared, it wouldn't be overly crowded, so he had to go to the library and research the history of the real estate around Bethel, New York, to find an appropriate place to make the jump. Getting back wasn't a problem—the sensor crystal would act as a beacon to the time machine. It would either bring him back after a pre-set length of time, or he could activate it earlier. As of now, he hadn't built in any way to override the return beam and let a traveler stay longer.

The more he thought about the trip itself though, the more problems seemed to crop up. He couldn't spend any money, as the dates would be all wrong; he'd have to try to find currency from the period. That was also a problem, as he wasn't sure that his clothing would make the trip. Because it was touching his skin, the sensor would be fine, but what else? It was all well and good to think about stealing what he needed, as *The Terminator* made it seem, but Ricky wasn't sneaky *or* confrontational.

How should he speak? Where should he go? Who was the president? As his set of notes got longer and longer, he finally decided that what he needed was a portable guidebook that he could bring with him, to give him all the information he would need about the time he was visiting, at the touch of a button. And where else did one turn these days for information but one's cell phone? With one final, loving caress, Ricky shut down the Time Jumper and sat down at his notebook. He began to program "The Time Jumpers Almanac".

When it was complete, he'd included the whole of *Wikipedia, the Encyclopedia Britannica*, and all the maps of North America he could find, going back as far as he could find. He coded page after page of dialects and idioms, customs, fashions, and—most importantly, what technology was available at any given time. These things would serve to help him blend in, and may even keep him alive, if it came to it. He didn't want to find himself arrested for treason just because he accidentally mentioned details of World War II in 1918 (not that *he* would, but he was convinced more and more that he was programming for the ages now).

That led to more questions. How accurate was the information he was putting in, anyway? Obviously Wikipedia had its limitations, but even "true" historical accounts were biased. How could he, in seeking to inform voyagers to the past, ensure that they would be prepared?

And that was when he knew what he had to do.

Ricky uploaded the applications in their present, half-finished state to his phone, uncovered the Time Jumper, and strapped the sensor to himself. There was only one way to tell what had really happened in the past, and that was to live it himself. He would write the most accurate account of history on record, because he would go there. It would be scary, and it would be dangerous—especially because he didn't have all the information he needed to blend in.

With his finger on the button to set his first destination, Ricky had to smile. What he was doing was also a stroke of genius. In writing the perfect traveler's companion to time travel, he was also going to become the undisputed master. There would be no refuting his results when he brought back photos and evidence from ages past.

He did a final check of his gear—the time sensor, the phone (with extra battery and solar charger). These were taped against his skin. It didn't make any sense to bring anything else with him, because he wasn't sure anything else would go. As it was, he'd made a new sleeve for his phone out of the same material as the sensor—just in case.

Keying in his first destination, Ricky pressed the button, and the green light came on.

> ### TIME TRAVELER'S COMPANION (excerpt)
> *Year: 1969*
> *Location: Bethel, New York*
> *Major Event: Woodstock Music Festival*
>
> *Culture Notes:*
> ### Dress
> *Casual – very casual. Blue jeans and a plain white or solid color shirt are okay. The longer your hair is, the better. If you*

have short hair, be sure to accessorize with beaded necklaces.
Wear the clothes for a week without bathing before you go.
Idioms
Intersperse your sentences with the following idioms: "man,"
"you know what I'm saying?" "peace."
Helpful Preparation
Watch: *Woodstock, (Dir. Michael Wadleigh)*
Listen to: *Get Together (Youngbloods), Are You Experienced*
(Hendrix)
Ricky's Notes
*When they say "do not take the brown acid." Do **NOT** take the*
brown acid. I was tripping so hard the time sensor thought I
was in distress and sent the signal to jump me home.

Bring your own birth control. It's way harder to find than
you'd think, and you're going to want it. My uncle Charlie was
right on this one. I haven't sorted out all the paradoxical
ramifications of interacting with the past, but to be on the safe
side, just assume that making babies in the past is a bad thing.

The message indicator on Ricky's phone was flashing, although he'd returned from 1969 within minutes of his departure—it was part of the machine's design, and meant to ensure the relative comfort and safety of the traveler. After all, Ricky reasoned, nobody wanted to come home to find that his apartment had been cleared out and someone else moved in while he was away. No—the reason his phone was flashing was that he'd gone immediately to the computer to start typing up his Woodstock notes.

He'd made sure to take lots of pictures, though he'd learned quickly to be extremely stealthy—the better to avoid awkward questions. As the party had gone on though, he'd gotten a little more reckless and ultimately, he'd wound up with the best shot of the bunch—himself on-stage with Crosby, Stills, Nash & Young. He'd convinced the roadie that took the shot that the device was a light meter for his film project. It was an insane thing to have done, but what the hell good was traveling in time if you couldn't have some *fun?*

Dialing up his answering service, Ricky heard his brother Joey's voice asking him where the hell he'd been. This couldn't have been about the Woodstock jump, he had to remind himself. Ricky had been out of touch with everyone since he'd gotten closer and closer to making time jumping a reality. He resigned himself to calling Joey back later and making dinner plans. It wouldn't do to get so caught up in the past that he forgot to live his own present life.

Then he started planning his next jump. On a whim, he punched in the Late Cretaceous period, entering it as "-65,000,000". He looked at Nico, winked, and hit the button.

> **TIME TRAVELER'S COMPANION (excerpt)**
> **Year: -65,000,000**
> **Location: New York (approx.)**
> **Major Event: Late Cretaceous Period**
> **Culture Notes**
> **Dress:**
> *Light. It's hot. If possible, stay close to areas of higher elevation to escape the increased humidity.*
> **Idioms:**
> *N/A*
> **Helpful Preparation**
> *Do Cardio. A lot of cardio. Scratch that, it needs to be more specific – running. Practice running as fast as you can.*
> **Ricky's Notes**
> *Okay, I had to look it up, because I hadn't even heard of a "Dryptosaurus" before I went back. Holy* shit*. The thing is like a cross between a Velociraptor and a T-Rex, and it's covered in purple feathers. Picture a Great White Shark, after it's eaten a flock of parrots. Dryptosaurs look like that. That's about the point where I hit the sensor to come home.*
> *Long story shor—don't go looking for dinosaurs. Your time jumper will end up bringing home a pair of bloody feet with a sensor attached.*
>
> *Also, I got bitten by a mosquito the size of my head. I put some peroxide on it. Hope it'll be okay.*

Ricky's heart was still pounding when he materialized in his living room. He went to the kitchen of his apartment and poured a stiff glass of scotch. His arm was throbbing where the monster insect had jabbed him. First things first, he thought, and downed the drink. After that, he went into the bathroom and tended to his arm. Not wanting to take chances, he took a razor blade and cut the bite open. It hurt like hell, but the alternative of having eons-old monster saliva coursing through his veins wasn't an alternative at all. He poured hydrogen peroxide right into the incision, and it foamed immediately, creating a foul smelling yellow froth that dripped into the sink. Repeating the ministrations until the bubbles were clear, Ricky bound his arm up with some bandages and went to record his notes.

Unfortunately, there wasn't going to be much he could add to the stock books of knowledge. He'd managed one clear photo of a two legged meat-eating dinosaur before it had smelled something new and appetizing and come after him—so there was that much at least. The rest of his notes could be summed up in four words—*don't mess with dinosaurs*.

* * *

As the weeks rolled by, Ricky found his motivations changing. He was finding he was no longer concerned with making his entries as lengthy and accurate as possible. Instead, he confined his writings to "Ricky's Notes." *That* was the stuff they couldn't find out in the books and websites. Let other people do some of their own work on the periods before they went back—if, that was, anyone else ever got the chance to go back. He was having too much fun jumping to worry about completing the discovery process. The information app had become an excuse for him to keep putting off sharing his results with the scientific community at large. And if someone else figured out the problem in the meantime? If someone else learned the secrets of bending and jumping through time? That was fine too. They wouldn't have his "Ricky-pedia," and they wouldn't have his experience.

He jumped, and jumped, and jumped again.

> **TIME TRAVELER'S COMPANION (excerpt)**
> **Year: 1692**
> **Location: Salem, Mass.**
> **Major Event: Witch trials**
> **Ricky's Notes:**
> *Be polite. Study the lingo. Under no circumstances should you ask ANYONE if they'd like to see you "pull a coin out of their ear."*

TIME TRAVELER'S COMPANION (excerpt)
Year: 1969
Location: New York
Major Event: Moon Landing on TV
Ricky's Notes:
Be polite. Don't show your phone to anyone. Everyone's so keyed up about technology that if they even get a glimpse of it you'll be explaining yourself for days. The best thing to do in this situation is to try and get to a bathroom and jump home.

THE TIME TRAVELER'S COMPANION (excerpt)
Year: 3199
Location: New York
Major Event: ???
Ricky's Notes:
Oh my God. What have I done?
If I'd known when I started this – if anyone had known... oh God, how could we?

I'm so sorry.
Time travel is... it's a horrible idea.

Ricky finished the last entry, and re-read it twice. He smiled, but it was a bitter, lifeless thing. Why had he even bothered writing in the log, when nobody was going to read it anyway?

He went to the closet, returned with a baseball bat, and smashed the Time Jumper into nothingness.

Before that final jump, Ricky's biggest challenge had been keeping good notes, and staying alive long enough to record them. Now, all he had to worry about was living with what he'd seen, and what he'd done—what *others* had done with his machine. He took the pieces of the machine's processor and burned them in a garbage can outside.

Hopefully, it would be enough. Time, it seemed, would tell.

ODIN'S SPEAR
BY SUSAN A. ROYAL

The sound of knuckles rapping against the frosted glass of my office door jolted me out of a particularly enjoyable dream, one that involved dancing girls. I opened my eyes and attempted to focus over the tips of my cowboy boots propped up on my desk, while the rest of me reclined in a perfectly serviceable executive chair snagged from Good Will.

"Are you in there, Boss?" The voice belonged to Charlene, my not-so-bright secretary.

"Where the hell did you think I'd be?"

She slipped inside and shut the door carefully behind her. "This is really important."

"It damn sure better be. You've interrupted my afternoon meditation."

She crossed her arms and glared at me over rhinestone-studded glasses. "You don't pay me enough to put up with that kind of talk."

"Aw come on, Charlene. It's not like you have that much to do. I haven't heard the phone all day."

She tapped a ruby red fingernail against her arm. "That's because it hasn't been ringing. No one's called in weeks, unless you count the bill collectors." Her pencil-thin eyebrows rose, and she nodded toward the outer office. "But it looks like your luck's about to change."

"Someone wants to hire me?"

"Yeah, can you believe it? I guess miracles *do* happen."

How long had it been since there'd been a paying customer on the premises? I yanked my feet down off the scratched mahogany desk. "Why didn't you say so in the first place? Who is it?"

Charlene handed me an expensive vellum card that read: Sir Dwight Winston, Esq.

"*The* Sir Dwight Winston?"

She nodded, ruby red lips pursed into a smirk.

Sir Winston was the stuff legends were made of. Archeologist, explorer, treasure hunter, you name it. He'd done it all and lived to tell about it. The man had gone on more quests than all the Templar

Knights put together and never once returned home empty-handed.

"Are you positive?"

"Of course I am. He looks just like his pictures on the cover of *World Geographic* and *Time*."

"Give me five." Charlene left, and I started scrambling. My office was a mess. Unpaid bills, candy wrappers, and old lotto tickets got shoved into an empty drawer. I used my shirt sleeve to wipe the top of the desk, and twisted the blinds nearly shut so all the dust motes in the room wouldn't be so obvious.

There was not enough time for a shave, but it took only a moment to dart into the tiny washroom to run my fingers through my hair and shrug on a jacket. A fine mist from the last of the air freshener filled the air to cover the lingering onion smell left over from lunch.

By the time Charlene had ushered my potential client in, he found me hunkered over my desk with my laptop open and frowning at the screen. "Please have a seat." Being in the same room with the famous Sir Dwight Winston filled me with awe, but I knew better than to appear overeager for his business. I pointed at the screen. "My apologies. This is something that can't wait. It'll only take a moment."

With a nod, Sir Dwight Winston lowered himself into one of my nicer chairs and waited. It couldn't hurt for me to look busy. Besides, there was no way he was going to know my internet had been shut off weeks ago.

Furtive glances in Sir Winston's direction while pretending to work gave me my first real impression of the man. He was distinguished, possessed with an air of vitality and authority. The suit he wore was undoubtedly custom-made and probably cost more than the rent on my office... for an entire year. His solid gold wristwatch winked at me, along with cufflinks sporting rubies the size of grapes. Sir Winston rested manicured hands on the expensive briefcase in his lap, showing not the slightest of tremors to betray his years.

I closed my laptop and rested my elbows on top of it, meeting his eyes for the first time since he'd entered the room. "What can I do for you today, Sir Winston?"

"Mr. Clanton, I've been told you are not one to shy away from dealing with the... unusual."

Who has he been talking to? "That all depends. What have you got in mind?"

"I was hoping to engage your services for a job that should take no longer than twenty-four hours to complete."

If the job were that simple, it had to be pretty cut and dry. "Tell me more."

Absently, he stroked the leather beneath his fingers. "First you must give me your word you will keep our little meeting to yourself."

"Discretion is my motto." I held up a hand as though taking a vow.

A knock on the door. Charlene again. She brought hot tea and a plate of stale-looking vanilla wafers. I knew what she was up to. If Sir Winston and I came to an agreement, it would mean she'd get paid for the first time in nearly a month, and she was going to do everything in her power to see that it happened. After plopping the tray on the corner of the desk, Charlene stood next to the chair as though expecting a tip.

"That'll be all, Miss Watkins." I used my most professional voice. "Hold all my calls until further notice."

She slammed the door when she left, and I turned to Sir Winston and shrugged. "She's a little slow, but she has a good heart. You were saying?"

He extracted rolled parchment from his briefcase, flattened it out on the desk, and slid it in my direction.

I found myself squinting down at a drawing of an ornate Viking spear. "What is this?"

"Do you know anything about Norse legends, those concerning Valhalla in particular?"

"You mean the Viking's version of heaven? Of course I do. I used to eat that stuff up when I was a kid... that is, until I realized Odin, Beowulf, and all the others were just stories people made up."

"What if I told you they actually *did* exist?"

I laughed, but his face stayed sober. "You're serious?"

"Indeed, and after a lifetime of research I've recently discovered Odin's dwelling, which also happens to be Valhalla, the resting place for fallen warriors and all their worldly goods. It is located high on a mountaintop in Norway." He leaned forward slightly. "*My* particular interest is in his spear."

I knew there was going to be a catch somewhere. "And you want me to get it for you?"

He fixed me with unwavering eyes. "Yes."

"If all you want is a lousy spear, why don't you go yourself?"

Sir Winston leaned back with a sigh. "There was a time when I would have jumped at the chance. In those days, danger meant nothing more than excitement to me. I'm a very wealthy man, Mr. Clanton, but I'm no longer young, and it would be foolish to throw away what years I have left—"

"When you could pay some idiot to take the risks for you?"

"Precisely. I'm not interested in any of the treasures carried to Valhalla with the bodies of the Viking warriors. Whatever you select as reward is yours for the taking. All I want is the credit for recovering Odin's spear." He sighed. "Consider it my swan song, if you must."

"Let me get this straight. You get the fame and I get the fortune?"

"While the expedition is not without possible risks, its rewards far outweigh the danger that might present itself. And it should take you a mere twenty-four hours to complete. Do we have an agreement?"

Even though I knew better than to be tempted, Sir Winston made it sound so simple. I glanced down at the drawing of the ornate spear and thought of all the *past due* notices crammed in my drawer. Who was I kidding? Business had been lousy for six months, ever since the fiasco with the Ogres. Instead of divorcing, the couple had not only reconciled, but threatened to sue me for defamation of character. It had dealt a real blow to my reputation. If I wanted to continue working as a private detective, I needed this job in the worst possible way.

"Count me in."

When we sealed the deal with a handshake, a strange tingling began in my fingertips and worked its way up my arms and across my shoulders until it had enveloped my entire body. Sir Winston didn't seem to notice. He retrieved the drawing, slid it back into his briefcase, and snapped it shut with an ominous click.

"It's a pleasure doing business with you. In one hour, Bruno will arrive to collect you and take you to the site. He will brief you on everything you need to know. The very best of luck, Mr. Clanton."

The minute he left, Charlene burst through the door. "Jeez, Boss!" Her eyes bugged, and she flattened a palm across her ample cleavage. "You really ought to warn a girl."

"What are you talking about?"

She led me into the washroom and pointed at the mirror over the sink. My rugged good looks—complete with stubble and bloodshot eyes—had disappeared, and were replaced with Sir Dwight Winston's face, right down to his aristocratic nose.

An identity veil. Sir Winston's way of ensuring he'd get all the credit for finding Odin's spear. "So that's what had happened when we shook hands." The old geezer had employed a little trick that gave the wearer someone else's appearance for roughly twenty-four hours. I'd had occasion to use them on occasion. Came in handy in my business.

I stood at my office window, focusing on the street six floors down, hoping for a glimpse of the man Sir Winston was sending. With a name like Bruno, I pictured him as a muscle-bound body guard type, arriving in a limo or maybe a Mercedes. Nothing wrong with enjoying the perks of being the famous Sir Dwight Winston, even if it was only temporary. He would no doubt brief me while he whisked me to the airport for a trip in Sir Winston's private jet to wherever the relic was hidden. With a little luck, I'd snag the spear, along with my reward, and return well within the twenty-four hours.

A beat up panel truck ground its gears and sputtered to a stop on the narrow street in front of my building. Right away traffic began backing up behind the vehicle, but the driver either didn't notice or didn't care. Just my luck. He was going to block the road and delay Bruno's arrival.

Aw, come on, moron. Can't you see you're holding up progress?

My office door opened. "Boss?"

"Damn it, Charlene. Can't you stay at your desk and at least *try* to look efficient?" I turned to glare at her and jumped like a scalded cat. A wizened little man, hardly tall enough to see over my desk, stood watching me out of beady little closeset eyes. He reminded me of a leprechaun, except he wasn't wearing green.

"Sir Winston sent me."

Where did he come from? I glanced through the window at the vehicle still blocking the street. "But... how did you... I mean..."

He didn't even blink.

"Um... you must be Bruno."

"This way, please. Time is of the essence."

Talkative little fellow.

On our way out, Charlene shoved my overcoat, hat, and an umbrella at me. Odd—it wasn't raining. It wasn't even cloudy. Charlene watched Bruno exit first, her eyes wide and her mouth open.

Her strange behavior made sense after I stepped through the door and found myself standing on the edge of a large body of water—in the middle of winter—and it was sleeting.

"Where the hell are we?"

"We are standing next to a fjord at the foot of snow-capped mountains, located in the Geirangerfjord region of western Norway."

"How did we get here... and why is it snowing?"

"The timer was set for the winter of 425 A.D. That's what it does here during this time of the year."

"You're kidding, right?" I'd expected to do some traveling for Sir Winston, but nothing like this. We'd gone from present day to the fifth century, just by stepping through a door.

So this was how Sir Winston had gained his unrivaled reputation. He'd found a way to travel back through time to obtain relics *before* they got buried under tons of dirt and rock or had sunk to the bottom of some ocean.

Bruno led me to an abandoned shelter on my left. Inside, he set fire to dry kindling stacked in a pit in the center of the room. The flames leapt high into the air. He shook a furry bundle at me. "Change into this."

Fingers numb with the cold left me fumbling. By the time I shook the garments out, the chill had spread to the pit of my stomach. The clothes he'd given me were made of leather, wool, and animal skins, and none of them looked any too clean.

"Why this getup?"

Bruno pulled a rough tunic over his suit and belted it. "When in Rome..."

I followed his lead, telling myself it was far too cold for any vermin to infest the clothing.

Dressed like Thor, complete with helmet, breastplates, and axes sharp enough to split hairs, we stepped back into the desolate landscape. The sleet had turned to snow and covered the ground with a mantle of purest white.

"Where do we go from here?"

"We are on the outskirts of Njord's stronghold." He pointed toward the snowcapped mountain range. From here you will need to make your way to the top of the mountain where Odin's dwelling lies."

"If we were going to travel through time, why couldn't you have zapped us a little closer... like on top of the mountain."

He shot me an exasperated look, as though I should know better. "This is as good at it gets."

"Figures." I scratched my chin, which reminded me of something. "Since we're going straight to the source to look for Odin's spear, why the identity veil? No one's going to have any idea who I am, not in this century, at least."

"There's always the possibility that some of Sir Winston's colleagues might have come up with the same theory. He didn't want to take the chance."

"I see." Bruno's boss was covering all his bases. I peeked at my watch hidden under the leather covering my forearm. Only twenty hours left. "We'd best get going."

We jogged at a brisk pace over the frozen turf. It pays for someone in my business to stay in shape. You never know when you might be testing your stamina. I wondered if this might be one of those days. I could end up carrying the little man before it was over.

Wood smoke filled the air before we glimpsed the crude stockade. A burly guard standing at the gate bellowed something in Old Norse. I had no idea what he was saying, but Bruno spoke the language like a native. Whatever he said worked, for the guard shouted again, and someone opened the gate. Once inside, we followed the crowd making their way toward the center of the settlement. It looked as though the entire town had gathered for some kind of meeting.

In the middle of the unruly mob, horses were hitched to a wooden cart laden with solid gold serving dishes, chalices and intricate candlesticks, along with ornate jewelry that spilled out of wooden chests. A dead man, dressed in full battle gear, his weapons at his side and golden coins on his eyes, lay on top of everything.

Most in the crowd were drunk. No doubt they'd been celebrating his demise in the traditional Viking manner. From the looks of things, the party had been going on for quite some time. Bruno eased over to one of the few spectators that was still sober enough to answer questions coherently.

After a lengthy discussion, he filled me in. "It seems Njord, the Earl of the village, has recently perished in a skirmish with another clan, and his subjects are giving him the kind of sendoff a Viking warrior deserves."

Someone thrust a cup of thick, dark mead into my hands that smelled strong enough to curl the hair on my chest and clean the tartar off my teeth. It seemed unwise to refuse, so I took a sample of the draught. It unsteadied my head, but I was still clear-headed enough to see a young woman being led through the crowd.

Talk about lusty Viking wenches. This gal had rosy cheeks, hair the color of golden grain, and smoldering dark eyes that put every other woman in the crowd to shame. She was drop dead gorgeous. Two guards accompanied her to a raised platform beside the wagon.

A barrel-chested man climbed up on a crate and held his arms up for silence. He launched into a long-winded speech that went on and on. The audience cheered and stomped and guzzled more mead. When he was finally done, the guards gripped the woman under her arms and hoisted her up into the wagon. She took a seat beside the dead man.

I frowned at Bruno. "What's going on?"

He questioned the man next to him, who gave another lengthy explanation—or maybe it just seemed that way because the words were so long.

At the end of it, Bruno nodded. "Ahhh, yes. Of course."

I was getting impatient. "What did he say?"

"The woman is Njord's wife and therefore considered part of his worldly goods. Lady Astrid is required to accompany him on his journey to Valhalla." The lovely lady sat next to her deceased husband, head down and hands folded in her lap as though resigned to her fate.

"Tell me you're joking."

Bruno shrugged. "It is the tradition of this clan, and while not every Viking custom is strictly adhered to, our intoxicated friend has informed me that it was one of her husband's last wishes." He leaned close and lowered his voice. "I gather Njord did not wish to leave the lovely lady behind for one of his kinsmen to enjoy."

"What a waste." My gut twisted uncomfortably until another thought came to me. "Don't Viking funerals consist of the dearly departed floating off into the sunset in a literal burst of flames? It's the dead of winter, and we're nowhere near a body of water that isn't frozen solid."

"That *is* mythology." He pointed to the icy ridge of the mountain in the distance. "Njord and all his worldly goods will be taken to Odin's dwelling place."

A plan began to form in my mind. "You know, we couldn't have come at a more opportune time. All we need are horses, and we can follow the wagon out of town, catch up with the driver and take his place. Once we get to Valhalla, all I have to do is find the spear and pick out my reward." Maybe, just maybe it would work.

"What do you mean 'we'?"

"Aren't you coming?"

Bruno narrowed his eyes. "Sir Winston hired you to retrieve the spear. I'm only here in an advisory capacity."

That figured. "Can you get *me* a horse, then?"

Farewells to Njord lasted another hour, until the mead finally ran out and people began to drift away. The driver took the last swig from his mug, climbed up on the wagon, and snapped the reins against the horses' rumps.

I frowned at the swaybacked horse Bruno had brought for me. "You couldn't do any better than this?"

"Don't look a gift horse in the mouth. He was wandering around the village after his owner drank too much to ride and fell headlong into a pig sty."

The wagon passed through the gates of Njord's settlement. Since it was moving at a snail's pace, the nag I rode managed to keep up, and the driver was still drunk enough not to pay me any mind. About the time we reached the foot of the mountain, the wooden wheels creaked to a stop. The driver climbed down from the wagon and stumbled on the other side of an oversized boulder to answer the call of nature. I slid off my horse, circled around behind, and took him by surprise, knocking him out with a rock.

A short sprint took me back to the wagon, and I climbed up and whipped the horses into a trot. Lost in her own thoughts, Astrid didn't seem to notice the change in drivers. Maybe she was pondering her fate when we reached Valhalla.

I wondered that myself.

The road zigzagged up the side of the mountain—steep at times, but not too difficult to navigate, especially since I was mostly sober. On the way up my thoughts alternated between feeling sorry for the lovely lady in the back of the wagon and how many different ways I could spend the money I'd get from my reward. By the time we reached the peak, the sun was setting. The fading light illuminated Odin's dwelling, a cave with massive stone columns on either side of an opening wide enough to accommodate the wingspan of a small jet.

I drove the wagon inside and helped Astrid to the ground. She stood with downcast eyes while I moved her late-husband's body and belongings onto the large, oblong slab in the middle of the room. What didn't fit on the slab, I stacked on the floor next to him.

There was no sign of Odin. Where was he? He should have been present to welcome his new arrival. This was "Valhalla," after all. Maybe he'd gone off somewhere with the Valkyrie or something.

I circled the room, in awe of its contents. All around me were elaborate objects made of gold and silver, set with precious stones that glowed like fire from the rays of the setting sun. Just the sight of everything made me breathless. This must have been an archaeologist's reaction when they first set foot in the tombs of the pharaohs.

A huge ivory throne stood on a raised dais at one end of the room. Did my eyes deceive me? Lying across the seat was Odin's spear, a shiny thing that appeared to be made entirely out of gold. I sprinted across the room for it, but before I could pick it up I heard the sound of wings—lots of them. The Valkyrie? *Oh, my God.* Odin could be returning. No time to waste. I grabbed the spear and spun around, my heart pounding.

Grab something and get the hell out of here, you idiot. Anything made of gold was far too heavy to carry while running. Should I grab a handful of jewels? *Come on, Clanton. Think!*

Just then, the answer was standing right in front of me...

* * *

The sound of knuckles rapping against the frosted glass of my office door woke me from a particularly enjoyable dream. Seriously? Was Charlene ever going to learn to follow directions? I yawned and squinted over the tips of my boots. The door opened just far enough for me to glimpse a flash of gold.

A vision of loveliness stood in the doorway. Astrid's shimmering blonde hair had been secured in a modest braid and she'd traded the rough tunic and cloak for tight jeans and a tee shirt that hugged every curve of her body. When our eyes met, her smile lit up the entire room.

No way could I have lugged solid gold artifacts down the mountain. And what would I have done with jewels the size of baseballs? I'd have had all kinds of trouble finding a buyer. Who'd have believed I'd gotten them honestly?

Astrid outshined any of the treasures in Valhalla. In the end, I'd made the right decision. My Viking princess was a diamond in the rough and worth far more than jewels or gold. Sir Winston could have his spear.

Life is good.

AMR-17
BY EDMUND WELLS

Ultraviolet scanners locked, AMR-17 squeezed off a pulse from his laser rifle. His target, a bulky yellow constructor robot with delusions of piratehood, flashed like a red neon bulb.

"Arr! Ye got me, matey."

Armand raised his rifle in triumph and glanced around at his teammates, AMR-3 and AMR-11, known among the other atmospheric maintenance robots as Omar and Mara. Their cobalt visual nodes shone with delight.

The constructor robot, CR-8, lumbered forth, followed by his two Cor union buddies, who swaggered from behind storage tanks. Each wore a regulation steel patch over one eye.

"Good game, Captain." Armand inclined his head.

"Lucky shot, Amir-17." The Cor's voice rumbled like an idling bulldozer. "Now we're tied—one for the Yellow Seadogs, one for you sneaky Amir bilge rats."

Omar stepped forward. "We're the *Molecule Jockeys*, damn you. Next round wins the match... and sixty extra hours on the gaming computers. Agreed?"

CR-5 nodded, pointing a thick iron finger. "And a tankard of grog. Arr."

Mara twirled her rifle. "Do you idiots even *know* how to use a computer?"

"Aye. And we're mighty fond of Pac Man," CR-4 said, flexing a steel bicep.

Life as a maintenance robot on Europa Colony was, Armand had come to learn, dull, dull, dull. If not for the games, the occasional "invasion defense drill," and his future role as Chief of Atmospheric Operations, he'd stuff himself in an airlock and switch the lights off. With the present Chief off-line for repairs, Armand was enjoying the perks of that position, making mandatory target practice a little more fun.

A tiny buzzer sounded in Armand's audio sensors. He heaved an electronic sigh. *Duty calls.* "Time to deploy the canisters, me hearties. I'll be back in twenty-two minutes."

The three Cor leveled their brushed steel rifles at him. "You've got fifteen minutes, lubber, or the rules state we shove off without you."

"But—"

Omar motioned with his head. "Go on."

"Hurry, Armand!" Mara shooed him away.

Cursing subvocally, Armand sprinted off. The biosphere's artificial atmosphere required regular injections of oxygen, drawn from Europa's own thin atmosphere, purified, and stored in pressurized canisters. Since the process was dangerous—and tedious—the colonists used robots to perform the tasks from a station adjacent to the biosphere.

Armand entered the security code to access the oxygen dispersion chamber. The heavy steel doors rotated open and he dashed inside. Using a grav-lift, he withdrew three canisters from cryo-storage and wheeled them to the bio-scanner.

He took note of his chronometer. Four minutes had already elapsed. Scanning for contaminants would take another five minutes per canister.

There wasn't enough time.

In nine years, only *once* had the bio-scan detected a potential hazard. To Armand, it seemed the greater risk was losing precious game time to the constructor robots, who already strutted around like they owned the station.

Drumming his fingers, Armand scanned the first canister—negative. The second canister—also negative. No surprises.

Fourteen minutes gone, damn those Cor and their union regulations. Why couldn't they be more like real pirates? Armand was usually one to follow orders, but if he was going to make it back in time, he'd have to omit canister 1121511229.

His first major executive decision as Chief.

Fingers flying, he entered the clearance code and all three canisters discharged their oxygen molecules into pipes that fed the biosphere of Europa Colony.

Humming a little tune, he disconnected the canisters and jogged back to Laser Tag Warehouse, as they'd re-named it. It was time to kick some constructor pirates in their afts.

* * *

Some time later, Armand slumped into a corner and let his visual nodes go dark. At times, life just wasn't fair. A jarring clang on the head caused him to jump. Warily, he re-activated one node.

"Optimal performance, Armand." Mara stood over him, fists on her hips. "You inspire me."

Omar lay flat on his back, the grinding of his mandible gears audible from across the room. "How could you let them sneak up on you like that?"

"They surprised me at an intersection." A patchwork of laser burns crisscrossed Armand's chest and arms. "They drill for an invasion from Titan all the time. I think they look forward to it."

Mara kicked him with another clang. "They're big, they're yellow and they stomp when they tiptoe. Are your sensors malfunctioning, or do you just need new batteries?"

"Hey. Is that any way to treat your Chief?"

A chime rang. High on the north wall, a panel opened, through which darted a gray shape: an automated courier pigeon. Tiny motors whirred as it alighted on the steel-plated floor, shaking snow from its wings.

"Greetings from Europa Colony, sixth moon of Jupiter. I am ACP-31." Its head bobbed as it eyed each of them. "Which of you is acting Chief of Atmospheric Operations?"

Omar and Mara thrust accusing fingers at Armand.

Armand rose to his feet. "That's me."

The pigeon scuttled nearer. "A message for you, Chief." Light streamed from the bird's eyes, raising a holographic image. A human female, her face twisted in an aspect of pain, spoke in a hoarse voice.

"Breach... in the oxygen filters... Organic... People are dropping... like lemmings." She drew a ragged breath even as her face turned a blotchy shade of purple. "Protocol One... lock down..." With a final desperate gasp, she collapsed onto her desk and lay still.

The three Amir shared a glance, shock reflected in each other's eyes. Protocol One was a general quarantine with a call for emergency assistance.

Armand sensed an alarming spike in his core temperature.

The holographic image now showed a pigeon's-eye view of Europa Colony. The dome had cracked in numerous places, exposing the biosphere to the frigid atmosphere of Europa. Snow and ice particles swirled in. Frozen bodies lay strewn everywhere, fallen where they had worked or played. Nothing moved, except for a few frost-rimed machines. The biosphere appeared to have been attacked, with devastating results.

The pigeon's eyes flickered and went dark. "Have a nice day!" It leaped into the air and flew off.

Mara strode to a computer access node and punched in a few commands. "Life signs register no readings. There are traces in the atmosphere of Yersinia anaeris, a bacteria that eats oxygen. It would have caused suffocation and then a vacuum inside the dome, resulting—"

"Yes, I can see the result." Armand peered over her shoulder, unable to believe his visual sensors. He rather liked human beings, despite their somewhat dismissive attitude toward worker robots. The colony was always in danger of attack from the neighboring moons of Saturn—Titan in particular, which was controlled by pirates. "There were twenty six thousand, five hundred and nine colonists in that dome!"

"They're still in there," Omar said. "They're just dead."

Mara poked Armand in the chest. "This is *your* fault."

"My fault?" His gyroscopes vacillated unpleasantly. "I ran the bio-scan. Well... most of it. You forced me to rush the procedure, as you'll recall."

Omar and Mara crossed their arms.

"Fine. But what were the odds the last canister would be contaminated with a lethal biohazard?"

"Apparently, one in one," Omar said. "So now what?"

Good question. Armand slumped back into his corner, head bowed in thought. It wouldn't be long before someone noticed and alerted Jupiter Station. The ensuing investigation would reveal he had neglected to scan the third canister. They weren't likely to fault the constructor robots for adhering to the fifteen-minute break rule. Instead, they would put him on trial, as a matter of bio-mechanical ethics, then disassemble him for parts. Or worse, banish him to a mining colony on Jupiter's seventh moon, Ganymede.

He needed time to think.

"Mara, Omar—I need you to create a diversion. Call a series of defense drills to keep everyone occupied, but nothing that involves interaction with the biosphere. Understand?"

The two Amir nodded.

"What do you intend to do?" Mara asked, her sarcasm circuits working overtime. "Go back in time to correct your mistake?"

Armand's head snapped up. An excellent idea, if only he had the means. With a flash of inspiration, he knew who he needed to talk to.

* * *

Flashing lights and sirens filled the corridors as robots rolled, ran or flew in response to a surprise defense drill. Blaring speakers announced that contact had been severed with the biosphere and Titanian space pirates were attacking the station. Surrender, as always, was not an option.

A bit overdone, but since such attacks happened often enough, the simulation was a credible excuse that would keep everyone busy.

Armand hurried along a series of side passages, making his way to the meteorological unit. He pressed a buzzer beside a dark metal door etched with a stylized golden sun.

The portal rotated open.

"Enter, friend." A deep, theatrical voice greeted him. "I have been expecting you."

Armand grimaced. "You say that to everyone, Michel."

At the center of the domed chamber sat a bright crystalline globe, three meters in diameter, raised on a clear pedestal. A ghostly light swirled within the sphere, pulsing as it spoke.

"What troubles you, AMR-17?"

"Please, call me Armand."

"Very well. And I will trouble you to call me Nostradamus, for thus am I known."

Armand bowed, knowing the pompous weather computer had an ego as vast as Jupiter. "Forgive me, esteemed Nostradamus. I come to you for advice."

"Naturally." The image on the globe's exterior coalesced to depict the frozen surface of Europa, with its cracked ridges and crisscrossing fault lines. A pair of red circles marked the site of the biosphere and the adjacent robotics station, while rotating blue and green swirls revealed the location and course of ion storms.

"Beautiful," Armand said, knowing the computer expected it.

"Thank you. Are you planning an excursion? A little hyper-skiing adventure, perhaps?"

"No, I have a more ... theoretical concern."

"Hmmm," Nostradamus intoned. "Do go on."

"How far into the future do your temporal circuits allow you to see?"

"My powers of meteorological prophecy extend twelve hours. Other areas of prophecy are variable. I am forsworn, just so you know, against gambling forecasts of any kind."

Armand shrugged. "Of course." *Now for the tricky part.* "My question is this, mighty Nostradamus: although you are a seer of the future, do your temporal circuits also enable you to peer... backwards?"

The computer hesitated. "Backwards?" His cavernous tone rose several octaves. "Meaning *into the past*? But that would merely be scrying upon a historical event. One does not *prophesize* the past!"

"Of course, but theoretically, *could* you? If you bent your formidable powers to the task?"

"Well, when you put it that way..." A deep hum filled the chamber as Nostradamus pondered for several long moments. "I've sent out a few feelers, and it appears I can, as you say, *peer* into the past, but I fail to appreciate the point."

Armand felt a tingle of electricity course over him. "Do you recall, dear friend, my gift to you from last Christmas?"

The great computer laughed, lights pulsing across its curved surface. "Of course! The complete, digitally re-mastered Farmer's Almanac series dating back to 1818, *and* a holo-image of Vilhelm Bjerknes, my favorite meteorologist from ancient Earth."

"That's right. And in return you promised me a favor, should I ever need one."

Nostradamus heaved a ponderous sigh. "I see where this is going, you know."

"I knew you would."

"Name your favor, friend Armand. If it lies within my power, I will grant it."

Armand began to pace. "I recently made a small mistake, you see. Small, but... far-reaching. It's vitally important I correct this mistake, for the sake of others as well as myself." He faced the swirling globe and balled his hands into fists. "To set matters straight, I need you to send me into the past."

A long pause. "Physically, you mean?"

"I assumed so, yes."

Nostradamus' lights swirled a long moment, stretching into several long moments.

"Hello?" Armand said. "Anyone there?"

"Hush! I'm thinking."

"Sorry." Another stretch of silence crept by. Armand began to fear

Nostradamus had lapsed into a prophetic trance, or dozed off, when the computer's voice rumbled forth.

"Although I admit to some reservations, I believe I can accommodate your request."

Armand nearly leaped for joy. "Huzzah!"

"I cannot, however, send you physically. I've consulted several engineering journals. One source claims to have connected temporal circuitry to a data transference device, in effect sending your consciousness back in time. In other words, I can project your present memory and cognitive array upon your past self."

"Neat. How far can you send me back?"

"Will three hours suffice?"

Armand nodded. He only needed twenty-two minutes.

* * *

Armand stood on the pad of a transference unit, which was normally used to transport heavy supplies and equipment from the moon's surface. As far as he knew, no one had ever cast their mind back to inhabit a past self.

Nostradamus' voice echoed through the room. "I must warn you, the test subjects reported a degree of disorientation from the memory transfer. You might want to write yourself a note or something."

"Good idea." Armand pressed a key on his forearm and whispered so Nostradamus couldn't overhear. "Imminent danger! Destruction of biosphere in 3 hours due to use of canister 1121511229. Urgent!" He straightened up. "I'm ready."

"Fare thee well, little friend. And Merry Christmas."

White light filled Armand's eyes, washing out the scene before him. A wave of dizziness spun him in circles, his body vibrating like a piano wire. A rising, operatic cry crashed over him, terminating in a crescendo of tinkling crystal.

All at once his vision returned. The scene wavered, as if his visual sensors had been... stretched. Blinking, he realized he was in Warehouse 3, standing on the matter transference pad.

What am I doing here?

A sense of urgency filled him. There was something critical he needed to do. But what? A flashing red light on his arm caught his attention. He tapped the button and a staticky message ran through his audio sensors.

Danger--biosphere--3 hours.

A danger to the biosphere? In three hours? The message was recorded in his voice pattern, but much of it was garbled and impossible to decipher. He put a hand to his head, trying to stop the sensation of spinning.

Disjointed sounds and images flashed through his memory. An announcement that the station was under attack by Titan, robots running through the halls. Sirens blaring. He glanced down and noticed laser burns lashed across his arms and chest. He'd been fired on, which would explain his various malfunctions. The immediate situation seemed clear enough.

Europa Colony was in danger.

Or would be. According to his own message, the danger would arrive in three hours. But how could he know such a thing?

He checked his chronometer, which caused him a jolt. Time was running *backwards*—inexplicably counting down from three hours. The readout indicated two hours and thirty one minutes remained.

Until the danger to the biosphere occurred.

Only one explanation fit. Somehow he'd gone back in time. But how? And for what purpose?

Moving on unsteady legs, vision flickering, Armand crept off the pad and through an open door. A trio of bulky yellow robots with eye patches huddled near the far wall, laser rifles slung over their shoulders. He recalled seeing such robots before...

The robots turned as one, raised their rifles, and opened fire. "Arr! Get him, me buckos!" They laughed and sang "yo-ho-ho" as spears of red light seared the air all around him.

Cursing, Armand ducked behind a bulkhead. *Space Pirates*! The situation was worse than he'd realized. The invasion had already begun.

He stumbled down an alternate corridor and locked an emergency hatchway behind him. His mind raced, stuttering to put the pieces together. Logically, the invasion had to be coming in two stages: first the station, and *then* the biosphere.

That had to be it. And yet ...

The corridor ended in another door, which parted as he approached: the Rec Room. Three ancient ore-smelting robots sat around a chess board, although it looked more like they were napping. Nearer, a pair of sanitation robots crouched before a gaming computer, remote controllers clutched in their dirty, oversized hands.

Armand jogged over to them. "What are you doing?" He shook a fist. "Shouldn't you be mounting a counter strike?"

The two Sar blinked their oversized LCD eyes. "Whaddya talkin' about?" SR-5 replied. "It's friggin' Mario Brothers, not Counterstrike. We're just jumpin' turtles, right, Tony?"

SR-6 snorted. "Yo, Vin. Maybe he means we oughta *mount* his sister." The pair laughed.

Armand stepped in front of the video screen. "Are your relays fried? The station is under attack by pirates. They just shot at me. We need to *do* something!"

The robot craned his head to see around Armand. "Pal, you need to move your friggin' ass, before somebody's *face* gets attacked. And by that, I mean you."

"Good one, Vin."

Armand turned and put a fist through the video screen.

The Sar stood, their heavy jaws askew. "That, my little friend, was a mistake." The sanitation robots each grabbed one of Armand's arms, dragged him to a storage room, and tossed him in like so much trash. The door rotated shut at his back.

"Let me out, you sanitation simpletons!" Armand pounded on the door. "You don't realize what you're doing!" After several minutes of fruitless shouting, he began tearing through the barrels and crates. Oil, spare robot components, batteries, and some simple tools—electron wrenches, force hammers, and ion drivers.

He tried each tool, but none enabled him to breach the door. Head in his hands, he slumped against a barrel to wait for someone to let him out. His vision continued to waver, making it hard to focus. Out of curiosity, he played his recorded message again. It sounded a little clearer.

Danger--biosphere--3 hours--canister--Urgent!

Canister? The danger related to a canister? It could be a bomb, or a biological weapon. He didn't know what the precise danger was, but he suddenly had a *very* bad feeling about it.

His chronometer indicated one hour and fifty five minutes remained. He needed to get out of this damned storage room.

Armand grabbed a force hammer and leaped to his feet. "Hey, garbage boys! You can be replaced by a vacuum hose, you know. Even though you suck twice as much."

The door rotated open and in strode an android made in the exacting image of a human colonist: a male, his round head all pink and shiny, tufts of white hair sprouting from his chin. It was the station's positronic matrix evaluator, or in human terms ... the psych counselor: Sigmund Droid.

He peered at Armand through little round eyeglasses. "Hallo. I am PME-1. A complaint has been filed against you, AMR-17. What seems to be troubling you, mein freund?" He clicked a pen, which he held poised over a cyber-clipboard.

Armand rose to his feet, eyeing the open door at the android's back. "What troubles me, Sigmund, is that the station has been invaded by enormous yellow pirates and no one but me seems to care. Excuse me, but I have to warn someone." He stepped toward the door.

"Halt." At a gesture from Sigmund, the door rotated shut. "We must first have a little chat, ja?"

The PME wielded the authority of law on the station, as well as the core program scripts to each and every robot. With a word, Armand could find himself re-assigned to the pigeon repair yard. He needed to tread lightly.

"Fine, but please hurry. We're all in imminent danger." Armand sat on a crate, tapping his force hammer.

Sigmund took a seat opposite. "Two Sar units have accused you of behaving in a strange, violent manner. Is this true?"

He suppressed an angry retort. "Atmospheric maintenance robots are not violent."

The counselor glanced at the hammer in Armand's hand.

Armand forced a casual laugh. "I'm interested in modern construction methods, that's all." He set the hammer down.

"Uh-hum." Sigmund jotted a note. "And does your *interest* in modern construction methods extend to the demolition of video monitors?"

Armand shot to his feet. "The station is under attack, Sigmund, and those idiot Sar were just sitting there pretending to be plumbers!"

Sigmund glanced around in an exaggerated manner, peering behind crates and barrels. "I see no evidence of an attack. Do you often feel you are under attack, AMR-17?"

This was not going well. Armand settled back onto the crate, trying to calm his resistors. "Not me personally, no, but—"

"Tell me, how long have you experienced this displaced hatred toward your mother?"

"My mother?"

Sigmund stood up. "I'm afraid you're going to require a lengthy course of psychoanalysis before you are fit to interact with your peers." He scribbled on his clipboard. "I recommend temporary deactivation until a suitable treatment schedule can be arranged, as well as a full diagnostic with a robotics engineer. And maybe a nice hot bath."

Before Sigmund could raise a hand to deactivate him, Armand snatched the force hammer, lunged forward and drove the tool onto the top of the android's head. A flash of light accompanied a small shock wave, and the lights went out in Sigmund's eyes.

"Sweet dreams, Herr Doktor. You'll thank me later."

Armand lifted Sigmund's hand and waved it toward the door a few times until it rotated open.

Omar and Mara would probably know what was going on. He sent a coded message asking they meet up with him. Meanwhile, there was someone he needed to speak with—someone he suspected would understand the reason for his time traveling.

* * *

Armand crept along darkened corridors, watching out for yellow pirate invaders and robots in white coats, and pressed a buzzer beside a metal door etched with a golden sun.

The portal rotated open.

"Enter, AMR-17." A deep, theatrical voice greeted him. "I have been expecting you."

Armand felt a wave of disorientation. This all seemed very familiar. At the center of the room, a bright crystalline globe rested upon a raised pedestal. A ghostly light swirled within the sphere, pulsing as it spoke.

"You have a question, AMR-17?"

He approached the weather computer. "I remember you. Your name is ..."

"Nostradamus."

"Of course. Are you responsible for sending me back in time, Nostradamus?"

"I will be, yes."

"Why?"

"You do not remember?"

"No. I recorded a message for myself, but it got corrupted. I only know the biosphere is in danger of destruction. Something to do with a canister."

Nostradamus seemed to consider this. "You informed me, or will do so, that you needed to correct a mistake having far-reaching consequences. No other details were provided."

"So the attack is somehow *my* fault." Armand paced, letting this realization sink in. All the diodes across his chest felt constricted. "Did I let the invaders into the station? Did a canister explode, destroying the colony's defenses? Whatever I did wrong, I traveled back in time to prevent it from happening. But I need your help to figure it out. My memory is all confused."

The great globe's swirling lights darkened. "It was a mistake for me to have sent you back." Nostradamus' voice took on a bitter tone. "One cannot tamper with time, AMR-17. It is not our place to play God. What will be, will be."

"But ... over twenty-six thousand colonists are in jeopardy. We have a chance to save them."

A bay door opened to Armand's left. A heavy repair machine rolled in, like a small tank with multiple arms ending in tools and claw-like pincers. It faced Nostradamus, apparently awaiting instructions.

A raw chill played over Armand's exterior.

"Alas, I now foresee that sending you back in time will result in my own destruction. Colonists are readily replaced, for they breed like vermin. Robots can be rebuilt, for parts are plentiful. There is, however, only one Nostradamus."

What an ego. "Please, you must help me. The colonists will be able to repair you, I'm sure. They built you, after all."

Nostradamus would not be swayed. "It would have been less unpleasant had you allowed Sigmund to simply deactivate you. I am sorry." He paused, as if to draw breath. "Repair machine—disassemble AMR-17!"

Armand backed away as the tank advanced. He was cornered.

A sudden barrage of laser fire streaked over Armand's head, blasting small pieces from the repair machine.

"Run, Armand!" Mara waved as Omar continued to lay down fire against the oversized robot, which recoiled in apparent confusion. It was not, after all, programmed for combat. "We heard the whole thing. Whatever's going on, finish it!"

Nostradamus' scream receded as Armand fled the chamber. He was going to have to fix things on his own. Since the danger involved a canister, Armand ran to the canister deployment area, still uncertain what he would do.

His chronometer showed only nineteen minutes remaining. He needed to act, before he was caught and destroyed by one of Nostradamus' minions or Sigmund's psych counselors. Thoughts racing in circles, he played the message one final time. Although still garbled, it was clearer than before.

Danger! Destruct--biosphere in 3 hours—use canister 1121511229. Urgent!

Use canister?

Armand secured canister 1121511229 from cryo-storage and ran a bio-scan, which to his surprise revealed a biohazard highly toxic to organic life.

I sent myself back in time to destroy the biosphere? But why?

He thought back on all that had transpired. Pirate robots from Titan had tried to kill him, damaging his systems, yet didn't seem to bother anyone else on the station. In fact, everyone denied there even was an invasion. Vin and Tony had locked him up, so that Sigmund Droid could deactivate him. Even Nostradamus had turned traitor. It was as if everyone had been against him from the start ...

And therein lay the answer.

When he'd gone back in time, the station had already been compromised—lost to the pirates of Titan. Sigmund could easily have re-programmed the station's robots to cooperate with the Titanians, whatever his reasons. That explained the lax attitude of the robots, the general acceptance of the yellow pirate invaders, and why everyone had acted against him—except for his true friends, Mara and Omar.

This changed everything.

He knew from the invasion drills that the biosphere must never be allowed to fall into enemy hands, for its strategic location and rich natural resources. Titan's control of Europa would re-open hostilities between Saturn and Jupiter, and lead to many more deaths than one medium-sized biosphere.

It all finally made sense.

In short, with the robotics station now under Titan's control, Europa Colony must be destroyed. A tragic, but necessary, casualty of war.

Diodes tightening across his chest, vision suddenly blurred, Armand punched in the security codes and canister 1121511229 released its deadly molecules into the biosphere.

One had to follow orders, especially one's own.

Burn it Up, Burn it Down
by Philip Overby

It's always a shame that I have to burn things to get what I want. But simplistic minds only deal in simplistic deeds. I am a dragon, therefore I must kill them. That's all they understand. I can't simply say "I'm looking for someone." They get out pitchforks, spew obscenities, or throw buckets of urine at me. I'm not sure what they think throwing urine on me does other than piss me off.

I burn because they push me. I don't enjoy it one bit.

In any case, I usually start with my memorized statement. "I'm looking for the Chosen One. The one who is supposed to slay me and end a thousand years of unyielding terror and destruction. I'd like to discuss our options for our final showdown. You see I'm quite tired and ready to die—"

That's about as far as I get.

All the screeching and hurling of various solids and liquids at me makes it nigh impossible for them to hear my monologue. So I resort to what they understand.

Burning.

Then, after I've scorched their homes, they listen better.

"So, have you heard anything about a Chosen One?" I say, shaking the ashes off my wings.

A crying man kneels before me, offering a butchered goat. "Please, take it. It's all we have left!"

"I don't want your goat." I give it a second look. "Not now anyway. Just listen to my—"

"We have more goats! Fatter and hornier."

"Hornier?"

"I'm sorry, I'll go find a better one," the man wails, scrambling up to fetch a better specimen.

"Wait!" I roar, breathing a gout of flame to block his escape. "I asked you a damned question!"

"We only have goats here," the man's lips tremble. "No Chosen

One."

"Good, that's all I wanted to hear. I apologize for the mess. I'll send a clean-up crew to take care of it for you."

"Clean-up crew?" The man blinks.

"Yes, I have a group of goblins that do work for me. They're a bit slow, but they'll—"

"Goblins!" The man yells and runs away, disappearing into the black smoke.

"Shit."

I take back to the air, soaring over the forests, lakes, and other natural splendors of my domain. All of it is just beautiful enough to keep me going for thousands of years. There are times when I want to curl up, shrivel, and die. My joints ache, some of my teeth are rotten and brittle, and I have trouble digesting the cows and stags I usually enjoy. I've seen my partners die, my children die; they fell victim to dragon slayers from Hasprig and Yarlingcoat or warlocks from the Grasping Isles, those Glazeen elves with their boomsticks full of brightly colored hissing sparks, raptors and razormouths, thibbering groths and shick-sathers—all variety of men and beasts claimed my kin, one by one. Not Chosen Ones, but hungry creatures and ambitious men. I cannot be harmed by such beings of infinitesimal power. I am the High Wyrm, hoary, the age of the first dusts and the Eternal Roach. My whiskers are longer than the reigns of most kings. My talons have not been trimmed since the last Hrungeld emperor ruled. My breath melts stone, flesh, and wood alike.

I whistle a tune to myself. The sound of air rushing in my ears gets rather tiresome. The sound of most things, even the chirping of birds, gets old when you've lived thousands of years. I almost wish that some other type of bird would migrate over. Just so I could hear a different song—or at least a slightly different flavor.

I spot the next village I want to interrogate, a fishing village called Blandwater. I've been there before, seems like twenty years ago. No Chosen One then, but maybe things have changed. Maybe a woman gave birth to him. The Chosen One would enjoy time fishing and playing, while elders warn him about the High Wyrm Aclexi. Twenty years of tales of warning and prophecies and training. Waiting but not waiting, living but not living. He can't truly begin living until I torch his town and he can come after me regaled in the armor of his dead father or uncle or some other such father-figure. We'll fight and he'll most likely win, cutting off my head or stringing out my guts with his bare hands. Some such grisly death that the bards love to sing about. Then he'll become a king or a prince or some other stupid title humans put on people. But I am the High Wyrm. The only title that matters in the scheme of the Grand Cosmos.

A familiar smell wafts up from the village. Smoke. "What the hell?"

Blandwater is already burning. Who could be the culprit? Bandits? Elves? Misguided goblins who cast off their rightful places as my janitors?

I swoop in lower to see what is going on. Whatever the struggle, no invaders are present. No horses, body carts, or fat, loping flies. None of the normal fare. I decide to land right outside the village, as not to induce further panic. I wait for a stray villager to come screaming out of the village, her hair aflame.

"Roll on the ground," I say bluntly.

When the woman sees me, her screaming and running both intensify. The flames, in turn, do the same. I swat her down gently, cupping my claw over her body. When the screaming stops, I lift up one talon to let her creep out. Her hair is singed but she is otherwise unwounded.

"May I talk to you now?"

The woman falls on her butt, trembling, her hair still smoking.

"Please, just a moment of your time. And don't panic or run away, or I'll pluck off your head like a grape."

The woman nods, her eyes blank, a nervous smile plastered on her face.

"I notice that your village is burning. Yet, I see no sign of an outside attack. Could you perhaps clue me in on what's going on?"

"W-what?"

I clench my teeth. "Why is the village burning?"

"Razik. It's the boy, Razik."

"Who is Razik?"

"A boy. " The woman's teeth chatter.

"Yes, we already affirmed that." I sigh. "Why did Razik burn the town?"

"He said he doesn't want to be the Chosen One. He said he wants to kill, maim, and torture like his grandfather before him, Morgath of Morgath."

I lean forward, my neck snaking towards the woman. "Is that so?"

I've often overheard tales of Morgath of Morgath, a wicked warlord who razed his way across my lands several years before, killing and destroying anyone and anything in his path. It was said he liked to juggle skulls, something that both delighted his men and horrified his victims. That was during my period of hibernation though, so I slept through the whole thing.

"And you're—you're a dragon!"

I glance down at my talons and shake my wings. "Yes, you are quite observant."

"It must be fate, then. Fate!" The woman got a far-off look in her eyes and clutched a pendant around her neck.

"Why is that?" I ask.

"Today is his seventeenth birthday. He was supposed to set out to kill a dragon. But he told his parents he didn't want to kill a dragon, he wanted to own one. When they told him no, he took his Blade of Ten Thousand Suns and started burning houses. Oh, it was so horrible. The cooking flesh, the dripping skulls, the—"

I burp. "That's enough. You're making me hungry."

The woman snaps her mouth shut.

"So, this boy—the Chosen One—doesn't want to kill me?"

She shook her head. "No, I suppose he'd be quite happy to see you, actually."

My lip curls back. "This Razik, where is he now?"

"Gone away. Riding a black horse north. He plans to keep killing until his parents get him a dragon."

"What a spoiled brat." I can't decide if this is the best or worst day of my life. "North, you say?"

"Yes, towards Tibblefoot. May I go now? I've soiled myself at least three times talking to you."

"Yes, go on. Get out of here."

I turn my head north. Tibblefoot, a small hunting village. They would probably be a little bit better prepared for this Razik. I flap my wings and shuttle back up into the sky.

As I soar overhead, the realization that the Chosen One doesn't want to kill me really sinks in. So no epic battle? No glorious death for bards to sing songs about and make into little storybooks? No final rest? The little bastard wasn't going to hand me my destiny?

I need this, my final stand. To die cold and alone in a cave wouldn't suit me.

Something pops into my head. That's it. It's times like these where I love having a humongous brain. My wings flap with great intensity, cracking and popping as I try to get my fat carcass going. I dive down, my flight knocking thousands of leaves from the trees below. My legs tear at branches, snatching them up and snapping the boughs in half. I roar, releasing a brilliant flame down into the forest. I see Tibblefoot, still intact, gentle smoke coming from the chimneys of the houses. I'd soon change that.

Screams rip through the air when the first hunters see me. Some scramble for their bows, men, women, and children all. I crash down into the village, landing in the square, dust rising up around me. The villagers let loose a volley of arrows. My scales reflect them harmlessly, so I just sit, waiting for them to run out. Once they do, I cock my head and look for someone who looks like a leader. A woman in a tall, multi-colored feathered hat seems important, so I focus on her.

"What's your name?"

The woman still has her bow hanging loose in her hand. "I am High Huntress Ezera, foul dragon. I will not allow you to—"

"Take it easy. I'm not going to kill you. Just burn your village, is all. I'm giving you the chance to leave now. Take what you can. Anything left will be burned."

The hunters all gawk at each other.

Ezera scowls. "You expect us to leave our homes for you to destroy? We will die fighting!"

The hunters all join in with rallying cries.

"With what?" I say.

They all stare at each other again.

Ezera snarls. "Our arrows are guided by the spirit of the Great Oaken Unicorn. We shall—"

"Come on. Seriously?" I laugh. "Are you really going to make me kill all of you?"

Ezera glances to her right and left. Her shoulders slump. "We have nowhere else to go."

"You're 'children of the forest' or some shit like that, right? You'll figure it out. Now get out of here before I change my mind."

The hunters mutter to each other at first. Their pace quickens once I start to breathe in and out. They grab what they can—food, horses, and carts, until only Ezera remains.

"We will not forget this, dragon."

"Yeah, yeah. Just get out of here." I shoo her away with my wing.

Grumbling, she dashes to catch up to the others.

I survey the town. Probably only about two dozen buildings altogether. Ten minutes to burn, most likely. I just hope Razik is a slow rider.

I burn, faster than I ever have before. I suck in air, breathe out. I cough up ash a couple of times. Fatigue sets in. Once the majority of the town is aflame, I sit back on my haunches and enjoy the view.

"My best work yet, I have to say."

Before long, a solitary black horse rides into the village in a slow gallop. The rider snorts and spits, a sword dancing with blue and black flames held in his hand. Razik, the Chosen One.

"You're the Chosen One?" I scoff.

The boy looks more a scarecrow than a Chosen One, with long, spindly limbs and a craning neck. Freckles cover his face and a mop of red hair flops about on his head as he rides forward. When he sees me, he brushes aside his hair, his eyes wide with delight. Not the usual expression I'm accustomed to.

"You're a dragon!" Razik squeals, his voice wavering between boy and man.

"That I am. And you're the Chosen One. Come to kill me, I suppose?"

Razik makes a face which could be either constipation or concentration. "Come to kill the villagers here, actually, but it looks like you've already done it." A cruel smile comes to the boy's face, his teeth so brown it makes me gasp.

"That makes you happy?" I say, trying to avoid looking at his disgusting teeth.

"Death and destruction make me very happy." Razik dismounts, waving his blade before him. "We should join together. We'd be unstoppable. The lands would all bow before us. Armies would crumble, kings would fall!"

"No thanks," I say.

"What?" Razik bristles. "What do you mean, 'no thanks?' It's a good offer. Better than me killing you, as I'm supposed to do, right?"

I shrug. "I think if I had to spend a long time ruling with you, I'd rather just be dead, if it's all the same."

"Oh really? Well, who says I need you anyway? There are other dragons about. I'll just go find one of them to ride."

"None around here." I look up at the sky. "They're all dead. You'd have to travel to Icewand to find one nowadays."

"Icewand? That's a month's ride away!"

"Guess you'd better start riding."

Razik brandishes his sword, barely able to keep it aloft with both hands. "Who cares about a stupid dragon, then. I'll just kill and raze, like my grandfather before me. He didn't need any dragons to help him."

"So are you going to kill me, or not?" I say. "I've been looking quite forward to this day. You're sort of ruining it."

Razik scrunches up his face. "I really want a dragon. Won't you change your mind?"

"I thought you said you don't need any stupid dragon."

Tears start to gush down Razik's face. "It's all I ever wanted, truly! Please, please!"

It took every drop of self control I had to quell the urge to incinerate the boy on the spot. He deserved no less, but that's not how it's supposed to go. The Chosen One kills me. That's how it ends. That's how I get my rest.

Razik's face trembles with rage. "Let me ride you! Now!"

I take off into the sky again, watching as Razik pounds his fists into the ground and curses up at me. I wait until he gets on his horse and starts riding off again until I see where it appears he's going. Crowhound. A bigger town, but mostly known for merchants and furriers. Razik rides strong, a black blur ripping down the roads. I watch as he slices off low-lying tree limbs as he goes, spitting and cursing all the way.

I soar down into Crowhound in mere minutes. Everyone screams per usual. I tell them to leave. They stare blankly. I tell them again by burning an abandoned cart. They get the hint and run.

I burn, burn, burn. Crowhound becomes a blackened husk within minutes.

Razik rides in, his horse lathered, the scowl on his face deeper than before. He dismounts the horse again, marching towards me as I sit in the smoldering rubble.

"What the hell do you think you're doing?" he asks.

"I'm a dragon. I burn towns. I'm quite good at this. You sure you want to compete with me?"

Razik looks back for his horse. It's not there.

"Looks like all the riding and flames finally spooked your horse," I say. "Best kill me now. It's your only way home. You'll be declared a hero and I'm sure they'll throw a big party for you in Gorren City. The king and all his daughters will be there. You know, like they've had planned for you since birth?"

"You piece of—" Razik drug his sword behind him, getting right in my face. I could smell his rank breath, smelling worse than any corpse I'd ever come across.

"Come on now. Kill me. Let us do battle, here in Crowhound," I said, goading him. I could feel his hatred seething out. This would be the moment. Our epic battle that would end with my head on some old king's wall. How it's supposed to be.

Razik smirks. "No."

"No?" I repeat.

"I'm not going to kill you, and that's that."

"Why?" I growl. "Just kill me already."

"I'm going to go to Gorren City, all right, but I'm going to go to turn myself in to the king. For killing dozens of people in Blandwater, I'll probably be sentenced to death. I'll be hanged by morning." Razik cackles, his brown teeth clicking.

"You wouldn't," I say, my eyes narrowing.

"Oh, yes, I would. What do I care? If I can't ride a dragon, then I don't want to live anyway."

I lean my head back, feeling the bones in my neck pop. So very tired. "If I let you ride me, will you kill me after that? In our promised, destined battle for the ages?"

Razik's eyes brighten. "Yes. I promise."

I squat down as far as I can. "Get on, then."

Razik squeals with glee and jumps onto my back. His feet dig into my sides and he grips too hard to my scales. His burning sword makes the nerves in my neck go haywire.

"This is perfect!" Razik shouts. "Now, take off. I want to soar above the kingdom."

"Fine. Hold on." I launch into the air, Razik holding on for dear life, screaming his head off all the way. Higher and higher I go, until Razik screeches for me to stop. I plateau off and settle into a easy glide.

"Ah!" Razik gasps.

"That good enough for you?" I await his tearful plea to be taken back to the ground.

"That was incredible!" Razik pats me on the neck. "I've never felt such a rush in all my life!"

I groan. "I'm glad you enjoyed it. So let's land now and we can fight to the death. We should do it somewhere public, so bards can wander in and record our glorious battle."

"What? No way. Not yet. I want to fly more."

"No, the deal was—"

Razik cut in. "The deal was that I promise I'll kill you. But we've just started. Let me enjoy this at least a little more."

I grit my teeth, but finally relent after he whines for several minutes. I soar over the stinking swamp of Gatheer and the many rivers of the Softlands. I swoop down near the Hattaka Mountains and dip down near the Thispen Wastelands. The whole time Razik croons and hollers, waving his flaming sword in the air.

We pass over Gorren City, the shimmering capital of the humans. I have to admit, it truly is a wonder to see. White spires jutting into the sky, piercing the clouds. The massive wall that surrounds a glistening moat of crystal clear water. Banners flapping in the breeze and men in pristine armor marching along the walls. I come here now and again to admire its beauty. Even with all the other wondrous sites in my lands, I come back to Gorren City the most.

"Gorren City," Razik whispers.

"You've been here before?" I ask.

"Never."

"Well, here we are."

Razik inhales deeply. "Go closer."

"I never get too close. Can't say they would like me flying overhead."

Razik laughs. A genuine laugh, not a cackle. "I imagine not."

"We should turn back now. I don't want to call too much—"

"Go closer," Razik says.

"I'm not going closer. Do you want to get plugged full of arrows?"

"Closer," Razik hisses.

"Fine, I'll go a little closer."

"It's been my dream. My life's quest to finally come here. To see Gorren City in all its beauty from up here in the sky. It's absolutely perfect."

If I could smile, I would. Finally the boy and I agree on something.

"Burn it," he says.

"Excuse me?"

"Swoop down there and burn it."

"I will not!"

"Then I won't kill you. Not if I live to be a hundred. I'll never let you rest!" Razik screams, holding his sword aloft. "Burn it! Burn it! Burn it!"

My mind shuts off, his chant reeling me in. I dart down, making the plunge toward the city gates. What's another city to burn? I've burned hundreds, thousands even. Just breathe in and breathe out. Ash, death, screaming. If it will make this rotten child fulfill his destiny—yet, how high a price to pay. Gorren City is such glorious splendor, and this despicable punk expects me to destroy it for a laugh!

I swoop back up.

"What are you doing? Go back! I want to burn it! Burn the shiny, perfect city! Watch their golden hair turn to a crisp."

I keep going up.

"Hey, I said go back! I swear to you, I'll never kill you. Go back!"

Higher and higher I go.

Razik's screams get higher and higher. The sun is blinding my eyes. But I keep going. I feel lighter, like I can fly into the sun, bathe in its warmth.

I crane my neck around. Razik plummets to the earth, his arms flailing, his legs kicking at nothing. I can still go back and catch him. Grab him with my talons or more preferably with my mouth. But I keep flying. Straight up.

I stop, letting my wings relax. My eyes blink away the purple and green sunspots.

I gaze down at Gorren City, now alive with commotion. I spot one of the white spires, now slick with red, Razik's arms splayed out to the sides. His horrid mouth is wide open. The crows already begin to gather. A horn blows.

"Dragon!" I hear. "Dragon!"

Archers raise up their bows. The horns blare even louder.

"Now I've done it," I say to myself. "Now I'll never get my glorious death."

A shrill voice rises over the rest. "Wait! That's Razik. The boy who's been burning villages!"

Others gather around, nodding their heads.

I just flap my wings, waiting for the archers to loose their arrows.

Maybe an arrow would pierce my eye and go straight into my brain.

Cheers rise up from the city instead. Some of the soldiers wave at me while others dance at their posts.

That's a first.

"All hail the great dragon!" One cry rings out. "Hip hip hooray! Hip hip hooray! Hip hip—"

I burn the tower Razik's body is impaled on. The crowd screams in terror as they rush to put the fire out. It's just enough. Just enough for them to keep hating me.

Maybe in another twenty or thirty years one will be born. Another Chosen One. And maybe, just maybe, then I can finally die.

Until then, I want some goat.

But I Know We'll Meet Again
Some Sunny Day
by Lauren A. Forry

London – October 1940

Penelope's feet landed on a pile of soggy sand. Had she miscalculated? The TT4500 remained strapped securely to her wrist, but her hands shook so badly she couldn't read the display. Bloody adrenaline, she thought. A red blur rumbled past, spraying her stockings with dirty water. She jumped back as the double-decker disappeared around the corner, her back colliding with a soft wall. Sandbags stacked four rows high. It was sand from a burst sack that littered the pavement. The TT buzzed—18 October 1940, 17:03. This was it. She was here.

The adrenaline fading, Penelope removed the watch-like device from her wrist and slipped it into her coat pocket as a gaggle of women in navy blue uniforms passed. Her eyes followed them, and she caught sight of the sign beside her: London Bridge. Damn it. She meant to land closer to Bermondsey. She could take the Jubilee... no. The Jubilee line didn't exist yet. She would have to walk, and daylight was fading.

Sandbags and barricades lined Borough High Street on either side, protecting the busy men in uniform and women in headscarves passing by. A roar sounded overhead. Penelope glanced up as a formation of Hawker Hurricanes streaked above floating, silver ovoids. The hydrogen-filled barrage balloons, anchored in place by heavy steel cables, littered the sky like bloated ticks. A little boy in short pants and cap regarded her strangely as his mother pulled him up the street, and Penelope realized she'd been standing there gawking like some stupid newbie. She hurried down Duke Street Hill, every step in her ridiculous wooden-soled shoes paining her. She used the sensation to anchor herself, keep her mind from thinking too much on her task. She couldn't get overexcited now that he was so close.

Many things about London had changed, more than she'd anticipated. As she made her way across Tooley Street, she occasionally passed a building that was vaguely familiar or an intersection she knew she had crossed before, in her own time, but the farther east she went, the less familiar the city became. When she reached Queen Elizabeth Street, she couldn't remember if she should follow it or stay on Tooley. She wanted to check the maps on the TT, but natives were everywhere. Yet, wasn't she a native? She'd been born here—had owned these streets when she was fourteen. Looking conspicuous in London had never been her problem, yet here she was now, her body language practically begging some stranger to walk up and offer directions. She could already feel many eyes on her.

Was she really so out of place? Her hair was permed perfectly to 1940s trends and her shoes handmade to match the Forties style. The plaid Eisenberg coat was a restored antique. Perhaps that was the problem. Perhaps her clothes were too perfect, her face too fresh. Everyone else looked worn and tired but Penelope, despite dehydration from the jump, was invigorated. Maybe that was enough to draw attention, and what if *he* noticed? Could he spot her in the crowd? If he did, she would lose the drop on him. He'd know where she was from, know enough to get out of her way, and all this would be for nothing. Another failure, just like her uncle predicted she would be, and that wasn't fair. Not after she'd spent so much time, had done so much research.

"Miss, are you all right?"

Penelope startled. The man wore a brown Army captain's uniform, and his blue eyes showed a kindness she could not accept. If it weren't for the pencil moustache it could be *him*. It wasn't; he was never a captain, but it could be, and that was enough. Her breath came in hesitant gasps and she could feel her carefully painted makeup erased by cold sweat.

"I'm fine, thanks. Thank you. I have to go."

Penelope hurried away and ducked round a corner. She held her breath, waiting for the captain to follow. When he didn't, she took the blister pack from her pocket, popped out a pill, and dry swallowed it. Her therapist told her not to do that, but Dr. Rosalind said a lot of things Penelope never listened to. She felt the pill crawl down her throat and settle in her stomach, then lifted her trembling hand. She watched until it was perfectly steady. The paranoia, again, that was all it was. She returned to the street, glancing at faces as she passed. That captain was gone. No one cared she was here. She was one of them, as far as they were concerned.

Penelope felt the trail of the pill as she swallowed and searched for a street sign. Where had she hid herself? The name Potters Fields was nailed above her on a brick building. A deep breath and she could smell the river. The river, of course. How could she be such an idiot? The Thames would guide her exactly where she needed to be.

Her feet traced the same route she and Mum took when they were housed in the old City Hall building. In 1940, that building wasn't even a thought in an architect's head, but Penelope felt compelled to head towards it, as if Mum were guiding her, telling her she was on the right path, that she was doing the right thing despite what her uncle and Dr. Rosalind said.

But, when she reached the river, any thoughts of her uncle or her mission were forgotten.

Tower Bridge was a fixture in her life. She saw it nearly every day and in every permutation—decked out in lights and fireworks for King William and Queen Catherine's Silver Jubilee or with the hanging murals memorializing those lost in the New World War.

Never had she seen it as it was now—with both the North and South towers intact. It was so much more beautiful in person than in archival footage. If the camera app weren't busted on her TT, she would've taken a thousand pictures. Then again, if the camera weren't broken, it wouldn't have been in the easily breachable repairs department in the first place.

"You there!"

An overweight man in uniform jogged towards her. Occupying soldier, she thought, and reached for her gun as if it were Mum's hand. A glance at Tower Bridge reminded her of when she was.

The man bent over to catch his breath. "Gasmask," he huffed.

"Sorry?"

"Don't be daft, girl. Your gasmask. Where is it?"

Girl? She was nearly twenty-four.

"Well?" As he coughed into his sleeve, Penelope read the white band on his arm—District Warden, Southwark.

"Oh. I forgot it?"

"You forgot there was a war on?"

"I'm really... I mean, terribly sorry."

"I should fine you, you know. Lucky for you, miss, I'm in a forgiving mood. Now, where're you headed?"

"The Parish of St. Mary the Virgin."

"Ain't that in Rotherhithe? You'll get caught out in the blackout, no doubt. Best you went home instead. Run along now."

"Please, it's really important. It's this way, isn't it?" She used the same voice and pleading eyes that had worked on Zeke in repairs. He eyed her up and down then sighed. Men never changed, no matter the year.

"About twenty minutes, if you hurry," he said. "But it ain't safe for a girl out there in the docklands."

"I'll be all right," she smiled. "For the first time in a while."

She passed under the bridge, berating herself for her foolishness. Gasmask, of course! No wonder every native was staring at her like an idiot. And if that man had seen her gun... It was an antique and the ammunition had taken two years to track down. Well, it didn't matter now, she thought, as she made her way around St. Saviours Docks. The gun was hers, and the Germans never used gas bombs in this war anyway, so it was the natives who were the real idiots.

Behind her, the sun dipped out of sight as she delved into the maze-like streets with their walls of towering warehouses. These buildings, still fulfilling their original purpose, were silent. If anyone were inside, heavy blackout curtains hid their movements. All of London was going dark. The TT could provide light, but wardens like the one she left behind would be on her in an instant, and she couldn't be caught. Not now. A flicker of fear rose up within her, but was smothered by her medication.

In the blackout, it was easy to ignore the differences between this time and hers. The fears which plagued her when she first landed trickled away, leaving her with only the purpose of her mission. She'd had to keep it hidden for so long—from her friends, her uncle... *especially* her uncle—that she was used to pretending it didn't exist, that it wasn't a part of her. But there was no need to keep pretending now. She let it out to play as she skirted the narrow streets, let her heart fill with the rage that had lived, sedated, inside her for so long.

Planes flew overhead, but Penelope could not see them now. She could see almost nothing in this darkness, not even Tower Bridge. She followed the cobblestoned street, keeping a hand on the brick buildings to guide her. Close. She had to be getting close. She could practically smell him. When the buildings disappeared, she risked a little light from the TT and recognized that grassy knoll beside her; King's Stairs Gardens. The adrenaline kicked in. The parish was less than five minutes away. The gun pressed itself, cold, against her thigh. Soon it would be warm.

If the parish had changed at all, Penelope could not tell. In the dim light of the TT, at least the church's iron gates seemed the same. Penelope hid the device as she walked through the open gate, then placed her hands on the heavy wooden doors. Behind them, James Cuttlethorpe was praying for his salvation. Well, today, she was here. Penelope pushed.

Inside, all the blackout curtains were drawn, hiding the light of the candles burning in the empty sanctuary. Penelope entered with caution, inhaling the scent of smoke and wood polish. Where was he? Was it a set-up? No. He couldn't know she would be here. Her heels echoed, clacking against the floor as she progressed up the aisle, past pew after empty pew. Had she gotten the date wrong after all? Was it 1941 not 1940? No. She was right. She had to be. James Cuttlethorpe came every Friday to this parish to pray for his dead wife. Penelope had researched this. She couldn't be wrong.

Penelope stood at the front rails, facing the altar. 'Worthy is the Lamb that was Slain' read the inscription. How many times had her uncle taken her here to church, where she'd been forced to stare at those words for the duration of the service? How many Sundays had she spent desperately, then angrily, asking what made Mum so worthy? She had forgotten them as soon as she turned seventeen, when her uncle could no longer force her to attend a service. Now, here they were again, providing no final answer, no actual relief.

Her hands were shaking again. Penelope popped another pill from the blister pack.

A door clicked open.

She dropped the loose pill and hid behind a pew.

In the shadows, the tall, silent figure of a man walked up the aisle and slid into the pew adjacent to Penelope's, where he bowed his head and began to pray. She could see the outline of his jaw, his nose—the profile that had haunted her dreams since she was thirteen years old. The realization that she was right negated the need for another pill.

Penelope rose from her hiding place, the gun warmed by her hand. He was too involved in his prayers to notice her. She wondered if it were a bigger sin to kill a man while he was praying than to kill him when he was not. Remembering Hamlet's mistake, she made her presence known.

"Why did you do it?" Her voice shot through the silence louder than any gun. James Cuttlethorpe startled and fell off the pew onto the floor.

"I... I beg your pardon? Hello? Who are you?"

She didn't let the stutter fool her. "James Cuttlethorpe?"

"Can I help you?"

"Yes, if you can tell me why." Penelope stepped forward. The metal of the gun glistened in the candlelight. He scurried backwards on his hands and feet, like a crab, trapped between the pews.

"In all my research—and I've done quite a bit—it's the one thing I've never been able to determine. I figured out the how, and that's really easy. She had a whole team that traveled back and forth to postwar London. No better way to research rebuilding efforts, that's what she always said. So you must have met one of her colleagues. Convinced them to give you a TT, teach you how to use it. But it's the why. I've never been able to sort that one out."

"I'm so sorry. I have no idea what you're on about. Please, my son is waiting outside. Please, let me..."

"No! You don't get to beg. She begged, too, but it didn't matter to you, so it doesn't matter to me. I can see you're confused, so let me tell you a story. No, no. Don't interrupt. I've been rehearsing it for a really long time. I'll start with a few spoilers. This war here? We win. Huzzah. But, many years later, turns out there's another, this time with an enemy who's not scared of invading our little island. England is the new France. Eventually it ends, and we start going about our normal lives. We start rebuilding. My mum is—was—one of the people in charge of rebuilding. We get a nice, new flat, my first real home outside of a refugee camp since I was born. But I think you've already guessed that this story doesn't have a happy ending. And the reason for that is *you*, Mr. Cuttlethorpe. You arrive in our flat at 178 Rotherhithe Street just as Mum finishes making dinner—Thai green curry. You land in our kitchen and you take out a gun and you shoot her."

"That's enough. This is ridiculous. Who put you up to this? The future? No one can predict the future. It's impossible."

"I don't predict the future, Mr. Cuttlethorpe. I am the future. Your future. See, the reason you're so confused is because you haven't done it yet. I wasted so much time trying to figure out the why, that I finally decided it didn't really matter, if I could stop you from doing it in the first place." She aimed the gun on the wrinkle between his eyes.

"Please, miss..."

An air raid sounded. Penelope fired. James Cuttlethorpe collapsed.

She stepped over to him and watched the blood pooling around his head. These antique guns were remarkably effective. She waited but felt nothing. She supposed she would have to wait until her medication wore off.

A small, choked cry sounded from the doorway. Penelope turned and saw a boy, eleven or twelve years old, standing there. She returned the gun to her pocket and walked towards him. The air raid sirens continued to blare.

"The bombs are about to fall," she said. "You better find cover."

She left him and walked calmly across the street to the empty cemetery watch house. The door was locked but easily forced. Inside, Penelope checked the TT. It needed two more hours to fully recharge before she could jump home. She crouched in the corner, knees to her chest, and listened to the bombs falling on London. Some sounds never changed.

She never thought she would feel so numb, but when anger drained away it left only a void in its place. Warmth, that was what she wanted, what she had always wanted. It must be the medication. Once it wore off, she'd feel warmth again. She took out the blister pack and popped out each pill one by one, and crushed them under her heel. She would never need them again. Another explosion far off, across the river maybe. Oh the things she could tell Dr. Rosalind at her next visit, if there was a next visit. Her whole past would be different now, wouldn't it? Her whole life? Penelope closed her eyes and focused on the moment she would return home, the moment when she would again see her mother's smiling face.

* * *

A pair of feet wearing his father's shoes lay in the aisle, the rest of the body hidden by the pews. The same hollowness that had come with Mother's death sat in Martin's stomach now.

"Father?" His voice was fragile, consumed by the bombs, and crying was useless. He knew the meaning of such stillness.

Martin ran to the doors. That woman, he should have stopped her. Why had he let her walk away? Where had she gone? He was going to find her. Find her and... and...

A glimmer of light came from within the watch house. But old Phil wasn't in tonight. Martin had seen him drinking in The Mayflower not ten minutes ago. Surely, it was her.

He ran. An explosion threw him back against the church.

He came to with a ringing in his ears and stinging smoke in his nose as fire lit up the night. The watch house was gone. As Martin limped towards the rubble, his foot kicked something in the road. First he thought it a brick, but when he picked it up he saw it was a gun like the one his uncle in the army carried. It was hot from the flames, but Martin held it and let it burn. Beside it was something else made of metal, something unlike anything he'd ever seen. It was like a wristwatch but with a larger casing and black glass where a clock face should be. It, too, was hot.

The fire wardens approached. Martin ran before they could catch him, and he crawled into the ancient ruins in King's Stairs Gardens. Safely concealed, he pulled out his torch. On the back of the odd device was a second square of black glass, but this one flashed green letters intermittently, like a flickering light bulb—*Username: Penelope Castlewaight*. Penelope Castlewaight was dead now, blown apart by the bombs like his mother. Dead, like his father, and as Martin realized that, the emptiness he felt changed to something else, something closer to the feel of the warm gun still clutched in his other hand.

* * *

London – March 2063

"Penelope, go wash up. Dinner's ready."

"I'm reading."

"You can read after dinner."

"Fine." Penelope tossed her e-book aside and loped down the hall to the bathroom. Mum called, but her voice was muffled by the running water.

"I can't hear you. I'm washing my hands like you said!" she shouted back. Penelope took her time, still in awe over indoor running water, private bathrooms, private anything really. She shut it off before Mum could yell at her for wasting water and dried her hands on the rough, purple towel. It needed to be washed. Mum was probably going to harp on about that, too.

With a sigh, Penelope took a moment to fix her hair, then went back down the hall.

"Mum, what..." She froze.

In the living room stood a man pointing an old gun at Mum's head. He was young, but his clothes were old—a long brown trench coat and one of those hats Granddad liked, fedoras.

"Please," Mum begged.

"You think I wouldn't remember you? Your face is burned into my memory, Miss Castlewaight. A face I've never wanted to remember but have never been able to forget."

Penelope cowered in the hall, wanting to help but terrified of being seen. She reached for her phone, but it wasn't in her pocket. She'd left it on the coffee table.

"My name is Mrs. Joyce..."

"I know exactly who you are. It's why I've come to return the favor."

"Please, tell me what's going on. Have I done something? Tell me what I did and I swear I'll make it right. I can make it right."

"Let me put it in your own words, Miss Castleweight. The reason you're so confused is because you haven't done it yet." He cocked the gun. "And now you never will."

"Please..."

He fired. Mum crumpled to the floor. The man pocketed the gun and tipped his hat.

"Courtesy of James Cuttlethorpe." As he moved for the hallway, Penelope ducked into her bedroom, too panicked to scream. The front door opened and shut. Body trembling, she ran to Mum, but there was no chance she was alive. Her eyes were as lifeless as Dad's after the Southbank Raids. Through the window, she saw the man leave her building and head towards St. Marychurch Street.

Penelope left her flat and ran out after him, weaving around bomb craters while keeping hidden behind corners. The man seemed stunned by the world around him, confused by buildings and the cars parked in front. He passed the parish then walked up Elephant Lane towards the river, pausing to stare at Tower Bridge.

There were no tears when he shot her mum, but there were some now as he gazed at the collapsed remains of the North Tower. Hand pressed against his head, he stumbled onward towards King's Stairs Gardens. Penelope kept back. Why would he be heading there? The mines weren't cleared yet. How could he not know?

He stumbled through the broken fence. Penelope waited, but not for long. An explosion shook the ground. She ran towards it. Debris was scattered outside the perimeter, thrown over the top by the force. Sirens rang out. Amongst the rocks and dirt, Penelope found the old gun clutched in the lifeless fingers of a detached hand. Beside it was another device.

It looked like the TT1000s Mum used for work trips to postwar London, but a much sleeker, more advanced model. She picked it up. It was still warm. Across the back was stamped TT4500.

Penelope ran away before the emergency crews arrived and hid in the watch house ruins, smelling the smoke as it drifted east. This device was damaged beyond repair, but her uncle was always building more. He kept saying he wanted to recruit Penelope into the family manufacturing business. Now she would agree. And when she was old enough, she would make her own trip. Penelope knew she would never forget that man's profile or his name. The numbness that she felt in the flat, the emptiness which prevented her from saving her mother melted away, replaced with a burning anger that would keep her heart beating for the next ten years.

The Temporal Element
ISBN#978-0-9887685-3-6

http://www.martinus.us/
books.html#temporalelement

Stories Included:

**A Thursday Night at Doctor What's Time and Relative
Dimensional Space Bar and Grill
—by Bruno Lombardi**

I'll Come Back For You—by A. C. Hall

The Long View—by William R. D. Wood

AMR-17—by Edmund Wells

Doing Time—by Barbara Austin

There's an App for That—by Chris Allinotte

Also Contains stories by Arthur M. Doweyko,
Paul Lamb, Carolyn M. Chang, James Hartley,
Tony Laplume, Martin T. Ingham,
Robert MacAnthony, Shawn Cook, Karl G. Rich,
Jeffery Scott Sims, Diane Arrelle, Steven Gepp,
Jon Wesick, and Lauren A. Forry

**Quests, Curses,
& Vengeance
ISBN#978-0-9887685-4-3**

http://www.martinus.us/
books.html#qcv

Burn It Up, Burn It Down –by Philip Overby

Quest through the Ages—by JL Mo

Hooked on Questing –by Gerald Costlow

Life or Death –by Stacey Jaine McIntosh

Odin's Spear –by Susan A. Royal

Wipeout –by A. C. Hall

Curse of the Bottle –by Nye Joell Hardy

Poetic Justice –by Edmund Wells

Abducted –by Shawn Cook

**But I Know We'll Meet Again Some Sunny Day
–by Lauren A. Forry**

Also contains stories by Mel Obedoza, Karl G. Rich,
Martin T. Ingham, Chris Allinotte, Bruno Lombardi

West of the Warlock
by Martin T. Ingham
ISBN#978-0-9887685-1-2
www.martiningham.com/westwarlock.html

Featuring:
Into the Thick of It

* * *

Also Available:

The Curse of Selwood
(A West of the Warlock Novel)
by Martin T. Ingham
ISBN #978-0-9887685-0-5

"The Curse of Selwood is back,
and it demands blood!"

Coming in 2014:

VFW:
Veterans of the Future Wars
ISBN#978-0-9887685-5-0

Sci-Fi Stories of the Future Wars,
and the Veterans who fight them!

Experience tales of valor, of brave men and women
standing their ground and serving their country in the world
beyond tomorrow.

http://www.martinus.us/books.html#vfw

Coming Soon:

We Were Heroes
A Super-Powered Anthology

How do heroes cope with aging? Do they ride gracefully into the sunset, or burn out in a blaze of glory? See what happens with these fantastic tales.